DEDICATED
TO
BYNG HUSBAND

*

KING ARTHUR
AND HIS
KNIGHTS OF THE
ROUND TABLE

NEWLY RE-TOLD
OUT OF THE OLD ROMANCES

BY
ROGER LANCELYN GREEN

AND ILLUSTRATED BY
LOTTE REINIGER

PENGUIN BOOKS

LONDON
MELBOURNE · BALTIMORE

FIRST PUBLISHED 1953

MADE AND PRINTED IN GREAT BRITAIN
FOR PENGUIN BOOKS LTD
BY THE WHITEFRIARS PRESS LTD

Contents

Illustrations

Author's Note

THE story of King Arthur and the adventures of his knights have been told so very many times that there seems at first sight little excuse for re-telling them yet again.

But, setting aside poetical versions of a variety of the legends made by such poets as Dryden, Morris, Tennyson, and Swinburne, scarcely any writer in English has done more than condense the narrative of Sir Thomas Malory, cutting and simplifying according to the age of their audience, but always following him with more or less exactitude.

Moreover, it has recently been shown that Malory himself did not write his Book of King Arthur as a single narrative, but merely as a collection of quite separate stories, based on a variety of old French romances. There is a certain coherence, but no fixed plan.

So now I have endeavoured to make each adventure a part of one fixed pattern – Arthur's Kingdom, the Realm of Logres, the model of chivalry and right striving against the barbarism and evil which surrounded and at length engulfed it. This is only the bare foundation, however; on it I have endeavoured to rear a fabric consisting of all the best-known adventures, exploits, and quests of the most famous Knights of the Round Table, and a few lesser-known stories which fit into the whole.

I have followed Malory in the main, except for certain isolated stories which he does not include; but I have not felt bound to follow him slavishly – any more than he scrupled to adapt or combine his many French sources.

Starting from the historical Arthur, the Leader or *Dux Bellorum* whose position in the Britain of the fifth century, when the Roman civilization made its last stand against the Saxons, is described by R. G. Collingwood in his *Roman Britain*, I have gone on to make use of the pseudo-history of

Geoffrey of Monmouth, and the verse chronicle of Layamon. These have given me a few ideas and details for Book One – but in essentials it is almost entirely Malory, except for the description of Balyn in the Grail Chapel which comes from the French *Merlin*, and of Nimue's imprisoning of Merlin from the Middle-English prose romance of *Merlin*.

In Book Two, *Sir Gawain and the Green Knight* is taken from the famous Middle English poem of that name; Launcelot's first quest is from Malory, but the account of his arrival at Camelot (which Malory omits) is from the French prose romance *Le Livre de Lancelot del Lac*. Sir Gareth, the next story, seems to be Malory's own invention, and I have followed him, condensing a little, and smoothing out the end. In dealing with Tristram I have deserted Malory and gone back to the earlier version (which he does not seem to have known) of Godfrey of Strasbourg. *Geraint and Enid* (not included by Malory) is adapted from the Welsh *Mabinogion*, with a detail or two from the *Erec et Enide* of Chrétien de Troyes. *Sir Gawain and the Lady Ragnell* (not in Malory) is based on a Middle English poem and a ballad, and seems never to have been retold; nor have the early adventures of Percivale, for which I have used another Middle English poem and many incidents from the French *Conte du Graal*. *Launcelot and Elaine* is directly from Malory; and so also is my Book Three, *The Quest of the Holy Grail*, except for Gawain's adventures at the Grail Castle which are from the German *Diu Crône* of Heinrich von dem Türlin, while the final adventures of Percivale are from the German *Parzival* of Wolfram von Eschenbach. (For synopses of both these poems I am indebted to the *Studies on the Legend of the Holy Grail* by Alfred Nutt.)

Book Four is directly from Malory, *The Last Battle* following him almost word for word in one of the finest tragedies in English literature. The death of Launcelot and Sir Hector's farewell is also Malory; but the account of the finding of the graves at Glastonbury is from a medieval Latin chronicle, and the story of the shepherd and the cavern is elaborated from the folk-tale preserved by Sir Edmund Chambers in his

Arthur of Britain, to which book, and to J. D. Bruce's magnificent work *The Evolution of Arthurian Romance,* I am deeply indebted.

These are my sources, and I have used them very much as Malory used his originals. In place of the French 'Arthurian Cycle' I have had Malory's own immortal book; like him I have drawn from the romances which he also used, but my net has been wider cast than his in my search for incidents and versions of one of the world's greatest legends. No writer can rival Malory as the storyteller of the *Morte D'Arthur* as he told it almost exactly five hundred years ago – but the great legends, like the best of the fairy tales, must be retold from age to age: there is always something new to be found in them, and each retelling brings them freshly and more vividly before a new generation – and therein lies their immortality.

ROGER LANCELYN GREEN

BOOK ONE

The Coming of Arthur

I

▰▰▰▰▰▰▰▰▰▰▰▰▰▰▰▰▰▰▰▰▰▰▰▰▰▰▰▰▰

The Two Swords

AFTER wicked King Vortigern had first invited the Saxons to settle in Britain and help him to fight the Picts and Scots, the land was never long at peace. Although so much of it was covered with thick forests, much also was beautiful open country, with little villages and towns, country houses and cottages, as the Romans had left it not many years before. Having once seen it, the Saxons could never again be contented with their savage, unfruitful homes in Germany and Denmark; and year by year more and more of them came stealing across the North Sea in their long ships, to kill or drive out the Britons and settle in their homes.

Vortigern was dead, and Aurelius Ambrosius, last of the Romans, was dead too, when Uther Pendragon, whom some call the brother of Ambrosius, led the Britons. He defeated the Saxons in many battles, and brought peace to the southern lands where he was king – to London, and to Winchester, which was then called Camelot, and to Cornwall where Gorlois his loyal follower was duke. But Uther fell in love with Gorlois's wife, the lovely Igrayne, and there was battle between them, until Gorlois fell, and Uther married his widow.

He visited her first in the haunted castle of Tintagel, the dark castle by the Cornish sea, and Merlin the enchanter watched over their love. One child was born to Uther and Igrayne – but what became of that baby boy only the wise Merlin could have told, for he carried it away by a secret path down the cliff side in the dead of night, and no word was spoken of its fate.

Uther had no other children, though Igrayne and Gorlois had three daughters: two of these were grown-up when

Igrayne became queen, and were married – Morgawse to Lot, King of Orkney, and Elaine to Nantres, King of Garlot: they had sons who in after days were among the bravest Knights of the Round Table. But the third daughter, Morgana le Fay, was still only a child, and she was sent to school in a nunnery; yet, by some means, she learnt much magic, which she used wickedly.

King Uther Pendragon had only a little while of happiness with the fair Igrayne, for soon the Saxons made war against him once more, and sent a traitor to serve him, who poisoned the King and many of his followers.

Then the land fell upon days more evil and wretched than any which had gone before. King Uther's knights fought amongst themselves, quarrelling as to who should rule; and the Saxons, seeing that there was no strong man to lead the Britons against them, conquered more and more of Britain.

Years of strife and misery went by, until the appointed time was at hand. Then Merlin, the good enchanter, came out from the deep, mysterious valleys of North Wales, which in those days was called Gwynedd, through Powys or South Wales, and passed on his way to London. And so great was his fame that neither Saxon nor Briton dared molest him.

Merlin came to London and spoke with the Archbishop; and a great gathering of knights was called for Christmas Day – so great that all of them could not find a place in the abbey church, so that some were forced to gather in the churchyard.

In the middle of the service, there arose suddenly a murmur of wonder outside the abbey: for there was seen, though no man saw it come, a great square slab of marble-stone in the churchyard, and on the stone an anvil of iron, and set point downwards a great, shining sword of steel thrust deeply into the anvil.

'Stir not till the service be done,' commanded the Archbishop when this marvel was made known to him. 'But pray the more unto God that we may find a remedy for the sore wounds of our land.'

When the service was ended the Archbishop and the lords

and knights who had been within the abbey came out to see
the wonder of the sword. Round about the anvil they found
letters of gold set in the great stone, and the letters read thus:
'WHOSO PULLETH OUT THIS SWORD FROM THIS STONE AND
ANVIL IS THE TRUE-BORN KING OF ALL BRITAIN.'

When they saw this, many and many a man tried to pull
out the sword – but not one of them could stir it a hair's-
breadth.

'He is not here,' said the Archbishop. 'But doubt not that
God will send us our King. Let messengers be sent through
all the land to tell what is written on the stone: and upon New
Year's Day we will hold a great tournament, and see whether
our King is amongst those who come to joust. Until then, I
counsel that we appoint ten knights to guard the stone, and
set a rich pavilion over it.'

All this was done, and upon New Year's Day a great host
of knights met together. But none as yet could draw forth the
sword out of the stone. Then they went all a little way off, and
pitched tents, and held a tournament or sham-fight, trying
their strength and skill at jousting with long lances of wood,
or fighting with broad-swords.

It happened that among those who came was the good
knight Sir Ector, and his son Kay who had been made a
knight not many months before; and with them came Arthur,
Sir Kay's young brother, a youth of scarcely sixteen years of
age.

Riding to the jousts, Sir Kay found suddenly that he had
left his sword in his lodgings, and he asked Arthur to ride
back and fetch it for him.

'Certainly I will,' said Arthur, who was always ready to do
anything for other people, and back he rode to the town. But
Sir Kay's mother had locked the door, and gone out to see the
tournament, so that Arthur could not get into the lodgings
at all.

This troubled Arthur very much. 'My brother Kay must
have a sword,' he thought, as he rode slowly back. 'It will be
a shame and a matter for unkind jests if so young a knight
comes to the jousts without a sword. But where can I find

him one? ... I know! I saw one sticking in an anvil in the churchyard, I'll fetch that: it's doing no good there!'

So Arthur set spurs to his horse and came to the churchyard. Tying his horse to the stile, he ran to the tent which had been set over the stone – and found that all ten of the guardian knights had also gone to the tournament. Without stopping to read what was written on the stone, Arthur pulled out the sword at a touch, ran back to his horse, and in a few minutes had caught up with Sir Kay and handed it over to him.

Arthur knew nothing of what sword it was, but Kay had already tried to pull it from the anvil, and saw at a glance that it was the same one. Instantly he rode to his father Sir Ector, and said:

'Sir! Look, here is the sword out of the stone! So you see I must be the true-born King of all Britain!'

But Sir Ector knew better than to believe Sir Kay too readily. Instead, he rode back with him to the church, and there made him swear a solemn oath with his hand on the Bible to say truly how he came by the sword.

'My brother Arthur brought it to me,' said Kay, with a sigh.

'And how did *you* get the sword?' asked Sir Ector.

'Sir, I will tell you,' said Arthur, fearing that he had done wrong. 'Kay sent me to fetch his sword, but I could not come to it. Then I remembered having seen this sword sticking uselessly into an anvil in the churchyard. I thought it could be put to a better use in my brother's hand – so I fetched it.'

'Did you find no knights guarding the sword?' asked Sir Ector.

'Never a one,' said Arthur.

'Well, put the sword back into the anvil, and let us see you draw it out,' commanded Sir Ector.

'That's easily done,' said Arthur, puzzled by all this trouble over a sword, and he set it back easily into the anvil.

Then Sir Kay seized it by the hilt and pulled his hardest: but struggle and strain as he might, he could not move it by a hair's breadth. Sir Ector tried also, but with no better success.

'Pull it out,' he said to Arthur.

And Arthur, more and more bewildered, put his hand to the hilt and drew forth the sword as if out of a well-greased scabbard.

'Now,' said Sir Ector, kneeling before Arthur and bowing his head in reverence, 'I understand that you and none other are the true-born King of this land.'

'Why? Oh why is it I? Why do you kneel to me, my father?' cried Arthur.

'It is God's will that whoso might draw forth the sword out of the stone and out of the anvil is the true-born King of Britain,' said Sir Ector. 'Moreover, though I love you well, you are no son of mine. For Merlin brought you to me when you were a small child, and bade me bring you up as my own son!'

'Then if I am indeed King,' said Arthur, bowing his head over the cross-hilt of the sword, 'I hereby pledge myself to the service of God and of my people, to the righting of wrongs, to the driving-out of evil, to the bringing of peace and plenty to my land ... Good sir, you have been as a father to me since ever I can remember, be still near me with a father's love and a father's counsel and advice. ... Kay, my foster-brother, be you seneschal over all my lands and a true knight of my court.'

After this they went to the Archbishop and told him all. But the knights and barons were filled with rage and jealousy, and refused to believe that Arthur was the true-born King. So the choice was put off until Easter; and at Easter once more until Whitsun, or Pentecost as it then was called: but still, though many kings and knights came to try their strength, Arthur alone could pull out the sword.

Then all the people cried: 'Arthur! We will have Arthur! By God's will he is our King! God save King Arthur!' And they knelt down before him, the noble and the humble together, the rich and the poor, and cried him mercy for delaying him so long. And Arthur forgave them readily, and kneeling down himself he gave the wondrous sword to the Archbishop and received of him the high and holy order of

Knighthood. And then came all the earls and the barons, the knights and squires, and did homage to Arthur, swearing to serve and obey him as was their duty.

King Arthur now gathered together all the hosts of Britain, and with the pick of the older knights who had served his father and the younger knights whose chief desire was to show their courage and loyalty, he set out to do battle with the Saxons and to punish all those thieves and robbers who had ravaged the land for many years, doing cruel and shameful deeds.

Before long he had brought peace and safety to the southern parts of Britain, making his capital at Camelot. But the other kings who ruled then in and about Britain – the Kings of Orkney and Lothian, of Gwynydd and Powys, of Gorre and Garloth – grew jealous of this unknown boy who was calling himself King of all Britain, and sent word that they were coming to visit him with gifts – but that their gifts would be given with sharp swords between the head and shoulders.

Then Merlin came suddenly to Arthur and led him to the city of Caerleon in South Wales, into a strong tower well provisioned for a siege. The hostile kings came also to Caerleon and surrounded the tower: but they could not break in, to kill Arthur and his faithful followers.

Merlin came out of the tower after fifteen days, stood upon the steps in the gateway and asked all the angry kings and knights why they came in arms against King Arthur.

'Why have you made that boy, that Arthur, our King?' they shouted.

'Be silent and listen, all of you!' commanded Merlin, and a great quiet fell upon all who were gathered together, an awe and a wonder as the good enchanter spoke to them.

'I will tell you of wondrous things,' he said. 'Arthur is indeed your King, the rightful King of all this land – yes, and of Wales too, of Ireland and Scotland and Orkney also, and of Armorica beyond the sea; and he shall rule other lands also. He is the true and only son of the good King Uther Pendragon! Of his birth and of the things which should befall when he was King, I knew by my holy arts. Uther came to Tintagel in the form of Gorlois three hours after Gorlois was dead: then and thus he comforted the Lady Igrayne and won her to be his wife. But, so my knowledge told me, their son, this Arthur, was born to great and wondrous things. A little while after his birth at dark Tintagel, Uther, who hearkened to my words, gave the child into my care, and I bore him to Avalon, to the Land of Mystery. And the Dwellers in Avalon – you know them not, but you would call them Fairies and Elves – cast a pure and great enchantment upon the child, a magic most strong. Three gifts they gave to Arthur: that he should be the best of all knights; that he should be the greatest king this land shall ever know; and that he should live long – longer than any man shall ever know. These, the virtues of a good and generous prince, the Dwellers in Avalon gave to Arthur. And in Avalon the elves are forging Excalibur to be the sword of his right – the clean, flashing blade that shall be raised only in the cause of right, shining on the earth until the time comes when they shall call it back again. ... Arthur is your King! Year by year as he reigns, his kingdom shall grow – not Britain, nor the islands of the seas, no, nor Armorica and Gaul, – but Logres, the land of blessing, God's Kingdom upon earth, which Arthur shall show you for a little space before the darkness falls again.'

There was silence for a while when Merlin had finished speaking, for all those who heard him felt that they were at the beginning of a time of wonders, and that Arthur was more than just a King who ruled because his father had been King, or because he was the strongest man amongst them.

Suddenly they all knelt before him where he stood above Merlin on the steps of the tower, and with one voice promised to be his true and faithful subjects all the days of their lives.

Then the Archbishop set the crown upon Arthur's head, and the people cheered him once more: and this was the real beginning of his reign.

'To-morrow we will begin to collect our forces,' said King Arthur. 'And when all are gathered together, we march to the north and to the east to do battle with the Saxons and drive them out of Britain. Then we will build castles and set guards along the coast so that never again may they invade us: we will rebuild the churches which they have destroyed, and build new ones to the glory of God; and our knights shall ride about the country punishing all those who break the peace and do ill to any. And if any man or woman, be he or she the greatest or the least of my subjects, be in any trouble, or have complaint against any man, let them come to me, and never shall their sorrow go uncomforted and their wrong unrighted.'

King Arthur feasted that day in the great castle of Caerleon: but before ever the feast was ended there befell the first of the marvellous adventures that were to happen in the wonderland of Logres during his reign.

Suddenly into the courtyard there rode a young squire, leading another horse, across the saddle of which lay the body of a knight but newly slain.

'Vengeance, lord King!' cried the squire, when Arthur came from the hall to learn what this might mean. 'Give me vengeance! Here lies Sir Miles, dead upon his steed, as goodly a knight and as brave as any in the land. In the forest not many leagues from here King Pellinore has set up his pavilion beside the high road, by a well of fresh water, and he goes about to slay all knights that pass this way. Wherefore I pray you that my master be honourably buried, and that some knight ride out to avenge his death.'

There was a certain squire in Arthur's court, whose name was Gryflet, no older than Arthur himself, and now he fell on his knees before the King and begged him for all his service to make him a knight so that he might go out and fight with Pellinore.

'You are not old enough yet for such a battle,' said King Arthur, 'nor have you grown great enough in strength.'

'Yet, make me a knight!' begged Gryflet.

'My lord,' said Merlin quietly to Arthur, 'it were a great pity to lose Gryflet, for he would be a passing good man when he comes of age, and would be your faithful knight all his life ... Pellinore is the strongest man in the world now bearing arms, and surely Gryflet will be slain if they come to sword strokes.'

King Arthur nodded, and turned again to his young squire: 'Gryflet,' he said, 'kneel, and I will make you a knight according to your wish.' And when this was done, he went on: 'And now, Sir Gryflet, since I have made you knight, surely you owe me a gift.'

'My Lord, whatever you shall ask is yours,' said Gryflet.

'Promise me then,' commanded Arthur, 'by your honour as a knight, that when you come upon King Pellinore by the well in the forest, you joust but with your spears and, on horseback or on foot, fight with him in no other wise.'

'That will I promise you,' said Gryflet; and then he took his horse in great haste, snatched up his spear, slung his shield on his left arm, and went off in a cloud of dust until he came to the well-side in the forest. And there he saw a rich pavilion, and before it a horse ready saddled and bridled, and at the side a tree on which hung a shield painted in bright colours, and by it a great spear.

Sir Gryflet hit the shield with the butt of his own spear so hard that it came clattering to the ground, and King Pellinore came out of the pavilion – a tall strong man as fierce as a lion.

'Sir knight!' he cried, 'why smote you down my shield?'

'Sir, for that I would joust with you!' answered Gryflet.

'It were better that you did not,' said King Pellinore. 'You are but a new, young knight, and not so strong as I!'

'In spite of that, I will joust with you,' repeated Gryflet.

'Well, this is by no desire of mine,' said King Pellinore as he buckled on his armour, 'but let things fall as they must. Whose knight are you?'

'Sir, I am one of King Arthur's court!' cried Gryflet. And with that they rode away in either direction along the road, then turned their horses, set their spears in rest, and galloped at one another as hard as they could. Sir Gryflet's spear struck the shield of King Pellinore and broke all to pieces: but King Pellinore's spear went straight through Gryflet's shield, deep into his side, and there broke off short. And Sir Gryflet and his horse fell upon the ground.

King Pellinore came and bent over Sir Gryflet, who lay still where he had fallen, and unloosed his helmet. 'Well, this was a brave youth,' said Pellinore, 'and if he lives, will be a mighty knight.' Then he placed Gryflet across the saddle, and the horse galloped back to Caerleon with none to guide it.

Arthur was very wroth when he saw how badly hurt was Sir Gryflet, and at once he put on his own armour, closed the vizor of his helmet so that no one could see his face, and with spear in hand rode hard into the forest to be revenged upon King Pellinore.

But on his way he found three robbers attacking Merlin, and they seemed like to beat him to death with great clubs.

'Fly, churls!' cried Arthur, riding at them furiously, and the three cowards turned and fled when they saw the knight charging at them.

'Ah, Merlin,' said Arthur, 'for all your wisdom and your magic, you would have been murdered in a few minutes if I had not come to your rescue!'

'Not so,' answered Merlin, smiling his mysterious smile. 'Easily could I have saved myself, had I willed it. It is you who draw near to your death – for you go towards it in your pride, if God does not aid you.'

But Arthur would not take heed of Merlin's wisdom, and rode fiercely on until he came to the rich pavilion by the well. And there sat King Pellinore upon his great war-horse, waiting for him.

'Sir knight!' cried Arthur, 'why stand you here, fighting and striking down all the knights who ride this way?'

'It is my custom to do so,' answered Pellinore sternly. 'And if any man would make me change my custom, let him try at his peril!'

'I will make you change it!' cried Arthur.

'And I will defend my custom,' replied Pellinore quietly.

Then they drew apart, and came riding together at full tilt, so hard that both spears shivered into little pieces as each hit the centre of the other's shield. Arthur would have drawn his sword then, but Pellinore said:

'Not so, let us run together with spears yet again.'

'So I would,' said Arthur, 'if I had another spear!'

'I have plenty,' answered Pellinore, and he shouted to his squire to bring two out of the pavilion.

Once more the two kings jousted together; and once more their spears broke into fragments without either of them being struck from his horse. A third time they jousted, and Arthur's spear broke, but King Pellinore's struck him so hard in the middle of the shield that horse and man fell to earth.

But Arthur sprang to his feet in a great fury, drawing his sword and shouting defiance at Pellinore, who thereupon came down from his horse and drew his own sword. Then began a fierce battle, with many great strokes; they hacked and hewed at one another, cutting pieces off their shields and armour, and suffering each of them so many wounds that the trampled grass in front of the pavilion was stained with red. They rested once, and then charged each other again: but their swords met together with so mighty a crash that Arthur's broke in two, leaving him with the useless hilt in his hand.

'Ah-ha!' cried King Pellinore. 'Now you are in my power, to slay or spare as I will! And I will kill you forthwith, unless you kneel and yield to me, confessing yourself to be a knight of little worth.'

'There are two ways with that,' cried Arthur, mad with shame and fury. 'Death is welcome when it comes; but to yield – never!' And with that he leapt in under Pellinore's sword, seized him round the waist and hurled him to the ground. They struggled there for a little while, but Pellinore was still the strongest, and presently he tore off Arthur's helmet and took up his sword to cut his head off also.

But Merlin came suddenly and laid his hand on Pellinore's shoulder: 'Knight,' he said, 'hold your hand and do not strike this stroke. For if you do the hope of Logres dies, and you put this land of Britain into the greatest ruin and desolation that ever a country suffered.'

'Who is it?' asked Pellinore.

'This is King Arthur!' said Merlin.

For a moment Pellinore was tempted to strike the blow: for

he feared that if Arthur lived, he would never forgive him for what he had done. But Merlin smiled quietly, and placed his hand on Pellinore's head. And at once all the anger and fear went from his mind, and he sank back quietly against the tree beside the well of clear water, and passed into a deep sleep.

Merlin helped King Arthur, who was sorely wounded, to mount his horse, and led him away into the forest.

'Alas, Merlin, what have you done?' asked Arthur; for now he had put from him all the pride and wilfulness which had so nearly caused his death. 'You have killed this good knight by your magic – and I would rather have lost my kingdom than that one so brave and mighty should die thus.'

'Cease to trouble,' said Merlin. 'For all things work by the will of God and to the glory of Logres. He is more like to live than you are, for you are sorely wounded, and he does but sleep ... I told you how mighty a fighter he was. This is King Pellinore who in time to come shall do you good service. And his sons, Sir Tor and Sir Lamorak, shall be among the bravest of your knights.'

Then Merlin brought Arthur to a hermitage where lived a good old man who was a clever leech, or healer of wounds. And in three days he was nearly cured, and could ride once more and fight as strongly as ever.

'Alas,' said Arthur as they rode through the forest. 'Now I have no sword.'

'Let not that trouble you,' said Merlin. 'There was no virtue in the sword which is lost: it has served its purpose. But near here your own sword awaits you: it was made in Avalon by fairy craft, made for you alone until you must return it ere you journey to Avalon yourself. It is called Excalibur, and none may stand against its stroke: and with it you shall bring freedom and peace to Logres. This is the hour appointed when Excalibur shall be placed in your hand – for now you will grasp its hilt in all humility, and draw it only to defend the right.'

Deeper and deeper into the forest they went, and before long the hills rose on either side until they were riding through a narrow valley that wound through dark mountains.

And at last they came to a narrow pass in the rocks, and beyond it, in a cup of the mountains, Arthur saw a strange lake. All around it the hills rose darkly and desolately, but the lake water was of the clearest, sunniest blue, and the shore was covered thickly in fresh green grass and flowers. Over the brow of a little rise beyond the lake, the mountains opened out into a great plain, and beyond it was water, half hidden in mist, and broken with many islands.

'This is the Lake of the Fairy Palace,' said Merlin, 'and beyond the lake, over the brow of the hill yonder, lies the plain of Camlann where the last battle shall be fought, and you shall fall beneath the stroke of the Evil Knight. And beyond the plain lies Avalon, hidden in the mist and the mysterious waters ... Go down now and speak with the Lady of the Lake, while I wait for you here.'

Leaving his horse with Merlin, Arthur went down the steep path to the side of the magic lake. Standing on the shore, he looked out across the quiet blue water – and there in the very centre of the Lake he saw an arm clothed in white samite with a hand holding above the surface a wondrous sword with a golden hilt set with jewels, and a jewelled scabbard and belt.

And then Arthur saw a beautiful damsel dressed in pale blue silk with a golden girdle, who walked across the water until she stood before him on the shore.

'I am the Lady of the Lake,' she said, 'and I am come to tell you that your sword Excalibur awaits you yonder. Do you wish to take the sword and wear it at your side ?'

'Damsel,' said Arthur, 'that is indeed my wish.'

'For long I have guarded the sword,' said the Lady of the Lake. 'Give me but a gift when I shall come to ask you for one, and the sword shall be yours.'

'By my faith,' answered Arthur, 'I swear to give you what-soever gift you shall ask for.'

'Enter into this boat, then,' said the Lady of the Lake. And Arthur saw a barge floating on the water before him, into which he stepped. The Lady of the Lake stood on the shore behind him, but the barge moved across the water as if unseen

The barge moved as if unseen hands drew it towards the sword

hands drew it by the keel, until Arthur came beside the arm
clothed in white samite. Leaning out, he took the sword and
the scabbard: and at once the arm and the hand which had
held it sank quietly out of sight beneath the blue waters.

Then the barge brought Arthur to the shore where the
Lady of the Lake had stood: but now she was gone also. He
tied the barge to a tree-root which curved over the waterside,
and strode joyfully up the steep path to the pass, buckling the
sword Excalibur to his side as he went.

Merlin awaited him with the horses, and together they rode
away into the forest, and back by many winding paths until
they drew near the river which lay between them and
Caerleon, and came to the straight, paved road leading to the
city.

'In a little while,' said Merlin, 'King Pellinore will come
riding towards us. For he has ceased to do battle with all who
pass through the forest, having seen a Questing Beast which
he must follow now for many years.'

'Then I will fight with him once more,' cried Arthur. 'Now

that I have so good a sword as Excalibur maybe I shall over-come and slay him!'

Merlin shook his head: 'Let him pass,' he said, 'for so I counsel you. He is a brave knight and a mighty, and in days to come he will do you good service, and he and his sons shall be among the bravest in your court.'

'I will do as you advise me,' said Arthur But he looked upon the sword Excalibur, and sighed.

'Which like you better, the sword or the scabbard?' asked Merlin.

'I like the sword!' cried Arthur.

'Then are you the more unwise,' said Merlin gravely. 'The scabbard is worth ten such swords: for while you wear that magic scabbard you shall lose but little blood, however sorely you are wounded. Keep well that scabbard, and have good care of it after I am gone from you, for a certain wicked lady who is nearly related to you shall seek to steal both sword and scabbard.'

They rode on, and in a little while met King Pellinore – who rode past as if he had not seen them.

'I marvel,' said Arthur, 'that he did not even speak to us!'

'He saw you not,' answered Merlin, 'for my magic was upon him. But had you striven to stay him in your pride, then he would have seen you well enough.'

Before long they came to Caerleon, and his knights welcomed Arthur joyfully. And when they heard of his adventures, they were surprised that he should thus have gone into danger alone. But all the bravest and noblest of them rejoiced exceedingly that they had such a king, one who would risk his life in an adventure as other ordinary knights did.

▰▰▰▰▰▰▰▰▰▰▰▰▰▰▰▰▰▰▰▰▰▰▰▰▰▰▰▰▰▰▰▰▰▰

Balyn and Balan

IN Caerleon King Arthur remained for many months, gathering his followers from all parts of the country, and preparing them for the great battles that were to come when they should go over all the island of Britain, and across the sea into Armorica, which we now call Brittany, to punish the cruel and wicked and drive out or bring to order the heathen Saxons.

And while he was still preparing for the war, King Ryon of North Wales, one of the proudest and cruellest of the enemies of Logres, sent a message to King Arthur. And this was the message: that Ryon had conquered eleven lesser kings and cut off their beards to make a border to his royal mantle; and he would spare King Arthur on condition that he sent his beard to make the twelfth on the mantle, as a token that Ryon should be his over-lord and his master. Otherwise, he would enter Arthur's lands to burn and slay, until he had by force not only Arthur's beard, but his head also.

'This is the most shameful and unrighteous message that ever I received,' said King Arthur to the messengers. 'Go back to Ryon the savage; tell him that I will come against him with all my knights and fight until *his* head is smitten off – unless he comes to do me homage. For I owe him none, who am by right king of all Britain, and by divine will the maker of the realm of Logres – in which realm there is no place for such a monster as this Ryon!'

The messengers went away, and before long news came that King Ryon was gathering together an army, and that bands of his wicked followers were already ravaging the lands of Arthur's true subjects, burning and slaying wherever they came.

But there were other powers of evil warring against Logres

– powers of magic harder to guard against and to overcome
than King Ryon or the Saxons.

As Arthur held court with his knights in the castle of
Caerleon, there came one day a damsel bearing a message to
him. And when she had delivered her message, she let the
cloak fall from her shoulders, and all could see that a great
sword was fastened to her side.

'Wherefore do you wear that sword, Lady?' asked Arthur.
'Such an instrument of war does not suit a fair damsel such
as you.'

'Now that you have asked me,' replied the damsel, 'I may
tell you. This sword I bear with me is a token of my sorrow.
I may not be free from it until I find a knight – a passing good
man in deed and thought, without wickedness or treachery
or evil thinking – who is able to draw it from the scabbard. I
have been to the Court of King Ryon, where I was told there
were good knights, but none might achieve the sword.'

'A great marvel indeed,' said Arthur. 'Yet not so strange
among the followers of Ryon. But now let one of my knights
set his hand to the hilt of it.'

Then a brave knight took hold of the sword and pulled
eagerly – but he could not draw it.

'There is no need to pull half so hard,' said the damsel.
'In the right man's hand it will come out at a touch. But he
must be a gentle knight, well-born and without evil in his
heart.'

One after another the knights tried to draw the sword, but
in turn each of them failed.

'Alas!' sobbed the damsel, 'I had thought that in the Court
of King Arthur I would have found one man true enough
knight to draw forth my sword!'

'By my faith,' said Arthur, half angered at her words, 'here
are knights as good as any in the world – but they are not
fated to help you, which troubles me sorely.'

But it happened that a young knight named Balyn, whom
no one thought much of, for he had lately been in prison for
killing a cousin of King Arthur's, came into the hall while all
this was going on.

K.A.K.   B

'Fair damsel,' he said presently, 'I pray you, of your kindness, let me try also to draw the sword. I am but a poor knight of Northumberland, but strong and passionate. And maybe these humble garments hide a better man than they seem.'

'You speak wisely,' said the damsel. 'Therefore try your fortune also.'

Then Balyn took the sword by the girdle and sheath, and drew it out easily. And when he looked upon the keen, shining blade, he loved it so much that it seemed worth more than the most precious thing in the world.

Many of the knights murmured, being jealous of Balyn, but the damsel said: 'Certainly this is a passing good knight, the best in all this land – and many great and wondrous deeds shall he do ... But now, kind and courteous sir, I beg you to give me back my sword.'

'Not so,' answered Balyn. 'With this sword I shall never part!'

'You are not wise to keep it,' said the damsel, 'for with it you shall slay the best friend that you have and the man you love best in the world. And that sword shall be your own destruction. ... It is a magic weapon which the Lady of the Isle of Avalon gave to me.'

'I will take my chances of what may come,' replied Balyn. 'But this sword I will not give up!'

Then the damsel made many lamentations, and departed from the Court in sorrow. And while Balyn stood to one side looking at his sword and rejoicing in it, and as the other knights crowded together talking of what had happened, the Lady of the Lake came suddenly into the hall and stood before King Arthur.

'Sire!' she cried. 'I hold you to your word! When I gave you your own sword you promised to grant me a gift.'

'That is true,' said Arthur. 'Therefore ask what you will, and you shall have it, if it is in my power to give.'

' Well,' said the Lady of the Lake, 'give me the head of this knight who but now drew the sword which the damsel brought. I had rather that you had cut off her head – but it is too late for that.'

'Truly,' answered King Arthur, troubled and surprised at her words, 'I cannot in honour grant you the life of either of them. Sir Balyn is my guest.'

'I will take nothing else!' cried the Lady of the Lake.

Now when Balyn heard this, a madness seemed to come over him: 'Evil woman,' he cried, 'you would have my head, would you? Rather, you shall now lose your own!' And there and then, in the presence of King Arthur, he sprang forward and cut off her head at a single stroke.

'Go from the realm of Logres for you are no true knight!'

'Alas, for shame!' said King Arthur, while all his knights murmured with reproach and disgust. 'Why have you done this? You have disgraced me and all my Court, for this damsel came to visit me, and was a lady of high worth. Therefore I will never forgive you for this deed.'

'Sire,' answered Balyn, 'be not displeased with me – for this lady was the falsest living, who had brought many brave men to their death, and women also.'

'Whatever the cause,' said Arthur, 'you have done a wicked and a shameful thing. Go now from my court, and from the realm of Logres, for you are no true knight unless you may redeem your honour by some brave deed or long penance.'

Balyn went with speed, mounted his horse, and rode out of Caerleon. Beyond the gate he commanded his squire to leave him:

'Go home to Northumberland,' he said, 'and tell them what has chanced. I myself shall ride in search of King Ryon and slay him, or die in the attempt: for if I slay Ryon, then surely King Arthur will be my friend again.'

But in King Arthur's court there was great wrath and uproar. And in the midst of it a proud knight of Ireland, Sir Launceor, who was jealous of Balyn for winning the sword, asked leave of King Arthur to ride after him and seek vengeance for the ill deed which had been done.

'Do your best,' said Arthur, 'for I am much angered with Balyn. I would that we might wipe out the shame that has fallen upon Logres by reason of that cowardly blow.'

Sir Launceor went from court with all the haste he might, and it was not long before he overtook Balyn.

But meanwhile Merlin came suddenly to the King and said:

'Evil has come into Logres and greater shall follow. The damsel who brought the sword has set the seeds of great and terrible things. That sword she had, by false means, from the Lady of the Isle of Avalon – and in that sword dwells a curse which must be borne to the end that in after days a blessing may come upon Logres by that sword in the hand of Galahad, truest knight of Logres. But alas for Balyn, for the curse is upon him who would have been of the bravest and best of your knights. He goes to his death, and naught can save him. ... Yet I will follow and see what good I may bring to him.'

While this was happening, Sir Launceor had come up with Balyn, who was riding up into the hills of Wales.

'Stay awhile!' he shouted as soon as he might be heard, 'or I will make you stay, whether you mean to or not! The shield you carry before you shall not help you – for I am after you!'

'Maybe you would have done better to stay at home,' said

Balyn, turning to meet him. 'Whence come you, and for what reason?'

'I am from the court of King Arthur,' answered Launceor. 'And I come to punish you for the evil stroke that you struck this day in his presence.'

'It grieves me much to have offended the best of kings,' said Balyn. 'But that damsel whom I slew was the wickedest in the world.'

'Make you ready, base knight!' was all that Launceor would reply. So the two of them fought there upon the hillside; and the end of it was that Balyn smote Sir Launceor through the body so that he fell to the ground dead.

Balyn stood beside him and was filled with sorrow at the death of a brave knight. But greater sorrow was to follow: for as he stood, a lovely maiden on a white horse came riding full speed up the hill. When she saw Launceor lie bleeding on the road, she cried aloud in great sorrow, and came and flung herself on the ground beside him.

'Ah, Balyn!' she sobbed. 'A sad stroke have you stricken! You have slain two bodies with one heart, and two hearts in one body, and two souls are lost by it!'

Then she took up Balyn's sword, which lay on the ground, and before he could stop her, flung herself upon the point of it and fell dead across the body of Sir Launceor whom she had loved better than life.

If Balyn was sad before, he was doubly sad now that he had caused the death of two such true lovers. And he would not be comforted, even when his brother Balan found him there – Balan whom he loved better than any in the world.

'Many sad things have indeed befallen you,' said Balan, 'but we must endure even the hardest adventures that God sends us.'

'That is so,' said Balyn. 'And now let us ride on, for I would find and slay the wicked Ryon of North Wales so that King Arthur may pardon me for the death of the Lady of the Lake.'

'I will come also,' said Balan, 'and put my body in adventure with you, as a brother ought to do.'

Deeper and deeper into the hills they went, through thick forests and by gloomy passes – and on a sudden they met Merlin, but Merlin disguised so that they did not recognize him.

'Whither do you ride?' asked Merlin.

'We do not tell our business to strangers,' said the two knights, Balyn adding: 'But tell us who you are that ask it.'

'At this time I will not tell you,' replied Merlin.

'That is an evil sign,' said Balyn. 'Surely you are no true man if you will not tell us your name.' And he put his hand to his sword.

'But I will tell you your name,' answered Merlin quietly. 'You are Balyn, the Knight of the Sword, and this is Balan your brother. And you go now to meet with King Ryon ... But your quest will be of little use unless you are advised by me.'

'Ah,' said Balyn, bowing reverently. 'You are Merlin! We will indeed be ruled by your wisdom.'

'Follow me,' said Merlin, 'and you shall do a knightly deed. ... But unknightly deeds have been done by the Knight of the Sword, yet good as well as evil shall come of them to Logres ... Sir Launceor lies dead, and with him his beloved, the Lady Columba: King Mark of Cornwall has found them, and will build a fair tomb above their bodies. And in days to come the greatest battle ever fought between two knights shall fall out just there – between Launcelot and Tristram, whom the land knows not yet – and King Mark shall find sorrow there also. But woe to you, Balyn, for you shall strike the Dolorous Stroke: yet for the healing of that stroke shall the Holy Grail come to Logres, and the good knight Sir Galahad shall achieve it: and thereafter shall the darkness fall once more upon Logres.'

These things which the good enchanter told to them filled Balyn and Balan with awe and wonder, and they rode on in silence until the fall of night.

'Dismount now,' said Merlin, 'unbridle your horses, leave them and follow me.'

In the midst of a dark wood they came to a little glade filled with soft moonlight.

'Abide hereby,' said Merlin, 'for at midnight King Ryon comes here secretly with but a few men to take by force the Lady of Vaunce who is to pass this way with two knights, in search of her lord.'

King Ryon came with twenty armed men, and Balyn and Balan attacked them with such fury that many were slain and the rest fled. But King Ryon turned to fight with Balyn, and after a great battle he fell wounded to the ground.

'Brave knights,' said Ryon, 'I pray you, slay me not. You may gain much by my life, but little by my death.'

'You speak truth,' said Balyn. 'You shall come yet living to King Arthur.'

'I will lead him to Caerleon,' said Merlin, 'for here you must abide till the great battle that is to be, when you shall do King Arthur good service.'

Merlin came to Caerleon as Arthur was about to march into North Wales. 'I bring you your worst enemy,' he said. 'But he was overcome and taken by two good knights whom you shall know at the great battle you go now to fight. It shall be before the walls of Castle Tarabil, and there you shall conquer twelve kings.'

King Arthur marched onward, and the twelve kings made ready for him. King Ryon was with them no longer, but Lot of Orkney had been persuaded by evil counsel to join them, which was a sad thing, for he was a brave man and a good and noble king, and the husband of Morgawse, Arthur's half-sister.

All through one long day the battle of Castle Tarabil was fought, and for long it seemed that Arthur must lose. But on a sudden two knights came riding out of the forest and entered the battle from behind, striking such blows and fighting so furiously, that the twelve kings thought that a new army was come against them, and broke and fled.

In the evening only King Lot remained alive of the twelve kings, and only his followers still fought on – for none could overcome King Lot. Then on a sudden came King Pellinore, following the Questing Beast across the world as his fate was, and he fought with Lot, and struck him such a mighty blow with his sword that Lot fell to the ground and died, and the hosts of Orkney fled into the darkness.

'You have won a great battle for Logres,' said Merlin, 'but the victory belongs to the Knight of the Sword and his brother, and to the Knight of the Questing Beast.'

'And who are these?' asked Arthur. 'King Pellinore I know, but not the others.'

'It is Balyn, who drew the damsel's sword,' said Merlin, 'and Balan his brother. Balyn you will meet once again, but Balan never. They shall die both on the same day, a sorrowful, unholy death. The tale of Balyn and Balan shall be the saddest of any, for he who drew that sword is the most unfortunate of all knights.'

'Alas,' said King Arthur, 'that is a pity indeed, for I owe him much gratitude for his deeds this day – and I have little deserved what he has done for me.'

After the battle Arthur marched on through the great forests which covered so much of Britain in those days, to make war against the Saxons in the north. And one day when they had pitched camp in the forest and King Arthur was resting in his pavilion in an open glade near by, he heard the sound of a horse's hooves, and looking out he saw a knight ride slowly by who sighed and lamented loudly as if some dreadful ill had befallen him.

'Stay a while, fair sir!' cried Arthur, 'and tell me wherefore you sorrow thus.'

'You can do nothing to help me,' said the knight, and he rode sadly on his way.

A little while later came Balyn, and knelt to King Arthur. 'Now by my head!' said the King, 'you are right welcome.'

'I may not abide,' said Balyn, 'for a sore curse is upon me and evil will come upon all those who are with me for long. But I pray you, my good lord king, give me some quest to follow, so that I may strive for the making of Logres before the evil overtakes me.'

'It grieves me that you cannot stay to follow me,' said King

Arthur. 'But Merlin has told me of your fate. And as for a quest – but now a knight rode by, crying and lamenting some great sorrow. Wherefore I desire you to follow him and bring him to me that we may help him if any help is to be found in man.'

Balyn rode on as fast as he could, and before long found the knight riding beside a damsel in the forest. 'Sir knight!' he cried, 'you must turn round and come back with me to King Arthur to tell him the cause of your sorrow!'

'That I will not,' said the knight, 'for it will harm me greatly and do me no good.'

'Sir,' said Balyn, 'I pray you, make ready to obey me, for otherwise I will fight with you, and bring you by force.'

'Will you promise me safe-conduct if I come?' said the knight. 'There is much evil abroad in this forest – yet from black enchantment I cannot fly.'

'Surely I will give you safety,' said Balyn, 'or else die for it!'

They rode back after this, the damsel waiting in the forest, until they came to the king's pavilion. But there, right in front of it, in the very presence of King Arthur, there came one invisible and smote the knight who rode with Balyn through the body with a spear.

'Alas!' said the knight, 'even under your safe-conduct am I slain. That was the false knight Garlon who, by black magic, rides invisible. The evil has come upon me as I feared it would. But mount now my horse, which is faster than your own, and ride back to the damsel in the forest and follow the quest that I was on as she will lead you, till you have avenged my death.'

Then the knight fell dead to the ground, and in great sorrow Balyn mounted his horse and rode to the damsel, whom he told of all that had happened.

Together they rode on towards the Castle of Meliot, but before they reached it they overtook another knight who was returning from hunting. They rode with him on his way, but in a little came Garlon the invisible knight and smote him as well, so that he fell down and died.

'For this also shall I do vengeance upon Garlon the coward and traitor,' said Balyn; and they came to the gateway of Castle Meliot. Balyn strode first over the drawbridge into the castle, with the damsel behind him: but as soon as he had passed under the gateway, the portcullis was let down, so that there was a grating of iron and wood between him and the damsel.

Then many men ran together and took the damsel, and it seemed to Balyn that they were about to kill her. He could not break through the portcullis, but instead he ran up the nearest stairway and jumped twenty feet from a window into the dry moat, and fell upon the men with drawn sword.

'Fair knight,' said the leader of them, 'we will not fight with you, nor would we do harm to you or to the damsel. But the lady of this castle has lain sick this many a year, and the custom of the land is that all damsels who pass this way must seek to heal her, which may be done with the blood of a pure maid of noble birth – and the maid shall not suffer therefrom.'

'Well,' said Balyn, 'if the damsel wills it, you may take blood from her: but do her no harm, for I would not for my life that any ill should befall her.'

Then they came within the castle, and the damsel gave of her blood in a silver dish: but it did not heal the lady, for only the sister of the pure knight Sir Percivale could do that when, in days to come, she and her brother should pass that way in quest of the Holy Grail.

After this, the Knight of Meliot, who was lord of the castle, made Balyn and the damsel welcome to a good feast and comfortable lodgings. But as they sat at supper, Balyn heard in the next room the sound of a man groaning as if in great pain.

'What is that noise?' he asked.

'But a little while ago,' said the Knight of Meliot, 'I jousted at Castle Carbonek, and twice I smote down a knight of King Pelles' following. Then this villain knight swore to be revenged by hurting the one I loved best; and the next day he rode invisible and smote my son, who may not now be healed of his grievous wound until I have that knight's blood – whose name even I know not.'

'Ah,' said Balyn, 'that knight is Garlon, who has slain two knights in like manner: indeed I am now in quest of him that I may slay him to avenge the wrong he has done to this damsel.'

'I will tell you how to find him!' cried the Knight of Meliot. 'King Pelles will shortly hold a great feast in Castle Carbonek to which any knight may come, but each must bring with him his chosen damsel. And there you shall find this Garlon – your enemy and mine.'

The very next morning they set out, and in fifteen days came to Castle Carbonek and were welcomed to the feast. But the Knight of Meliot was made to remain outside, since he had brought no lady with him.

Balyn was led to a fair chamber where he was unarmed and clothed in rich robes. Now his sword was taken from him, for the custom was that no man might come armed to the feast: but Balyn hid his own long dagger beneath his robe, and so came down with his damsel into the great hall where the other knights and ladies were gathered.

Presently Balyn asked: 'Is there not a knight in this court whose name is Garlon?'

'Over there you may see him,' he was told, 'the knight with the cruel, dark face. But indeed he is the most marvellous man now living, for he can ride invisible and slay whomsoever he will.'

'Indeed,' said Balyn, 'so that is Garlon.' And then he thought to himself: 'If I kill him here where all these knights and ladies may see, I shall not escape with my life; but if I leave him now, I may never find him again – and he will do much harm if he lives.'

Now as he sat looking at him and wondering what to do, Garlon saw him, and coming over, struck him in the face, saying: 'Knight, why do you stare at me like this? For shame! Eat your meat, and do what you came for!'

'It were shame indeed not to avenge this insult – and all the other ill deeds which you have done,' cried Balyn springing up. 'And as to what I came for – it was to do this!' And as he spoke, he drew his dagger and stabbed Garlon to the heart, so that he fell down dead.

Then there was a great commotion in the hall. 'Sir, where-fore have you slain Garlon who was my guest?' cried King Pelles. 'For this evil deed, surely you shall be slain before you depart from the Castle of Carbonek!'

'Well,' cried Balyn, 'come and kill me if you dare!'

'Yes,' said King Pelles, 'no man shall do it but I, for Garlon was my knight.' And as he said this, King Pelles snatched a great sword from the wall and struck fiercely at Balyn, who guarded the blow from his head with the long dagger. But so mighty a stroke had King Pelles stricken, that Balyn's dagger flew into small pieces.

Balyn ran seeking for a sword

When Balyn found that he was weaponless, he turned and ran, seeking for a sword or a spear with which to fight; and King Pelles followed him, still in a great rage.

Away went Balyn out of the hall with King Pelles behind him, along stone passages, up dark spiral staircases, and through room after room of that great, mysterious castle. And at last he came to a great tower far away from the part where anyone lived, or had lived for many centuries: and still up and up the tower he went, until, near the top, he paused at a closed door, and a great feeling of awe and fear began to creep over him. But he heard King Pelles clattering up the stone steps behind him, so he pushed open the door and sprang into the room.

As Balyn stepped across the threshold a Voice said to him: 'Enter not into this room, for you are unworthy!' But there was no one in the room.

Balyn looked about him, and saw a table made of silver standing in an alcove under an archway of the most beautiful carved marble; the table was spread with a fair white cloth which showed no sign of dust or age, and on it stood a great cup under a silken cloth – and it seemed to Balyn that the cup was filled with light, so that he could hardly bear to look at it.

He was trembling now, he did not know why, and he seemed to wish nothing so much as to kneel before that table and the cup upon it and pray for the blessing of God. But he saw above the table a strange spear which hung point downwards with nothing to support it: and once more he heard King Pelles behind him, stumbling over the threshold of the room.

Then Balyn leapt forward to seize the spear: 'Sinner, touch it not!' cried the Voice again. But he did not heed it, for now he seemed to wish for nothing but to turn and slay King Pelles.

King Pelles stood in the doorway, and he had dropped his weapon and all the hate had gone from him. But Balyn, in his madness, took the spear and struck the Dolorous Stroke, wounding King Pelles deeply in the side.

Then the Castle of Carbonek shook and rocked: all became dark, and a great wind seemed to seize Balyn and whirl him about and cast him bleeding and senseless on the ground, while a terrible cry of woe rang in his ears and went echoing away across the distance.

Three days Balyn lay senseless among the ruins which alone remained of much of the castle; and on the fourth Merlin came, and drew him out, and set him upon a horse.

'Sir, I would have my damsel,' said Balyn feebly, as he came to himself again.

'See,' answered Merlin, 'where she lies dead, and many

another with her. You have struck the Dolorous Stroke and laid waste three counties. For the cup you saw was the Holy Grail wherefrom our blessed Lord Jesus Christ drank the wine at the Last Supper; and the spear which you laid impious hands upon, once pierced His side as He hung upon the Cross for all our sins. Now Pelles the maimed king lies wounded with a wound unhealable in the hall of Castle Carbonek, until Galahad the pure knight shall come to cure him after many years ... Joseph of Arimathea, in whose tomb Our Lord was laid ere He rose again, brought them to Britain and died yonder in Castle Carbonek. The spear has accomplished the evil that must fall upon Logres, but the Grail awaits the truest holiness and purity wherewith Logres shall be blessed for a little while before the end ... But ride on now, for your fate calls you ... And my own fate draws near also.'

Sad at heart, Balyn rode forward through the Waste Lands, and as he passed the people cried to him: 'Ah, Balyn, you have brought great sorrow upon this country: doubt not but that vengeance shall fall upon you!'

At last he came out of those desolate fields and villages into the deep forests, and rode through them eight days until he came to a castle set on the bank of a fair, broad river. And as he came out of the forest, he heard a hunting-horn blow the *mort* – which is the call blown ever at the death of a deer.

'That blast,' said Balyn, 'is blown for me; for I am the prize, and yet I am not dead.'

A long bridge led across the river to the castle; and as Balyn drew near, a great company came riding across it to meet him: a hundred maidens singing more sweetly than the plaintive nightingale, and a hundred knights richly dressed riding gravely behind them.

The Lady of the Castle came to Balyn and said:

'Sir Knight, welcome are you to my castle: here you may rest in peace after your toils and sorrows. But first, for so the custom is, you must fight with the Knight of the River, for he is our champion who dwells upon the island in midstream, and all who enter the castle must pass him.'

'It is a bad custom,' said Balyn, 'that a knight may not pass this way without doing battle with a stranger.'

'You need but this one battle,' said the Lady.

'Well,' answered Balyn, 'since I must fight, I am ready now. My horse is still fresh, though my heart is weary and I long to sleep.'

'Noble Sir,' said a knight to Balyn, 'I think that your shield is too small for such a battle: use mine, I beg you.'

Balyn thanked the knight, took his shield and rode down towards the river, looking to his armour as he went to see that he was well prepared for the fight.

As he came to the ford of the river, a damsel leant over the side of the bridge nearby and said:

'Oh! knight Balyn, why have you left your own shield? Alas, you have put yourself in greater danger yet, for by the painting on your shield you would have been known. Alas, of all knights surely you are the most unfortunate!'

'I am sorry that ever I came within this country,' said Balyn, 'but I may not turn back now, or all would think that I was afraid.'

He came to the island, and there was a knight in black armour waiting for him, with vizor closed and no coat-of-arms upon his shield.

In silence they set their spears in rest, and rode at one another so hard that their spears were shattered and each flung from his horse so hard that they lay insensible for a few minutes. But soon they were on their feet again and fighting fiercely with their swords. First Balyn smote the Black Knight with his unhappy sword, so that the blood ran down to the ground; and then he was himself smitten until he fell.

As he rose to fight on, Balyn saw that the bridge and the castle walls were crowded with fair knights and sweet ladies who watched there in silence while the battle was fought. To it again they went, striking great strokes that might each have killed a weaker man: on and on until much of their armour was smitten away, and each was wounded with seven cruel wounds from which the life-blood ran down on to the grass.

And at last the Black Knight sank to the ground, unable longer to stand on his feet. Balyn stood leaning on his sword, but without it he too would have fallen.

'What knight are you?' he asked hoarsely. 'For never till this day did I meet with one so brave, except only my brother.'

'My name,' said the Black Knight, 'is Balan, brother to the good knight Balyn!'

'Alas that ever I should have lived to see this day!' cried Balyn, and he fell to the ground in a swoon for loss of blood and in horror of what had chanced. Very slowly and painfully, crawling on his hands and knees, Balan drew near to Balyn, unlaced his helmet and looked upon his face. And Balyn awoke and cried:

'Oh Balan, my brother whom I love better than any man in the world, you have slain me, and I have slain you also – and men shall speak in sorrow of our deaths for evermore!'

'Alas that ever this should be!' sobbed Balan. 'Had you but carried your own shield, I would have known you by the arms upon it! And had I not overcome and slain the knight who kept this island in past times, I would not now have been its keeper armed all in black.'

Then the Lady of the Castle and her followers came to them, and Balan said: 'Lady, the same mother bore us who now die in the same hour, slain each by the other unknowing whom we struck. Bury us, I pray you, in the same tomb, and write upon it that here lie two brothers who slew one another by mischance, so that all who pass by may pray for our souls.'

Then Balan died, and Balyn a little later, and the Lady of the Castle caused their tomb to be made there upon the island in the river. And she set Balan's name upon the tomb, but his brother's she did not know.

When this was done, Merlin came suddenly to the place, and bade them write the name of Balyn, and that he was the unhappy knight who struck the Dolorous Stroke. Then he took the unlucky sword which had been broken in the fight, and set a new blade in the hilt, and laughed softly as he did so.

'Why do you laugh?' asked the Lady of the Castle.

'For this cause,' said Merlin. 'No man shall handle this sword now, save only Launcelot, and Galahad his son. And that shall be when the knights of Logres seek for the Holy Grail ... In the castle, also, you have a bed: but none shall lie in it without going mad, save Launcelot alone ... But in the end Launcelot shall use this sword, and the bravest knight of Logres, the man he best loves in the world, shall fall beneath it. And that shall be Gawain ... But soon thereafter shall come the last battle on the Plain of Camlann, and the darkness shall fall once more upon Logres.'

Merlin left the scabbard of Balyn's sword in the castle, where Galahad should find it. But the sword with the new blade he set with its point in a great stone which floated by magic upon the water: and no one knew whither it went until on the day appointed it should come to Camelot.

When all these things were done, Merlin came to King Arthur and told him of the Dolorous Stroke that Balyn had given King Pelles; and of how Balyn and Balan had fought and died upon the island in the river.

'Alas!' said King Arthur. 'This is the greatest pity that ever I heard tell of two knights. And two such knights as these I have as yet never known in Logres.'

3

The First Quest of the
Round Table

WHEN King Arthur had conquered Ryon of North
Wales and the other rebel kings, he marched to the
north and to the east with his knights, and defeated the
Saxons in six great battles. And the Saxons throughout the
whole of Britain, and in Scotland also, fled away in their ships,
or else swore to be King Arthur's loyal subjects. They could
not stand against him any more, for they never knew where
he was, nor when he and his knights would ride suddenly out
of the forest and attack them – just when they had certain
news that he was resting after a battle hundreds of miles
away.

In this way peace came to the whole island for a great many
years: though still there were robbers and outlaws, cruel
knights and evil magicians dwelling in the depths of forests
and deep among the mountains, ever ready to break the peace
and stain the realm of Logres in one wicked way or another.

King Arthur marched south through a land of peace, and
made his capital in the town of Camelot, which now we call
Winchester, and the best and bravest of his knights gathered
there about him.

But on the way he passed through Camelerde where dwelt
his friend King Leodegraunce, who had a beautiful daughter
called Guinevere; and Arthur loved Guinevere the moment
he saw her, and for thinking of her he could hardly rest or eat
when he came home to Camelot.

'The land is at peace,' he said to Merlin, 'and my wars are
ended for a little while. Is it not right that I should marry?'

'It is right indeed,' answered Merlin. 'A man of your

bounty and nobleness should not be without a wife, nor should the realm of Logres lack a queen ... But tell me now, is there any princess whom you love more than another?'

'Yes, indeed there is,' said Arthur. 'I love Guinevere, King Leodegraunce's daughter. And she is the fairest, sweetest, loveliest, and purest maiden in all the world. Her will I wed, or die a bachelor!'

'Certainly she is among the fairest,' said Merlin. 'Yet I would that you loved another; for by her very beauty shall come the end of Logres – when the best knight of your court shall love her, bringing shame upon her and upon himself; bringing war between you and him; bringing in the day when the traitor of Camlann shall triumph, not long after the coming of the Holy Grail, which shall be a sign that the glory of Logres is at hand, and its passing also ... Yet Guinevere is the fairest lady in all the world – and when a man's heart is set upon such a damsel as yours is upon her, he will not be turned.'

'There you speak truth,' said Arthur. 'For Guinevere I will have to be my Queen.' Merlin went to King Leodegraunce and told him of Arthur's love.

'To me,' said King Leodegraunce, 'this is the best news I have ever heard, that so noble and worthy a king should love my daughter. Now all my lands shall be King Arthur's, and all my followers his knights. At the Feast of Pentecost we shall bring Guinevere to him, and that day shall be the wedding.'

Meanwhile at Camelot King Arthur held a feast at Easter: but before the knights of his court would be seated at the long table in the hall, a great strife broke out between them as to where they should sit – for they counted it a greater honour to be near the head of the table than near the foot.

'We shall amend this at Pentecost,' said Merlin when he heard of the quarrel. 'On that day I will set a table here in the hall which shall be the centre of the glory of Logres, a table whose fame shall live while the world endures.'

The Feast of Pentecost drew near, and many knights gathered together, and some young men also who wished to become knights, among whom were Gawain, King Arthur's nephew, and Tor the son of King Pellinore. And these King Arthur knighted on his wedding morning, and decreed that these, his newest knights, must do some great deed to show their worth – the first quest that should be brought before him.

The wedding was a very splendid ceremony indeed, with two Archbishops to join their hands and four kings to bear golden swords in front of them as Arthur and Guinevere marched out of the abbey where the people were waiting to cheer them.

They came at last to the banqueting hall, and there Merlin awaited them, standing before a great round table of stone and wood which filled it almost from side to side.

'Hail, King and Queen of Logres!' cried Merlin. 'Your places wait you at the table, and seats also for one hundred and fifty knights – the Knights of the Round Table. Upon every siege – for so the seats at this table are called – you shall find in letters of gold the name of the knight whose place it is. And when a knight is slain in battle or dies, when you have made a new knight, his name shall appear in the siege. But the name of the dead man shall fade when the man dies. Yet the names of the Knights of the Round Table shall live for ever. Sit down all of you, for at a round table no man may complain that he is set at the lowest end, or that another is placed above him. ... But of the high honour of the Table you shall hear before long.'

'There are four places still empty,' said Arthur, when all his knights had found each their siege.

'Doubt it not,' said Merlin, 'for so shall the greater honour be to Logres. King Pellinore comes this day to rest him from the pursuit of the Questing Beast, and one place is for him. Behold how his name grows in letters of gold upon the siege! And for the three remaining, read now the names of Sir Launcelot of the Lake and Sir Percivale of Wales upon two of them. Launcelot shall be with you at the next feast of Pentecost: Sir Percivale is not yet born, but the bravest knight now sitting here shall be his father; but when Percivale

Round the table ran a white hart

comes, you will know that but one year waits before the coming of the Holy Grail to Camelot. As for the last place, that is the Siege Perilous, and it is death for any man to sit therein, save he for whom it is made – the best knight of all. And he shall come at the time appointed.'

Then Merlin went to the door and led in King Pellinore, who knelt to King Arthur and was made a knight before taking his place at the Round Table. Gawain sat upon one side of the three empty sieges, and Merlin led Pellinore to the other side, saying:

'This is your place, for you are more worthy to sit there than is any other now present. Howbeit, on a day to come Sir Tristram shall sit there.'

Then the great banquet began: but before it was ended Merlin stood up in the midst of the feasters, and all were silent as he spoke.

'To-day,' said Merlin, 'is the day of the first Quest. Many strange adventures in the years to come shall begin as you sit at meat here about the Round Table: but I shall not be here to see them ... But now be still, for you shall see a strange and marvellous thing.'

As they sat, waiting in silence, a white hart came running into the hall, and behind it a white brachet or small hunting dog, and behind them a pack of sixty great black hounds baying loudly. Round the table ran the white hart, and as it drew near the door again, the brachet came up behind and snapped fiercely at its flank, so that it gave a great leap to one side, knocking over a knight called Sir Abelleus who sat eating at a small table. At once this knight seized the brachet and strode quickly out of the hall, where he took his horse and rode away still carrying it. The black hounds went away into the forest after the white hart; but before the bell of their baying had died away in the distance, there came riding into the hall a damsel on a white palfrey, and cried aloud to King Arthur, saying:

'My lord King, suffer me not to be robbed in this way; for the brachet is mine which yonder knight has taken with him!'

'But this is no affair of ours!' said King Arthur, who feared very much that he himself might be called upon to ride after Sir Abelleus, then and there on his wedding day.

Hardly had he spoken when a stranger knight, fully armed and riding a great horse, came into the hall and by force led the damsel away with him, however loudly she cried and complained.

Arthur was glad when she had gone, for she had made such a noise. But Merlin rebuked him:

'You may not let this pass so lightly,' he said. 'Such an adventure must be followed to the end – else it were shame to Logres, and to you and your knights.'

'I will do as you advise me,' said King Arthur.

'Then send Sir Gawain to bring back the white hart,' directed Merlin. 'And Sir Tor to bring the brachet and the knight, if the knight be not slain by him. And let King Pellinore bring the damsel, and the knight, living or dead, who forced her away. For these three knights shall have marvellous adventures ere they come again. And when they return, I will have more to tell you concerning the Round Table. But after that, I must go from you, for the damsel is the Lady Nimue, who calls me to my long sleep. ...'

The three new knights, on receiving each their orders as to their quest, armed and mounted and rode away into the forest.

Sir Gawain took with him his young brother Gaheris to be his squire, and before they had gone far, they found two knights on horseback fighting fiercely with their swords.

'Stay!' cried Gawain, riding between them. 'For what cause are you fighting?'

'Sir,' answered one of the knights, 'a white hart came by not long ago, with a cry of black hounds close behind it. Now we knew, my brother and I, that this was an adventure made for the high feast of King Arthur's wedding, and each of us desired greatly to follow the Quest of the White Hart. Then we fell to quarrelling as to which of us was the better knight, and of that quarrel grew many blows. . . .'

'Shame be upon you, brothers and knights, thus to fight!' cried Gawain. 'Go now and render yourselves prisoners to King Arthur.'

'And if we do not?' said the younger knight.

'Why then, I will fight you until you do, or lie dead!' cried Gawain.

'We will go straightway to King Arthur,' they said, 'and tell him that the knight who follows the Quest of the White Hart has sent us!' Then they bowed to him and departed towards Camelot: but Sir Gawain went forward on his Quest.

Deep into the forest he went, with Gaheris riding close behind him; and before long they could hear the bell of the black hounds in front of them, and knew that they were going in the right direction.

Presently they came out of the forest, on to the banks of a wide river, and saw the white hart swimming across it, with the hounds still following. And as Sir Gawain would have ridden into the water, a knight rode up on the further side and shouted:

'You there! Come not over after the white hart, unless you want to fight with me!'

'I do not fear to do that,' answered Gawain. 'Fight I will, rather than turn aside from my quest!'

He splashed across the river, and on the further side they drew apart and came together in so mad a rush that Gawain smote the knight over his horse's tail.

'Yield you now!' cried Gawain.

'Not I!' answered the knight, struggling to his feet. 'I am Sir Allardyne of the Outer Isles, and never will I yield with life to a raw young knight like you.'

So Gawain leapt down from his horse, and to it they went with their swords, striking mighty blows. But in a little while Gawain smote Allardyne of the Outer Isles such a slash across the head that his helmet split in half, and his head also – and that was the end of him.

'Ah,' said Gaheris proudly. 'That was indeed a mighty stroke for so young a knight.'

After the white hart they went, following six of the black hounds which still were hot on its trail. And at length they came into a great castle, and in the courtyard the hounds overtook and slew the white hart. Then the Lord of the Castle, a mighty man with an evil face, came out of his chamber, roaring with rage, and began slashing at the hounds with his sword, crying:

'Alas for the white hart that I gave to my lady and I kept so badly! A cruel death shall they die who have killed you!'

'Cease from this!' cried Gawain, angrily. 'Satisfy your anger upon me rather than upon dumb beasts – for the hounds did only what their nature prompted.'

'You speak the truth!' yelled the Lord of the Castle. 'I have killed your curs – now only the cur their master remains to slay!'

Then he and Gawain set to fiercely with their swords, the Lord of the Castle striking many cowardly strokes which angered Gawain sorely. But at last, after several wounds given on either side, Gawain struck so hard that the other came clattering down at his feet, crying for mercy and calling Gawain a sweet, gentle knight instead of the unpleasant names he had used a little while before.

'You shall die!' cried Gawain, mad with rage, and he whirled round his sword and struck at the Lord of the Castle, meaning to cut off his head. But at that moment the Lady of the Castle, who had been watching the battle, ran out and flung herself upon her husband's body. And her neck came in the way of Gawain's whirling sword, so that before he could stop he had smitten off her head instead of his enemy's.

Then Gawain was filled with horror and shame for what he had done, and he let the Lord of the Castle rise unhurt, and said that he would spare his life.

'I would not mind if you killed me now,' he said, 'for you have slain my lady love whom I loved better than anything in the world.'

'What is your name?' asked Gawain.

'I am Sir Blamoure of the Marsh' was the answer.

'Then go you to King Arthur's court: tell him truly all that has happened. Say that the Knight of the White Hart sent you.'

Sir Blamoure mounted his horse and rode away; but Gawain went sadly into the castle with Gaheris.

'I am a shamed knight,' he said, 'for I have slain a lady. Had I been merciful to Sir Blamoure, this would not have happened!'

'We are in danger here,' said Gaheris. And even as he spoke four armed knights came striding into the hall and attacked Gawain fiercely. 'You, a new-made knight,' they cried, 'have shamed your knighthood! A knight without mercy is dishonoured: but to kill a fair lady is shame unto the world's end! Doubt not that you shall have great need of mercy before you depart from us!' Then they made at Gawain so fiercely that in the end they wounded him sorely, and took him and Gaheris prisoner.

They would have been slain there and then, had not four fair ladies come and begged for their lives.

'Now what cheer, sir knight?' one of the ladies asked Gawain.

'Not good!' he answered.

'Why so? The fault is your own, for you did a passing foul deed in slaying this lady ... But tell me, are you not of King Arthur's court?'

'Yes, truly. I am Sir Gawain, son of King Lot of Orkney, and my mother is Morgawse the sister of King Arthur.'

'Get you back in peace to the court,' said the ladies, 'but

we lay this penance upon you, that you bear the body of the
lady whom you slew, and her head also: tell King Arthur all
that has come to pass, and give her honourable burial.'

So Gawain and Gaheris rode sadly back towards Camelot.

But meanwhile Sir Tor had ridden another way after the
knight who stole the brachet. And he had not gone far before
he met suddenly with a dwarf who struck his horse such a
blow on the head with his staff that the poor beast went
staggering back a spear's length.

'Why do you strike my horse?' asked Sir Tor angrily.

'Because you shall not pass this way unless you joust with
the knights in yonder pavilions!' answered the dwarf.

Then Sir Tor perceived that by the roadside stood two
pavilions, with a great shield hanging on a tree beside each of
them, and a great spear leaning beside each shield.

'I may not tarry for jousting,' said Sir Tor, 'for I am upon
a quest which I must not delay in following.'

'Nevertheless, you shall not pass!' cried the dwarf; and
seizing a great horn, he blew it loudly.

At once a knight strode out of the nearest pavilion, took
his shield, vaulted upon his horse, caught up his spear, and
came thundering down upon Sir Tor, who had scarcely time
to set his own spear in rest and spur forward to meet him.
Nevertheless, he rode so well that he caught the stranger
knight fairly in the centre of the shield and sent him flying
over his horse's tail. And in the same way he smote the
second knight, laying him flat on the ground beside his
companion.

'Now,' said Sir Tor, looking down at them both, 'Get you
both up and go to the court of King Arthur, and say that I
sent you – the Knight in Quest of the Brachet. Otherwise, I
will slay you where you lie!'

Both of them swore to obey him, and Sir Tor was turning
to ride on his way, when the dwarf came up to him. 'Sir,' he
said, 'grant me a boon, I beg!'

'I will indeed,' answered Sir Tor. 'What is it that you wish
for?'

'I ask only that you will let me be your servant,' said the

dwarf. 'Let me follow you now – for I will no longer serve these cowardly knights!'

'You are welcome,' said Sir Tor. 'Take now a horse, and come with me.'

'You ride after the knight with the white brachet, do you not?' said the dwarf. 'I shall bring you to where he is!'

Through the forest they went, and came before long to where two silken pavilions stood beside a priory, with a white shield hanging outside one of them, and a red shield outside the other.

Then Sir Tor dismounted, and while the dwarf held his horse and spear, he went to the white pavilion and looked inside. And there he saw three damsels lying asleep on rich couches. Without waking them, he went to the other pavilion, where he found but one damsel lay sleeping – but by her side was the white brachet, and when it saw him it barked so loudly that the lady woke.

Sir Tor picked up the brachet, which had come running at him, and handed it to the dwarf.

But a moment later the lady came out of her pavilion, with the three damsels who had been wakened by the noise, and she said to him:

'Knight, why do you take my brachet from me?'

'I must,' answered Sir Tor, 'for I have come in quest of it from King Arthur's court.'

'You shall not go far without suffering for this unkind deed,' said the lady.

'I shall bear quietly whatever adventure may befall me,' said Sir Tor, and turning, he rode back the way he had come.

They had not gone far on the road to Camelot, however, when they heard the sound of hooves behind them, and the voice of Sir Abelleus, the knight who had first taken the brachet, shouting:

'Knight! Wait awhile, and give me back the brachet which you have stolen from my lady!'

Sir Tor turned at this, and set his spear in rest. Then Sir Abelleus did likewise, and they rode together with a great crash which flung them both from their horses. Then they drew their swords and fell to the battle, striking great strokes until the armour flew from them in fragments like the splinters beneath a woodman's axe. At last Sir Tor struck Sir Abelleus to the earth.

'Yield now!' he cried.

'Never!' gasped Abelleus. 'Never while I live, unless you give me back the brachet.'

'That will I not,' said Sir Tor, 'for it was my quest to bring it back to King Arthur, and to send you thither as a vanquished knight.'

At that moment a damsel on a palfrey came riding up as hard as ever she could.

'Sir knight! Sir knight!' she cried to Sir Tor. 'For the love of King Arthur and the glory of his court, give me the gift that I shall ask you! As you are a gentleman, grant me that which I shall ask!'

Now when Sir Abelleus saw the damsel, he started to tremble; and very slowly he rolled over and began to crawl away.

'Well,' said Sir Tor, 'ask a gift, fair damsel, and I will give it you.'

'I thank you,' she answered. 'And now I shall ask you for the head of this false knight Abelleus, for he is the most outrageous knight living, and the wickedest murderer.'

'Now I repent me of my promise,' said Sir Tor. 'Cannot he make amends for any wrong that he has done you?'

'Not possibly,' said the damsel, 'for he slew my own brother before mine eyes, and would not spare him, though I knelt half an hour in the mud begging him for mercy. So strike off his head quickly, I beg of you – or else I shall shame you as a false knight at the court of King Arthur.'

Sir Abelleus heard all this, and now he stood a little way off and begged Sir Tor to spare his life.

'I may not now,' said Sir Tor, 'or I should be false to my promise. Moreover, I offered you mercy a little while ago, and you would not yield.'

Then Abelleus turned and ran, but Sir Tor overtook him quite soon, and smote off his head at a single blow.

'Now sir,' said the damsel, 'come and rest a little while at my manor which is near by.'

So Sir Tor went with her, and was entertained well by the good old knight her husband, who thanked him for having avenged the murder, and told him that he would ever find a welcome with him and his wife.

Then Sir Tor rode towards Camelot in the cool of the evening, the dwarf carrying the brachet behind him; and before long he found his father, King Pellinore, weeping over a dead knight and lady beside a well.

'Alas, my father,' said Sir Tor, 'what sorrow has befallen you here?'

'This shame is mine,' said King Pellinore; 'when I rode out from Camelot to bring back the Lady Nimue, I was so eager in my quest that I would not stay for any. As I came past the well, this lady called to me: "Help me, knight, help me for Christ's sake!" But I would not stay. And now she has slain herself, for grief as I perceive, for this knight who has died of his grievous wounds.'

Then the Lady Nimue came from the edge of the forest and asked King Pellinore the cause of his sorrow.

'Now do as I advise,' she said, when he had told her. 'Take up these bodies and bear them with you to Camelot that they may have honourable burial.'

'How did you fare in your quest?' asked Sir Tor when he had told his father of the quest of the brachet.

'It was not hard,' answered King Pellinore. 'When I had ridden some way through the forest, I came upon the Lady Nimue held by two squires.

'"Fair lady", said I, "you must come with me to King Arthur."

'"That would I gladly," she answered.

'"You may not have her," said the squires, "until you have spoken words with the two knights who fight for her yonder."

'Turning, I saw two knights battling furiously with swords, until all the grass of the glade was trampled and bloody. Riding to them, I asked why they were fighting.

'"For this lady!" they said. "And you shall not have her!"
Then, without more ado, they both turned and attacked me.
And before I had time to dismount, one of them leapt forward and killed my horse, laughing: "Now you are on foot as
well as we are!"

'"Guard yourself!" I cried in a great rage, "for I will give
to you such a buffet for slaying my horse –" Then I struck –
and split his helmet, and his head to the chin at one blow!

'But the other knight did not try to fight with me. "I am
Sir Meliot of Logure," he said, "and I did but strive to save
the Lady Nimue from this man whom you have slain. Take
now his horse, since he has slain yours, and ride with my
cousin the Lady Nimue to King Arthur's court. And one day
you will see me there also." Then we rode back slowly – and
met you beside the well.'

A little nearer to Camelot they overtook Sir Gawain, riding
sadly with the lady's body across the saddle before him. And
together they came through the streets in the soft evening
light and into the great hall of the castle where Arthur and his
knights were sitting at supper about the Round Table.

Then, before they could sit down in their places, each of
them was bidden to tell of their adventures on the quest
which had been set him.

'Ah, King Pellinore,' said Queen Guinevere, 'you were
greatly to blame that you saved not the lady's life beside the
well.'

'Alas,' said Pellinore. 'I was so fierce on my quest that
nothing could stop me – but I shall blame myself all the days
of my life.'

'Well may you,' said Merlin gravely, 'for the lady was your
own daughter Alyne whom you have sought these many years,
and her husband was the good knight Sir Miles of Llandys.'

'Your son, Sir Tor, has done well,' said Arthur gently,
striving to sooth King Pellinore in his grief. 'Right gladly do
I welcome him to his place at my Table, and sit you also – for
you will not again ride past those who beg you for help. But
what of my nephew Gawain? Why does he look so full of
sorrow, and carry the headless body of a damsel?'

'I slew her,' said Gawain sadly, and he told all the tale of his adventures, hiding nothing. 'This has come upon me as a punishment for that I would not show mercy to the vile knight whom I meant to slay,' he ended. 'Hereafter I swear always to be merciful, and to spare all those who ask for mercy. Moreover I set this penance before myself: Ever in especial to fight for all damsels and all ladies who seek my aid, and to be their knight in all humbleness and honour.'

'Well have you all learnt,' said Merlin gently. 'And Sir Gawain has suffered the cruellest lesson, even as he shall be in days to come the noblest, the bravest and the most merciful of knights.

'But, behold now, on this the first day of the Round Table, I lay upon you all the Order of Chivalry. All of you, and those who shall sit afterwards at this Table, are the Knights of Logres, and for the glory of Logres the Realm of Righteousness, do not ever depart from the high virtues of this realm. Do no outrage nor murder nor any cruel or wicked thing; fly from treason and all untruthfulness and dishonest dealing; give mercy unto those that seek it – or sit no more at this Table. And always give all the help in your power to ladies and damsels, go out to succour gentlewomen and widows, turn from all else to right any wrong done to any woman in the world – and never, on pain of death and eternal disgrace, do you any ill thing to a woman, or suffer it to be done. Nor, for love or gain, fight in any quarrel that is not just and righteous.'

'To these things you shall swear upon the Blessed Sacrament,' said King Arthur. 'And every year, upon the feast of Pentecost, see that you all come hither to Camelot to swear that oath anew. Then shall we take our places all together at the Round Table. But I swear not to eat that day until some quest or some adventure has come to us.'

'Do you even so,' said Merlin, 'that the realm of Logres may endure for many years as an example to all the men of after time. For be you sure that, though you all die, its fame and its example shall live for ever ... But now I must depart from among you, to sleep my long sleep until the time appointed, when the next Circle of Logres shall again be formed upon the earth ... These are things that you may not understand: but this you may: Break not your oaths of chivalry, nor fail in your allegiance to King Arthur, the symbol and the ruler of the realm of Logres.'

Then Merlin passed slowly down the hall and away into the night; and the Lady Nimue, she whom King Pellinore had brought to Camelot, rose quietly from her place in the hall and followed him.

4

The Magic of Nimue and Morgana le Fay

ON the day following that feast of Pentecost on which the Round Table was set up in Camelot, King Arthur rode alone in the forest, sorrowing for the strange words of Merlin. And as he rode, suddenly Merlin himself stood before him.

'I come to bid you farewell,' said the good enchanter, 'and to speak my last word of warning ... Have good care of the sword Excalibur, and of the magic scabbard of it – and beware of the evil woman who shall steal it from you, she who shall be the mother of the Evil Knight who shall strike you down upon the Field of Camlann. Yet she shall be with you at the last, her evil purged away, and she, with others, shall bring you to Avalon ... Of these others, the Ladies of Avalon, one awaits me, even the Lady Nimue. She shall bury me in the earth while I yet live ...'

'May not you escape her by your magic arts?' asked Arthur. 'Oh Merlin, I would not lose you!'

'Nay, it is my fate,' answered Merlin. 'It is to the glory of Logres ... And for you: now you must show your worth and stand alone!'

Then Merlin went on his way deeper and deeper into the forests, following the Lady Nimue; and they came to the land of Gwynedd where Pant was king, and lodged in his castle And on the morrow, before they went on their way once more, Merlin spoke with King Pant's wife, whose name was Elayne.

'You have a son,' said he, 'a marvellous youth whom the Lady of the Lake took from you when he lay in the cradle, so that he dwelt with her many years. I would see this boy before I pass from the ways of men, for his name is Launcelot, and another Elaine in the times to be shall bear him a son called Galahad – and these two knights shall be the best of all the Round Table, and the chiefest glory of the Realm of Logres.'

And when Merlin saw Launcelot, he blessed him, and bade him ride to the court of King Arthur before the next feast of Pentecost, and ask to be made a knight, saying that it was Merlin's last wish before he laid himself living in his own grave.

And then, while King Pant and Queen Elayne and young Launcelot marvelled at his words, Merlin departed from among them and went away into the hills of North Wales, while Nimue went before him, playing upon the cwyth, the magic harp of Wales, and singing strange songs of weird and wonderful enchantment.

At length they came to the place appointed, and there under the shadow of a fair white hawthorn covered in flowers Nimue sat down, and Merlin laid his head upon her lap. Then, singing and playing, she wove a great magic round about him in nine circles, round Merlin and round the haw-thorn bush. Merlin slept, and woke again: and now it seemed to him that he dwelt in the fairest tower in the world and the most strong. 'Lady,' he said, 'you have taken from me all my magic, so that never may I come out of this tower. Stay but with me, and leave me not alone in these enchantments.'

'I shall go forth before long,' answered Nimue, 'for King Arthur is in great danger, and, now that you may stand by him no longer, I must go to his aid. Morgana le Fay is weaving her wicked spells to entrap him – I must leave you and go speedily ... But first I will give you rest, that you may sleep through many centuries until the day dawns when you shall wake.'

Then, as if walking in his sleep, Merlin rose to his feet and went down a narrow stairway which opened in the ground before him: down and down he went into a dark stone room beneath a great rock; and he laid himself upon a great slab of stone like a table, and fell asleep. Then Nimue by her magic closed up the passage leading to the light, and went her way swiftly towards Camelot, leaving Merlin to rest in his dark tomb. And there he lies until the day of his awakening, when the Circle of Logres shall be formed once more in this island – but whether he rests in the magic Forest of Broceliande, or in the Isle of Bards in Cornwall Crag, or beneath the Wood of Bragdon, no one can tell until that day.

Meanwhile, King Arthur hunted in the mysterious forests of South Wales with Sir Urience his brother-in-law, the

Singing and playing, she wove a great magic round about him

husband of Morgana le Fay, and with the brave knight Sir Accolon of Gaul. Far and fast they followed a certain great hart, mile after mile until they were quite lost in the forest, so fast that at length their horses fell dead under them: and still they followed that hart, for it too was now so weary that it could hardly move.

They came out from under the trees, down a grassy bank, and saw the hart fall to earth and die. And then, looking round, they discovered that the bank sloped down to a great sheet of water, and that a small ship, all hung with rich silks, was drawing in beside the shore. The ship came right to them, running in against the sands so that they could step aboard:

but there was no living thing to be seen anywhere upon that ship.

'Sirs,' said King Arthur, 'let us enter this strange barque and dare the adventure of it.'

So they went aboard, and found it a passing fair ship, very richly furnished and draped with rare silks. It was evening when they came down the bank to the water-side – and the night fell rapidly after they had stepped on to the ship – so rapidly that in a few minutes it was pitch dark. Then suddenly great torches appeared all along the bulwarks, so that the decks were brilliantly lit: the ship moved across the still, dark waters, while twelve fair damsels came out from the cabins and served them with all the meats and wines that ever a man could desire. Sweet music played softly all the while, and the whole ship was fragrant with the heavy scent of strange flowers.

The King and his two companions were weary after their day's hunting; and after they had supped and enjoyed the cool night air on the deck of that strange vessel, each of them was led below to a rich cabin prepared for him alone. And before long each one of them was laid in a soft, comfortable bed. And that night they slept most marvellously deep.

On the morrow Urience woke to find himself at Camelot, in his own bed beside his wife the enchantress Morgana le Fay: and much he marvelled how he came two days' journey during one night's sleep. His wife smiled deeply and mysteriously, a strange, evil light glimmering behind her great dark eyes – but she said nothing of the matter, though well she knew.

King Arthur, however, woke to find himself in a dark and dismal prison, a damp, unwholesome dungeon beneath some great castle. And he heard in the darkness the groans of twenty knights who were also held there in cruel captivity.

'Who are you that so complain?' asked King Arthur.

And one of them replied: 'We are twenty knights kept prisoners here, and there are some of us who have been here as long as eight years.'

'How does this happen?' asked Arthur.

'The lord of this castle,' answered the knight, 'is an evil man called Sir Damas, who wrongfully holds the castle and lands from his elder brother the good knight Sir Outlake. And he takes captive all those who come to the castle and shuts them in this miserable dungeon ...'

As they were talking, there came a damsel bearing a lamp, and said to King Arthur:

'What cheer, sir?'

'I hardly know,' he answered. 'Nor can I tell how I came to be in this evil place.'

'Sir,' said she, 'you shall be set at liberty, and win the freedom of all these knights also, if you will but fight for my lord. For his brother will this day send a champion to do battle for him, and whoso wins shall become lord of all these lands.'

'Now,' said Arthur, 'you have set me a hard question. Your lord, Sir Damas, is an evil knight, and I would not strike a blow in his defence. Yet had I rather die in battle than linger to my death in this dungeon ... If Sir Damas will release all those who lie prisoned here, I will do battle to the death in his quarrel.'

'It shall be so,' said the damsel.

'Then I am ready,' said Arthur, 'if I had but a horse and armour.'

'You shall lack neither,' she assured him. 'Do but follow me.'

They came up from the dungeon and out into the clear sunlight of the courtyard ...

'Surely, damsel, I have seen you before,' said King Arthur. 'Were you ever at King Arthur's court?'

'No,' answered the damsel, 'I never came there in all my life. I am but the daughter of Sir Damas, lord of this castle.'

But she spoke falsely when she said this, for she was one of the damsels who served Queen Morgana le Fay.

At the same moment that Arthur found himself in the dungeon beneath Sir Damas's castle, Sir Accolon of Gaul woke also from his charmed sleep, and found himself lying in a pleasant courtyard, but at the very edge of a deep well so that if he had moved but a little he would have fallen into it and found his death many, many feet beneath.

When Sir Accolon found where he was, he blessed himself and said: 'Now may God save King Arthur and King Urience – for those damsels in the ship have betrayed us. Surely they were fiends and not women: if ever I escape from this adventure I will slay all women who deal thus in black magic and wicked enchantments.'

While he was thinking this there came a dwarf with a great mouth and a flat nose, and saluted Sir Accolon, saying: 'I come from your lady, Queen Morgana le Fay, and she greets you well as her dear love, and begs you for her sake to fight for her this day with a strange knight. And for this she sends you King Arthur's own sword, Excalibur, and its scabbard, and bids you fear not, but do battle to the death without any mercy as she has instructed you ... She bid me also tell you that her husband lies dying, wounded to the death by a traitor's hand, and that you shall wed her and be King of Gorre in his stead.'

'I did indeed promise to fight for her,' said Sir Accolon, 'and you come truly from her, since you bear the sword Excalibur. All these enchantments must be her doing, so that I might do battle against her unknown enemy and slay him.'

'Sir, it is even as you say,' answered the dwarf. 'And you do well to fight in this battle.' Then he drew Sir Accolon from the side of the well, and afterwards led him to the hall of the castle, where Sir Outlake awaited him with six squires. When Sir Accolon had eaten and drunk, these armed him in strong armour, set him upon a mighty war-horse, and led him to the field of battle, midway between the castles of Sir Outlake and Sir Damas, in a fair green meadow.

Meanwhile six squires of Sir Damas had led Arthur also to the hall of their master's castle, given him food and drink, armed him well, and led him out of the gate. As Arthur rode from the castle another damsel came to him, bowed low, and said:

'Sir, your sister, my mistress, Queen Morgana le Fay, greets you. And she sends me to bring you your sword

Excalibur which you left in her keeping, for she hears that this day you must engage in battle. Here is the sword, and the scabbard also: and my mistress kneels even now in prayer for your safety.'

King Arthur thanked the damsel, and went towards the battle with a lighter heart now that he had his own sword, and the magic scabbard the wearer of which would never lose much blood, however sorely he was wounded.

These two knights, King Arthur and Sir Accolon, in strange armour with closed vizors and no devices on their shields to show who they were, met together in the green meadow, neither knowing the other. They jousted with their spears first of all – so mightily that neither might sit his horse. Then they drew their swords, and went eagerly to battle, smiting many great strokes. But always King Arthur's sword failed to bite as Accolon's did: for Accolon's sword bit through King Arthur's armour at every stroke, until his blood ran down and dyed all the meadow. But Accolon bled scarcely at all, though Arthur had wounded him once or twice.

And when King Arthur saw his blood upon the grass, and felt how the sword in his hand bit not into the steel as it was wont to do, while Accolon's drew blood at every stroke, he felt that there had been treason and black magic used to change the swords. For he became more and more certain that in Accolon's hand gleamed the true Excalibur.

'Now, sir knight, beware, for I am going to hit you again!' taunted Sir Accolon. Arthur, without replying, struck so hard that he went staggering back; but Accolon struck once, and Arthur fell to the ground.

He was soon up again, however, and they struck many more great strokes at one another: but always King Arthur lost so much blood that it was a marvel that he still stood on his feet – and only so brave a knight could have fought on while enduring such pain.

At last the two of them paused to rest, and all those who had gathered to watch the battle spoke well of them, but lamented that one of two such brave knights was doomed to die. And amongst those who watched was the enchantress, Lady Nimue of Avalon, she who had put Merlin under the stone, and who had arrived only after the battle had begun.

'This is no time for me to suffer you to rest!' exclaimed Sir Accolon suddenly; and thereat he came fiercely against Arthur once more. But Arthur, wild with rage and pain, whirled up his sword and smote Accolon so hard upon the helmet that he fell to earth. But at that stroke the sword broke to pieces in his hand, leaving only the hilt and cross bar.

Accolon sprang up again and rushed at King Arthur, who defended himself with his shield, though certain that now there was no escape.

'Knight!' jeered Accolon. 'Yield you to me as craven and vanquished – or else I will smite off your head with my sword!'

'Nay,' said Arthur. 'I cannot so shame my vows. If it were possible for me to die a hundred times, I would rather that. For though I lack weapon, yet shall I lack no honour – and if you slay me weaponless, it is you who will be shamed.'

'I'll take the risk of that!' cried Accolon. 'Run away now – for you are no better than a dead corpse already!' He slashed at Arthur again; but the king took the blow on his shield, and hit Accolon across the vizor with the broken sword so hard that he staggered back three paces.

And as he did so, Nimue by her magic loosened the scabbard at his side, so that it fell to the ground in front of Arthur, who caught it up and buckled it to his belt. Accolon came on once more, struck a stroke that might have cleft Arthur's head to the chin: but Nimue waved her hand once more and the sword twisted from Accolon's fingers and landed point downwards in the ground.

Arthur leapt forward, took the sword in his hand – and knew at once by the feel of it that it was his own Excalibur. 'Ah-ha!' he cried. 'You have been from me all too long, and you have done me much damage.' And then to Accolon:

'Sir knight, it is you who stand near to death – for this my own sword shall reward you well for the pain I have endured and the blood I have lost.'

Therewith he leapt at Sir Accolon and smote him to the ground so hard that the blood burst out from his mouth and nose and ears; and he stood over him with Excalibur raised to strike, crying: 'Now will I slay you!'

'Slay me you well may,' gasped Accolon, 'for never will I yield. I also vowed by my knighthood never to yield with life. Slay me therefore, since I will not live shamed.'

'You are a brave knight, and an honourable,' said Arthur, lowering his sword. 'Tell me of what land you are, and who you serve.'

'Sir, I am of the royal court of King Arthur, and Accolon of Gaul is my name.'

'Tell me – who gave you the sword?' asked the king, much dismayed as he remembered the magic of the ship.

'A sorrowful sword it has been,' said Accolon, 'for by it I have got my death.'

'That may well be,' said the king. 'But how came it into your hands?'

'From Queen Morgana le Fay,' answered Accolon sadly. 'I have loved her long, and she me. And I promised to fight and slay whom she would, even though it were Arthur the King: for which reason she sent me the sword this day, telling me that her husband King Urience was dead, and I should be king indeed if I conquered in this battle. But tell me, who are you that she would have had me slay?'

'Ah, Accolon,' said Arthur, 'do you not know that I am the King?'

When Accolon heard this, he cried out aloud: 'Fair, sweet lord King Arthur, have mercy on me, for I knew you not!'

'Mercy you shall have,' answered Arthur, 'for I see that this battle was not your doing, but my sister's. Ah, Accolon, she has deceived me also by her beauty and her magic wiles: the good Merlin warned me, but I would not take warning. Now will I send her from my court, or slay her if she bring any man to his death.'

Then King Arthur made peace between Sir Damas and Sir Outlake; and when he had done this their squires carried him and Sir Accolon, who was even more badly wounded, to an abbey near by in the forest. And Nimue came with them and tended on them. Sir Accolon died of his hurts before the next sun rose, but Arthur recovered slowly.

Meanwhile Queen Morgana le Fay, thinking him to be dead, was continuing at Camelot with her wicked plans. On the very day of the battle she found her husband King Urience lying asleep on his couch; and at once she called one of her damsels to her and said:

'Go, fetch me my lord's sword, for I never saw a better moment than this wherein to slay him!'

'Ah, Madame!' cried the damsel. 'Do not do this thing – you will never escape if you murder your husband!'

'That is no concern of yours,' answered Morgana le Fay. 'This day have I decreed that he shall die – so fetch me the sword quickly!'

Away went the damsel, but she sought out Prince Uwaine first of all, and said:

' Sir, come quickly and wait on my lady your mother, for she is just going to murder the king your father – I am fetching the sword for her to do it.'

'Bring her the sword quickly,' said Sir Uwaine, 'or she will slay you also!'

With trembling hands the damsel brought the sword to Morgana le Fay, who went swiftly to where King Urience lay sleeping. But as she raised the sword to strike, Sir Uwaine sprang out from behind the hangings and seized her arm:

'Ah, fiend,' he hissed. 'What wickedness are you at? Were you not my mother, I would kill you here and now: I think you are a devil, and not a woman!'

'Have mercy on me,' begged Morgana. 'It was the devil who tempted me to this deed: the fiends of darkness are ever ready to lead astray those who know too much of their secret arts.'

'You shall vow upon the Holy Sacrament never to attempt such a deed again,' said Uwaine. And to this oath Morgana le Fay pledged herself.

And a little while later one of her damsels came to tell her that Accolon was slain, and King Arthur resting at the abbey in the forest.

'When he returns to Camelot,' she thought, 'he will surely slay me for striving to bring about his death. I will go speedily from the court before he comes . . .'

Then she set out with her men-at-arms and her damsels: but she told Queen Guinevere that she was going riding in the forest.

She raised the sword to strike

On her way Queen Morgana le Fay came to the abbey where Arthur lay recovering from his wounds; and suddenly she thought that now at least she could steal his sword Excalibur.

'The King lies sleeping on his bed,' she was told, 'and gave command that no one was to wake him.'

'I am his sister,' answered Morgana very sweetly. 'Let me come just to watch by his side for a little while, there to pray for his speedy recovery.'

So they brought her where he was, and left her with him. She found Arthur lying asleep with the sword Excalibur naked in his right hand: but the scabbard leant against a chair at his bedside.

'At least I can take this from him,' she thought, and hiding it beneath her cloak, she went quietly out of the abbey, mounted her horse, and rode on her way.

Presently King Arthur woke and missed his scabbard. Then he was very angry and asked who had been there while he slept, and they told him that it was Queen Morgana le Fay.

'Alas,' said Arthur, 'falsely have you watched me.'

'Sir,' they answered, 'we durst not disobey your sister's commands.'

Then Arthur called for horses, and he and Sir Outlake went galloping through the forest after Queen Morgana le Fay and her attendants.

Before long they saw them, and the chase became fast and furious. Nearer and nearer came Arthur and Outlake, until at last she realized that there was no escape. Then she rode to a deep lake in the forest and threw the scabbard into the middle of it, crying: 'Whatever happens to me, I will at least make sure that my brother never has his scabbard again!' And it sank, for it was heavy with gold and precious jewels.

After this Queen Morgana led her followers into a valley filled with great stones, and by her magic turned herself and all of them into stones also, so that when King Arthur and Sir Outlake came among them a few minutes later, neither Morgana le Fay nor any of her people was to be seen.

'Here has been an evil magic,' said Arthur, crossing himself. And when they had searched long and vainly for the scabbard, they rode back to the abbey, and thence to Camelot, where Guinevere and all the fellowship of the Round Table rejoiced greatly to see them.

But as they sat at meat in the great hall that evening a damsel came in and bowed low before King Arthur.

'My lord,' she said, very humbly, 'I come from your sister Queen Morgana to beg her pardon of you for the wickedness that she has done. Never again after this day will she strive to hurt you – for the fiend has gone from her which tempted her to evil. And in token of her great love and true repentance she sends you this mantle, the fairest in the world: and whoso wears it shall never suffer pain any more.'

When all saw the mantle they marvelled at it – for indeed it was passing fair, set all with precious stones and embroidered with gold and silver. And King Arthur was happy in the gift of the mantle, and put out his hand to take it. But the Lady Nimue, who had returned to Camelot with him, cried out suddenly:

'Lord King, put not on the mantle until you know more of it! Let this damsel set it upon her own shoulders ere it come on yours or any other's in this hall.'

'It shall be as you counsel me,' said King Arthur. 'Damsel, I would see the mantle upon you!'

'Sir,' she said, 'I am not worthy to wear a king's robe!'

'Nevertheless, you shall wear this!' commanded Arthur. And so perforce the damsel drew the mantle close about her – and immediately there was a bright burst of flame, and she fell to the ground, a heap of smouldering ashes.

And after this Queen Morgana le Fay dared never again enter the realm of Logres, but went to her own castle in the land of Gorre, and fortified it strongly.

BOOK TWO

The Knights of the
Round Table

I

Sir Gawain and the Green Knight

KING ARTHUR'S adventures did not end when he had defeated the Saxons and brought peace to Britain: for though he had set up the Realm of Logres – the land of true good and piety, nobleness and right living – the evil was always breaking in to attack the good. It would need many books to tell of every adventure that befell during his reign – that brief period of light set like a star of Heaven in the midst of the Dark Ages: and we cannot, for example, tell here how Arthur himself fought with the Giant of St Michael's Mount who carried off helpless wayfarers to his dark and evil castle; nor how he made war against the Emperor Lucius and was received in Rome; nor even of his fight with the dreadful Cat of Losane.

But year by year the fame of his court grew, and spread far and wide, and the bravest and noblest knights in the world came to his court and strove by their deeds of courage and gentleness to win a place at the Round Table.

Many stories are told of these knights also – of Launcelot and Gawain, of Tristram and Gareth, of Percivale, Ywain, Marhaus, Cleges, Agravaine, and many, many others – and more adventures that befell the most famous of these than may possibly be told in one book.

One of the first and bravest of the knights was Sir Gawain – and it was said indeed that only Sir Launcelot, Sir Galahad, and Sir Percivale could surpass him. He had many exciting adventures: but now only one of them can be told.

King Arthur held his Christmas feast at Camelot one year, with all the bravest of his knights about him, and all the fairest ladies of his court – and his chief celebrations fell upon New Year's Day. Queen Guinevere, clad in fair, shining silk, sat beneath an embroidered canopy studded with gems: fair was she to look upon, with her shining eyes of grey, and each knight bent in reverence before her ere he took his place. Beside her sat King Arthur, well pleased to see the noble gathering and the joy that was in the hall: but he would not begin the feast, for such his custom was, until he had been told of some knightly deed, or set before his knights some strange or terrible new quest.

The minstrels had stopped playing and the whole company sat quietly in the great hall, only the roar and crackle of the log fires in the wide hearths breaking the silence – when suddenly there rang out the clash and clang of iron-shod hooves striking upon stone: the great doors flew open, and into the hall rode a strange and terrible figure.

A great man it was, riding upon a huge horse: a strong-limbed, great-handed man, so tall that an earth-giant almost he seemed. Yet he rode as a knight should, though without armour, and his face, though fierce, was fair to see – but the greatest wonder was that he was green all over. A jerkin and cloak of green he wore above green hose gartered in green, with golden spurs; in the green belt round his waist jewels were set, and his green saddle was inlaid richly, as were also his trappings. But his hair, hanging low to his shoulders, was bright green, and his beard also; green was his face and green his hands; and the horse was also green from head to foot, with gold thread wound and knotted in the mane.

He had no weapons nor shield save for a great axe of green steel and gold, and a bough torn from a holly tree held above his head. He flung the branch upon the inlaid floor of the hall and looked proudly on every side; at the knights seated about the Round Table, and the ladies and squires at the boards on either side, and at Arthur where he sat with Guinevere above the rest. Then he cried in a great voice:

'Where is the governor of this gang? With him would I speak and with none other!'

All sat in amazement gazing at the strange knight: some

dire enchantment it must be, they thought – for how else could there be such a man sitting there on his horse, as green as the grass – greener than any grass on this earth?

But at length Arthur, courteous ever, greeted the Green Knight, bade him be welcome and sit down to the feast with them.

'Not so!' cried the stranger in answer. 'I come not to tarry with you: and by the sign of the green bough I come not in war – else had I clothed me in armour and helmet most sure – for such have I richly stored in my castle in the north. But even in that land have I heard of the fame and valour of your court – the bravery of your knights, and their high virtue also.'

'Sir,' replied the king, 'here may you find many to do battle and joust if such be your will.'

'Not so,' cried the Green Knight in his great booming voice. 'Here I see only beardless children whom I could fell with a stroke! Nay, I come rather in this high season of Our Lord's birth to bring Yule-tide sport, a test of valour to your feast. If any man in this hall is so brave and so courageous as to exchange stroke for stroke, I will give him this noble axe – heavy enough truly to handle as he may desire: yes, and I myself will stand here on the floor and receive the first stroke of the axe wherever he may smite me. Only he must swear, and you, lord king, to give me the right to deal him such another blow, if I may, a twelve-month and a day from now.'

More silent still sat the knights; if they had been surprised before now their amazement was greater still. But none dared answer his challenge, so terrible was the man and so fearsome the great axe which he held in his hand.

Then the Green Knight laughed aloud in mockery: 'Is this indeed the court of King Arthur?' he cried, 'and are these the far-famed Knights of the Round Table? Now is their glory laid low for ever, since even to hear tell of blows makes them all grow silent in fear!'

King Arthur sprang up at this. 'Fellow,' he cried, 'this foolishness of yours shall have a fitting answer. If none other will take your challenge, give me the axe and make ready for the blow!'

But at this Sir Gawain rose to his feet and said:

'My lord king and noble uncle, grant me a boon! Let this adventure be mine, for still there is my old shame unhealed: still have I to prove my worth as a Knight of your Round Table, still to fit myself to be a champion of Logres.'

'Right happy I am that the quest shall be yours, dear nephew,' answered Arthur. And the Green Knight smiled grimly as he sprang from his horse and met with Gawain in the middle of the hall.

'I too am overjoyed to find one brave man amongst you all,' he said. 'Tell me your name, Sir Knight, ere we make our bargain.'

'I am Gawain, son of King Lot of Orkney, and nephew to royal Arthur,' was the answer. 'And here I swear by my knighthood to strike but one blow, and bravely to endure such another if you may strike it me a twelvemonth hence.'

'Sir Gawain,' cried the Green Knight, 'overjoyed am I indeed that your hand shall strike this blow. Come now and deal the stroke: thereafter shall I tell you who I am and where you may find me. Take now the axe and let us see how well you can smite.'

'Gladly will I,' said Gawain, taking the axe in his hands and swinging it while the Green Knight made ready by kneeling on the floor and drawing his long hair on to the crown of his head to lay bare his neck for the stroke. Putting all his strength into the blow, Gawain whirled up the axe and struck so hard that the keen blade cut through flesh and bone and set the sparks flying from the stone paving, while the Green Knight's head leapt from his shoulders and went rolling across the floor.

But the knight neither faltered nor fell: swiftly he sprang forward with hands outstretched, caught up his head, and turning with it held in his hand by the hair mounted upon the waiting horse. Then, riding easily as if nothing had happened, he turned his face towards Gawain and said:

'See to it that you keep your oath and seek me out a year

The Green Knight mounted, his head in his hand

hence. I am the Knight of the Green Chapel, and as such men
know me in the north. Through Wales shall you seek me,
and in the Forest of Wirral: and you will not fail to find me
there if you be not a coward and a breaker of your knightly
word.'

With that he wheeled his horse and galloped out of the
door, the sparks flying up round his horse's hooves, and away
into the distance, his head still held in his hand, swinging
easily by the hair.

But all at the feast sat astonished beyond words at this
strange adventure, and it was a little while before the hall was
filled once more with laughter and the joy of that festal
season.

The year went by full swiftly; the trees grew green with
spring, the leaves fading through the bright summer days,
turned to red and gold in the early autumn; and upon

Michaelmas Day King Arthur held a feast at Caerleon with many of his knights, in honour of Sir Gawain who must on the morrow set forth upon his dreadful quest. Ywain and Agravaine and Erec were there; Launcelot and Lionel and Lucan the Good; Sir Bors and Sir Bedivere and Baldwin the lord bishop; Arthur and Guinevere to bless him and wish him God-speed. Gawain donned his armour, curved and shining and inlaid with gold; he girt his sword to his side and took the Green Knight's axe in his hand; then he mounted upon Gringalet his war-horse, and rode into the forests of South Wales, the shield held before him with the device of the Pentangle, the five-pointed Star of Logres, emblazoned in the midst.

So Sir Gawain set out, and rode through the realm of Logres, seeking for no joy but a deadly danger at the end of his quest. After many days he came into the wild lands of North Wales, and fared through lonely valleys and deep forests, forced often to sleep out under the stars by night, and to do battle by day with robbers and wild men.

Grim winter had closed upon him when he came to the northern sea, left the islands of Anglesey upon his left, and came by Clwyd to the Holy Head, near Saint Winifred's Well on the shore of the wide river Dee. Near to the mouth he forded the stream at low tide, and came across the desolate sands into the wild Forest of Wirral. Here were many more robbers and evil men, lying in wait by forest path and lonely stream, by rocky defile and by green valley – and he must fight with all who stayed him.

Everywhere he went he asked tidings of a Green Knight and of a Chapel also of Green near which was his dwelling: but none in the forest could help him in his quest. Only a brave knight could have passed that way, and Gawain endured all – foes to overcome, and the bitter weather of mid-winter.

On Christmas Eve he rode upon Gringalet through marsh and mire, and prayed that he might find shelter. And on a sudden he came through open parkland to a fine castle set on a little hill above a deep valley where flowed a wide stream.

A fair lawn lay in front of it, and many great oak trees on either side; there was a moat before the castle, and a low palisade of wood.

'Now God be thanked,' said Sir Gawain, 'that I have come to this fair dwelling for Christmas, and may He grant me to find an honourable welcome herein ... Good sir!' he cried to the porter who came to the great gate when he knocked, 'Grant me entrance, I pray you, and tell the lord of this castle that I am a knight of King Arthur's court passing this way upon a quest.'

With a kindly smile the porter opened the gate, and Gawain rode over the drawbridge and into the courtyard. And there were squires and serving-men waiting who helped him to alight, led Gringalet away to the stable, and brought Gawain into a goodly hall where a fire burned brightly and the lord of the castle came forth from his chamber to greet his guest, saying:

'Welcome to my dwelling, sir knight: all that I have is here at your service, and you shall be my honoured guest for as long as it shall please you to remain in this castle.'

'I thank you, noble sir,' said Gawain. 'May God bless you for your hospitality.' With that they clasped hands as good friends should; and Gawain looked upon the knight who greeted him so warmly, and thought what a fine warrior that castle had as its lord. For he was a tall man and broad of shoulder, with an open, honest face tanned red by the sun, with red hair and beard, a firm hand-clasp, a free stride, and a straightforward speech: just such a man as was born to be a leader of valiant men and a lord over wide estates.

The squires led Gawain next to a fair chamber in the keep, where they helped him to lay aside his armour, and clad him in rich, flowing robes lined softly with fur. Then they led him back to the hall and set him in a chair near to the fire, beside the lord of the castle. They brought in the tables then, set them upon trestles, covered them with fair white cloths, set thereon salt cellars and spoons of silver, then brought in the dishes and the goblets of wine. The lord of the castle drank to Sir Gawain, and rejoiced with all his followers that chance had brought so far-famed a knight to his lonely dwelling.

When the meal was ended the two knights went together to the chapel of the castle, where the chaplain celebrated Even-song and the whole service for Christmas Eve.

Then the knight brought Sir Gawain into a comely closet and sat him in a chair by the fire. And there the lady of the castle came to visit him, accompanied by her handmaidens – a very lovely lady, fairer even than Queen Guinevere. So the evening passed in jest and joy, and they brought Gawain to his room with bright tapers, set a goblet of hot spiced wine at his bedside, and left him there to his rest.

Three days were spent in feasting and in Christmas rejoicings – dancing and carol-singing, and much merriment. And ever the lady of the castle sat by Gawain, and sang to him and talked with him, and attended to his comfort.

'Tarry with me longer,' said the lord of the castle on the evening of the fourth day. 'For while I live I shall be held the worthier because so brave and courteous a knight as Sir Gawain has been my guest.'

'I thank you, good sir,' answered Gawain, 'but I must away to-morrow on my high quest. For I must be at the Green Chapel upon the New Year's day, and I would rather keep mine oath than be ruler of all this land. Moreover as yet I have found none who can instruct me as to where the Green Chapel is.'

The lord of the castle laughed happily. 'This is indeed good news!' he cried. 'Here then you may stay until the very day of your quest's ending. For not two hours' ride from this castle you shall find the Green Chapel – a man of mine shall bring you to it upon the first day of the new year.'

Then Gawain was glad, and he too laughed joyously. 'I thank you, sir, for this news – and greatly also for your kindness. Now that my quest is achieved, I will dwell here in all joy and do what you will.'

'Then these three days,' said the lord of the castle, 'I will ride out hunting in the forest. But you, who have travelled far and endured many things, shall abide in my castle and rest at your ease. And my wife shall attend on you, and entertain you with her company when I am out hunting.'

'I thank you indeed,' said Gawain. 'And in no other wise could I pass with greater joy the three days before my meeting with the Green Knight.'

'Well,' said the lord of the castle, 'so let it be. And as this yet is the festive season of game and jest, let us make a merry bargain together, I vowing each day to give you whatever I may win in the wood, and you giving in exchange anything that may come to you here in the castle. Let us swear to make this exchange, for worse or for better, whatever may happen.'

'With all my heart,' laughed Gawain. And so the oath was sworn.

Next morning the lord of the castle hunted the deer through the forests of Wirral and Delamere; and many a hart and hind fell to his keen arrows.

But Gawain slept long in a soft bed hung about with curtains, and dreamt of many things 'twixt waking and sleeping, until the lady of the castle, stepping silently as a sunbeam, came and sat upon his bed and talked with him merrily. Long they spoke together, and many words of love did the lady utter; but Gawain turned them all with jest and courtesy, as a true knight should who speaks with the lady of his host.

'Now God save you, fair sir,' she said at length, 'and reward you for your merry words. But that you are really Sir Gawain I misdoubt me greatly!'

'Wherefore do you doubt?' asked the knight anxiously, fearing that he had failed in some point of courtesy.

'So true a knight as Gawain,' answered the lady, 'and one so gentle and courteous unto damsels would never have tarried so long with a lady and not begged a kiss of her in parting.'

'Faith, fair lady,' said Gawain, 'and you bid me to it, I will indeed ask a kiss of you: but a true knight asks not otherwise, for fear to displease you.'

So the lady kissed him sweetly, and blessed him and departed; and Gawain rose from his bed and called for the chamberlain to clothe him. And thereafter he ate and drank, and passed his day quietly in the castle until the lord of it came home in the grey evening, bearing the spoils of the chase.

'What think you of this game, sir knight?' he cried. 'I deserve thanks for my skill as a huntsman, do I not – for all of this is yours according to our bargain!'

'I thank you,' answered Gawain, 'and I take the gift as we agreed. And I will give to you all that I won within these walls.' And with that he put his hands on the lord of the castle's shoulders and kissed him, saying: 'Take here my spoils, for I have won nothing but this: if more had been mine, as freely would I have given it to you.'

'It is good,' said his host, 'and much do I thank you for it. Yet would I like to know whence came your kiss, and how did you win it?'

'Not so,' answered Gawain, 'that was no part of the bargain!' And thereupon they laughed merrily and sat down to a fine dinner.

Next morning the lord of the castle went forth down the hillside and along the deep valley-bottoms to seek out and slay the wild boar in the marshes.

But Gawain abode in his bed, and the lady came once more to sit by him; and ever she strove to wheedle him into speaking to her words of love unseemly for the lady of a Knight. But Gawain the courteous turned all into jest, and defended himself so well by his wit that he won no more than two kisses, given by the lady ere she left him laughing.

'And now, Sir Gawain,' said the lord of the castle when he came home that night and laid the boar's head at his feet. 'Here is my spoil of the day which I give you according to our bargain: now what have you won to give me in exchange?'

'I thank you,' said Gawain, 'for your just dealing in this game. As truly will I give you all that I have gained this day.'

Thereat he took the lord of the castle by the shoulders and gave him two kisses, saying: 'Now are we quits – for this and no more have I got me to-day.'

'By St Giles!' laughed the lord of the castle, 'you will be rich in a short time if we drive such bargains!' Then they went to the feast, and sat late over their meat and wine, while the lady strove ever to please Gawain, making fair, secret glances at him which, for his honour, he must not return.

The morrow would be the last day of the year. Gawain was eager to ride forth in quest of the Green Knight; but the lord of the castle stayed him with hospitable words:

'I swear by mine honour as a true knight that upon New Year's Day you shall come to the Green Chapel long ere the hour of noon. So stay in your bed to-morrow and rest in my castle. I will up with morning and ride to hunt the fox: so let us make once again our bargain to exchange all the winnings that may be ours to-morrow. For twice have I tried you and found you true; but the next is the third time, and that shall be the best.'

So once more they swore the oath, and while the lord of the castle went forth with his huntsmen and his pack of music-mouthed hounds, Gawain lay asleep, dreaming of the terrible meeting with the Green Knight so close before him. Presently the lady came in, blithe as a bird; she flung up the window so that the clear, frosty sunshine streamed into the room, roused Gawain from his slumbers and claimed of him a kiss.

She was fairer than the sunshine itself that morning, her hair falling each side of her lovely face, and her neck whiter than the snow gleaming between the fur of her gown. Sweetly she kissed Gawain and chid him for a sluggard.

'Surely you are a very man of ice that you take but one kiss! Or is it that you have a lady waiting for you in Camelot?'

'Not so,' answered Gawain gravely, 'no lady yet has my love. But it may not be yours, for you have a lord already – a far nobler knight than ever I shall be!'

'But this one day we may love,' she said. 'Surely it may be so? Then all my life-days I may remember that Gawain held me in his arms.'

'Nay, for the sake of mine oath of knighthood and the glory of Logres, I may not do so – for such were shame indeed.'

Then she blamed him and besought him, but ever he turned aside her words courteously, and ever held true to his honour as a knight of Logres should. At last she sighed sweetly, and kissed him a second time, saying: 'Sir Gawain, you are a true knight, the noblest ever. So give me but a gift whereby to remember you, that by thinking of my knight I may lessen my mourning.'

'Alas,' said Gawain, 'I have nothing to give. For I travel without baggage on this dangerous quest.'

'Then I will give you this green lace from my girdle'

'Then I will give you this green lace from my girdle,' said the lady. 'Wear that for my sake at least.'

'It may not be so,' answered Gawain, 'for I cannot be your knight and wear your favour.'

'It is but a little thing,' she said, 'and you may wear it hidden. Take it, I pray you, for it is a magic lace and while a man wears it he may not be slain, not even by all the magic upon earth. But I charge you to hide it, and tell not my lord.'

This proved too great a temptation for Gawain, and, mindful of his ordeal with the Green Knight next day, he took the lace and promised never to reveal it. Then the lady kissed him for the third time, and went quickly away.

That evening the lord of the castle came home from the hunt bearing with him the skin of one fox. In the bright hall where the fire shone warmly and the tables were all laid richly for dinner, Gawain met him merrily:

'I come with my winnings, and I will be the first giver this night!' he cried gaily; and with that he kissed him solemnly three times.

'By my faith,' cried the lord of the castle, 'you are a good merchant indeed: you give me three such kisses – and I have only a foul fox-skin to give you in return!'

Then with laughter and jests they sat down to the feast, and were merrier that night than on any of the others. But Gawain spoke no word of the green lace which the lady had given him.

The day of the New Year came in with storm: bitterly the winds howled and the sleet lashed against the window pane, and Gawain, who had slept but little, rose at the first light. He clothed himself warmly and buckled on his armour, setting the green lace about his waist in hope that its magic might protect him. Then he went forth into the courtyard, the squires brought out Gringalet, well fed and well groomed, and helped him to mount.

'Farewell,' he said to the lord of the castle. 'I thank you for your hospitality, and pray Heaven to bless you. If I might live a while longer I would reward you for your kindness: but greatly I fear that I shall not see another sun.'

The drawbridge was let down, the gate flung wide, and Gawain rode out of the castle, with a squire to guide him. Through the bitter dawning they rode, beneath trees dripping drearily, and across meadows where the wind moaned as it bit them to the bone, and they came to a great valley with cliffs at one side of it, all filled with mist.

'Sir,' said the squire, 'go no further, I beg of you. Near here dwells the Green Knight, a terrible and a cruel man. There is none so fierce or so strong in this land – and no man may stand against him. Over yonder at the Green Chapel it is ever his custom to stay all who pass by, and fight with them, and kill them – for none can escape him. Flee away now – and I will not tell ever that you fled for fear of the terrible Green Knight.'

'I thank you,' said Gawain, 'but I must go forward. I would be a coward and unworthy of knighthood if I fled away now. Therefore, whether I like it or not I must go forward ... And God knows well how to save His servants if so He wills.'

'Well then,' said the squire, 'your death be your own doing. Go down this path by the cliff, into the deep valley, and upon the left hand, beyond the water, you will find the Green Chapel. Now farewell, noble Gawain, for I dare not come with you further.'

Down the path rode Gawain, and came to the bottom of the valley. No chapel could he see, but only the rugged cliff above him, and high, desolate banks in the distance. But at length he saw, under the dripping trees, a low green mound beside the rushing stream; and he heard a sound as of a scythe upon a grindstone coming from a deep hollow in that mound.

'Ah,' said Gawain. 'This must be the Green Chapel! A very devil's oratory it is, and green indeed – a chapel of mischance! And within it I hear the knight himself, sharpening a weapon to smite me this day. Alas that I must perish at his hands in this cursed spot ... Yet will I go on boldly, for my duty is so to do.'

Gawain sprang from his horse and strode down to the streamside:

'Who waits here,' he cried, 'to keep tryst with me? I am Gawain, who have come to the Green Chapel as I vowed.'

'Wait but a little,' came a mighty voice out of the hollow beneath the mound. 'When my weapon is sharp, you shall have that which I promised you!'

Presently the Green Knight came out with a new, shining axe in his hand. He was as terrible as ever, with his green face and his green hair, as he strode down the bank and leapt over the wide stream.

'You are welcome, Gawain!' he cried in his great voice. 'Now will I repay the stroke you dealt me at Camelot – and none shall come between us in this lonely valley. Now off with your helmet, and make ready for the blow!'

Then Gawain did as he was bidden, bending his head forward, with his neck bare to the stroke.

'Make ready to strike,' he said quietly to the Green Knight, 'for here I shall stand and do nought to stay the blow.'

The Green Knight swung his axe round so that it whistled, and aimed a terrible stroke with the sharp blade of it: and try how he might, Gawain flinched at the sound of it.

'Ha!' grunted the Green Knight, lowering his axe and leaning on the handle of it: 'You are surely not Gawain the brave, thus to fear even the whistle of the blade! When you struck off my head in King Arthur's hall I never flinched from your blow.'

'I shrank once,' said Gawain, 'but I shall not a second time – even when *my* head falls to the ground, which I cannot replace as you have yours! Come now, strike quickly, I will not stay you again.'

'Have at you then!' cried the Green Knight, whirling his axe. He smote once more, and once more stayed his hand ere the sharp blade drew blood. But Gawain stirred not a jot, nor trembled in any limb. 'Now you are filled with courage once more,' he cried, 'and so I may smite bravely a brave man. Hold aside your hood a little further, I am about to strike my hardest.'

'Strike away,' said Gawain. 'Why do you talk so much? Are you perhaps afraid thus to smite a defenceless man?'

'Then here is the blow I promised!' cried the Green Knight, swinging his axe for the third time. And now he struck truly, yet aimed with such care that the blade only parted the skin at the side of his neck.

But when Gawain had felt the wound and the blood over his shoulders, he sprang away in an instant, put on his helmet, drew his sword, set his shield before him and said to the Green Knight:

'Now I have borne the blow, and if you strike again it is beyond our bargain and I may defend myself, striking stroke for stroke!'

The Green Knight stood leaning on his axe. 'Gawain,' he said, all the fierceness gone out of his voice, 'you have indeed borne the blow – and no other will I strike you. I hold you released of all claims now. If I had wished it, I might have struck you a crueller stroke, and smitten your head off as you smote off mine. The first blow and the second that struck you not – these were for promises truly kept, for the one kiss and the two kisses that my wife gave you in the castle, and you truly rendered to me. But the third time you failed, and therefore had the wound of me: you gave me the three kisses, but not the green lace. Oh, well I know all that passed between you – she tempted you by my will. Gawain, I hold you to be the noblest, the most faultless knight in all the wide world. Had you yielded to dishonour and shamed your knighthood – then would your head be lying now at my feet. As for the lace, you hid it but for love of your life – and that is a little sin, and for it I pardon you.'

'I am ashamed,' said Gawain, handing him the green lace. 'For cowardice and covetousness I betrayed my oath of knighthood. Cut off my head, sir knight, for I am indeed unworthy of the Round Table.'

'Come now!' cried the Green Knight, laughing merrily, so that Gawain knew him indeed to be the lord of the castle. 'You have borne your penance, and are quite absolved and forgiven. Take and keep this green lace in memory of this adventure; and return to my castle to end the festival in joy.'

'I must back to Camelot,' said Gawain, 'I may not bide longer. But tell me, noble sir, how comes this enchantment? Who are you that ride in Green and die not when beheaded? How come you to dwell, a noble knight in a fine castle, and also to strike axe-blows, the Green Knight of the Green Chapel?'

'My name is Sir Bernlak, the Knight of the Lake,' answered he. 'And the enchantment comes from Nimue, the Lady of the Lake, the favoured of Merlin. She sent me to Camelot, to test the truth of the renown that is spread abroad concerning the valour of the Knights of the Round Table, and the worth of Logres.'

Then the two knights embraced one another and parted with blessings. Gawain rode back swiftly through the Forest of Wirral, and after many more adventures he came to Camelot, where King Arthur welcomed him, marvelled at his tale, and set him with honour in his place at the Round Table. And of all the knights who ever sat there, few indeed were so worthy as Gawain.

2

▰▱▰▱▰▱▰▱▰▱▰▱▰▱▰▱▰▱▰▱▰▱▰▱▰▱▰▱▰▱

The First Quest of
Sir Launcelot

ON the day before the Feast of Pentecost one year after
Merlin had made the Round Table, King Arthur with
some of his knights rode out early from Camelot to hunt in
the forest. Before they had ridden far they met with a
wounded knight, carried in a litter by four squires; the knight
groaned like one in great pain, and as he turned upon the
litter, all might see the broken blade of a sword standing out
from a grim wound in his head.

'Now tell me,' said King Arthur, 'wherefore you rest thus
in the litter, and do you seek for a leech or a priest?'

'Sir,' groaned the knight, 'I seek for neither. But I would
come to the Court of King Arthur, for only there may I be
cured of my grievous hurt. For there I shall find the best
knight of all Logres, and he shall be known by his first deed
of knighthood which shall be the healing of my wound with
the touch of his hand, and the drawing forth of the steel. And
such a healing shall be his last deed also, after many years,
before the night falls upon Logres. These things the Lady
Nimue of Avalon revealed to me.'

Then Arthur bade all his knights try, each in turn, to heal
the wound: but none of them might do it, no, not even
Gawain, the best knight among them.

'To-morrow is the Feast of Pentecost,' said King Arthur,
'and on that day all my Knights of the Round Table shall be
met together as upon their oath. Then shall we seek for this
knight: but I know not who it shall be if my nephew Gawain
were not worthy.'

Then the wounded knight was carried into the great hall

at Camelot and well tended there all that day, while Arthur rode on into the forest.

And on the morrow all the knights were met together at the feast, each in his place at the Round Table: but some places stood empty, for there were knights who had fallen in battle since the year before.

When those who came had told each of his deeds during the year and sworn himself afresh into the high order of Knighthood, they laid hands in turn upon the wounded man in the litter, but none might heal him.

'Now,' said King Arthur, 'this is a great wonder: and I know not if greater still there is to be ere we eat our meal this day.'

Hardly had he spoken these words when there came a trumpet call from without, and into the hall rode Nimue, the Lady of the Lake of Avalon, she who had laid Merlin to his long rest. And behind her came three young men, squires in white array, very goodly to behold. But the first of them was so fine a man – golden haired, broad of shoulder, open of face – that all were silent to see the goodliness of him: and Queen Guinevere sighed, and the colour fled from her face for very wonder.

'I come to you, my lord king,' said the Lady Nimue, 'to bring this man, my foster child, the son of King Pant of Gwynedd. I come to bring you Merlin's last behest: for ere he went living into the earth, he sought out this youth and bade him come to your court upon this feast of Pentecost and ask you to bestow upon him the high order of knighthood. My lord Arthur, this is Launcelot, called "of the Lake" for that he dwelt with me in my faerie dwelling many years when the wicked King Ryon ravaged his land of Gwynedd: Merlin has spoken his name to you – and see, that name grows in letters of gold upon the empty siege on the right hand of the Siege Perilous!'

Then Arthur rose and came down into the hall: drawing the sword Excalibur, he laid it upon Launcelot's shoulders, and bade him rise a knight. And, as there were three places still empty at the Round Table where knights now dead had

sat, he knighted also the two squires who came with Launcelot, his half-brother Hector and his cousin Lionel.

Now all this while the wounded knight had lain in his litter
near the fire. And when Arthur had returned to his seat the
Lady Nimue took Launcelot and led him over to the place.
Then Launcelot stretched forth his hand and drew out the
sword-blade very gently: and when it was out the wound
closed up and all pain forsook the knight so that he rose from
his litter, and was given the last place at the Table.

Then the Lady Nimue curtseyed low to King Arthur,
kissed Sir Launcelot very tenderly on the brow, and went
swiftly from the hall. But some of the older knights thought
it wrong that this boy Launcelot should win such honour and
be set beside the Siege Perilous when he had done no deed
and followed no quest; and they murmured unkind things
about Launcelot and about Sir Hector and Sir Lionel as
well.

However, both King Arthur and Queen Guinevere made
much of Sir Launcelot, and believed at once that he was
indeed the peerless knight of whom Merlin had spoken. But
they did not know that another new knight, Mordred the son
of Queen Morgana le Fay, who also sat that day at the Round
Table, was to be the Traitor of Camlann at the still distant
hour when the darkness should fall once more upon Logres.

Now although Launcelot seemed not to hear the unkind
things which some of the knights who sat near Mordred were
saying, he knew none the less, and was sad. And so, early the
next morning, he arose and called to him his cousin Sir
Lionel:

'Make you ready, fair cousin,' he said, 'for this day we ride
upon our first quest. Doubt it not that we shall find adventures full many ere we come again to Camelot.'

Away they rode into the forest fully armed, in and out of
the early morning shadows, as fair knights as ever there were
in the world. Higher and higher rose the sun and hotter it
grew, until Sir Launcelot grew so sleepy that at length he told
Sir Lionel that he must stop and rest.

'See,' said Lionel presently, 'yonder is a fair apple tree

standing by a hedge: under its shadow both we and our horses may find rest.'

'In good time,' said Launcelot, 'for truth to tell I have not been so weary these seven years!'

So they tied their horses to trees, and while Sir Lionel stood on guard against any attack by robbers, Launcelot laid himself down, with his helmet under his head for a pillow, and fell into a deep sleep.

The day was very hot and still, and Lionel was nodding over his sword as he stood leaning on the hilt of it, when suddenly he heard the jingle of armour, and on the plain at a little distance he saw three knights riding their hardest, with one passing strong and mighty knight pursuing them. Anon as he watched, the strong knight overtook first one and then another of them, and in turn smote each down on to the cold earth. Then he dismounted, flung each knight across his own saddle, tied them there with the horses' reins, remounted his own horse, and rode away driving the three horses with their shameful burdens before him.

When Sir Lionel had seen this he thought to himself: 'Here may I win great honour!' So, without waking Launcelot, he sprang upon his horse and rode after them at full speed. Very soon he came up with the strong knight and bade him turn and defend himself or straightway release the three whom he had so shamefully bound. Then the strong knight turned round, set his spear in rest, and came against Lionel so fast that he flung both horse and man to the ground. Then he dismounted, tied his hands and feet, threw him over his own horse, just as he had served the three other knights, and rode on his way, driving them before him.

Meanwhile at Camelot, Sir Hector de Maris missed his half-brother Launcelot and his cousin Lionel, and thinking that they must have set out in search of adventures, made himself ready also and rode into the forest.

For a long way he rode without finding any trace of them, and at last, seeing an old forester, he stopped and said to him:

'Fair fellow, know you of any place hereby to which knights seeking adventure might have turned?'

'Yes, sir knight, indeed I do,' answered the old man. 'Scarcely a mile from here dwells Sir Turquyn in a strong castle by a ford. Over that ford stands a great oak tree, and from its branches hang the shields of many good knights whom he has overthrown and cast into a deep prison. Thereon also hangs a great basin of copper: strike upon it with the handle of your spear and Sir Turquyn will come forth and do battle with you.'

'Gra'mercy,' said Sir Hector politely, and set spurs to his horse. Soon he came to the castle by the ford; and there, sure enough, hung a gay collection of shields on a great tree – and among them Sir Hector recognized that of his cousin Sir Lionel. Then in a fury he struck the copper basin until it boomed like a great bell, and turned to let his horse drink at the ford.

'Come out of the water and joust with me!' cried a loud voice behind him, and turning quickly Sir Hector found a huge knight, with spear already in rest, waiting for him.

Out of the water he came in a great rage and charged the knight so mightily that both horse and man spun round twice.

'That was well done!' roared Sir Turquyn. 'You hit me as a brave knight should, and such as you rejoice my heart exceedingly!' And with that he charged Sir Hector, caught him under the right arm, lifted him clean out of the saddle on the point of his spear, and carried him away into his castle, where he threw him down on the floor.

'I'll spare your life,' said Sir Turquyn, 'for you joust mightily!' Then he pulled off Sir Hector's armour and flung him into the deep dungeon with the other knights.

'Alas,' said Sir Hector sadly when he found Lionel also a prisoner there, 'how has this happened to you? And where is Sir Launcelot? – No one but he could save us, for none other is strong enough to fight and overcome Sir Turquyn.'

'I left him sleeping under an apple-tree,' answered Lionel sadly. . . .

And there Sir Launcelot still lay, peacefully and comfortably asleep, without any idea of what had happened to his cousin and his brother. But when the noon was passed there

came four queens riding on white mules, with four knights
who held a green silk awning above them with a spear at each
corner so that the sun should not fall upon them too hotly.

As they rode thus they heard a war-horse neigh, and looking saw it tethered to a bush, and beside it under an apple-
tree a sleeping knight armed completely except for his helmet.

Quietly they rode near to look: and the knight was so fair
that all four queens loved him at once.

'Let us not quarrel over him,' said one of them, who was
Morgana le Fay, King Arthur's wicked sister, 'I will cast an
enchantment upon him so that he shall sleep without waking
for seven hours: then we can have him carried to my castle,
and when he wakes, he shall choose one of us to be his love –
or else die some dreadful death in my dungeons.'

So this enchantment was cast upon Sir Launcelot; and
when he woke, it was to find himself lying in a cold stone cell
where a fair damsel was setting supper for him.

'How now, sir knight,' said she when she saw that he was
awake. 'What cheer?'

'But little,' answered Launcelot, 'for methinks I have been
brought into a gloomy prison by some cruel enchantment.'

'Make now what cheer you may,' said the damsel, 'and I
will tell you more to-morrow morning. There is no time now
for words.' And she went away quickly, sorrowing to herself
that so fine a knight should be the victim of the wicked Queen
her mistress.

Next morning early Launcelot was brought before the four
Queens, and Morgana le Fay said to him: 'Right well we
know that you are Launcelot of the Lake, King Arthur's
knight, whom Nimue the Lady of the Lake fostered in
Avalon to be the best knight of Logres and the noblest
knight living; right well we know that of ladies you serve
Queen Guinevere alone: yet now, in spite of fate, she shall
lose you – and you her, or else your life. For living you go not
from this castle unless you take one of us to be your lady and
your love.'

'A hard choice indeed,' said Launcelot, 'to die or to choose
one of you to be my love ... Yet it is easily answered: I

Quietly they rode near to look . . .

would rather die than shame my honour and my vows of knighthood. I will have none of you – for you are all false enchanters! As for Queen Guinevere, I will prove it in battle with any man alive that she is the truest lady to her lord of any living!'

'Then you refuse us?' asked Morgana le Fay.

'Yes, by my life – I refuse the lot of you!' cried Launcelot.

The four queens went away threatening terrible things, and Launcelot was left to grieve alone in his cold dungeon, and wonder what cruel death they would make him die.

By and by he heard light footsteps down the stone stairs; the door opened gently and there stood the damsel who had spoken to him on the previous night, carrying food and wine for him.

She set these down on the stone table and asked him as before how he fared.

'Truly, damsel,' answered Launcelot, 'never so ill as now.'

'Alas,' sighed the damsel, 'it grieves me much to see so noble a knight held thus cruelly and wickedly . . . Maybe I could find some help for you – for indeed I love not these queens whom I serve, nor do any oaths bind me to them.'

'Help me but to escape, fair damsel,' exclaimed Launcelot eagerly, 'and I will promise to repay you in any way that is not against my honour.'

'I would ask you then, sir, to do battle on Tuesday next for my father King Bagdemagus in a great tournament. For thereat many of King Arthur's knights shall fight, and at the last tournament three of them overcame him.'

'In truth, your father is a goodly knight,' said Sir Launcelot, 'and gladly will I do battle for him.'

'Then sir,' she went on, 'I will lead you out of this castle early to-morrow morning, giving you your armour, shield and spear, and your horse. Ride then through the forest and meet me at an abbey you will find not far distant: and there I will bring my father to you.'

'All this shall be done,' said Sir Launcelot, 'as I am a true knight.'

Before the sun was up the damsel came to him again and led him through twelve locked doors out of the castle. 'Damsel, I shall not fail, by the grace of God,' said Launcelot, and rode away into the morning, the white ground mist floating up nearly to his saddle, until he seemed almost to be gliding

. . . and all loved him at once

across the waters of the Lake of Nimue, and was lost in the shadows of the forest. And the damsel sighed as she turned back into the castle, and there were tears in her eyes: for not many women could look upon Launcelot without loving him.

Not many days later Sir Launcelot met the damsel and King Bagdemagus at the abbey, and on the Tuesday he rode to the tournament carrying a plain white shield with no coat of arms on it so that no man might know who he was.

And there he fought right nobly, and with one spear smote down Sir Madore and Sir Mordred and Sir Gahalantyne, and spared their lives when they swore to come before King Arthur at the next Feast of Pentecost and tell how they had been overthrown by the Nameless Knight.

Then, without waiting for any thanks from King Bagdemagus, he rode into the forest once more and continued there many days, until on a sudden he was aware of a great knight riding a mighty horse, who jousted with Sir Gaheris, Gawain's brother, a Knight of the Round Table. And the great knight smote Sir Gaheris to the ground, picked him up, threw him across his horse, and went on his way, driving the horse and the wounded knight in front of him.

Sir Launcelot set spurs to his horse and rode after them, crying:

'Turn, sir knight! Put down that wounded man to rest awhile, and let us try one another's strength in battle! For I hear it said that you have done great shame and despite to many Knights of the Round Table. Therefore – defend yourself!'

'Ah-ha!' cried Sir Turquyn, for it was he, 'If you are a Knight of the Round Table yourself, so much the better! I defy you – and all your fellowship!'

'You have said enough for now,' cried Launcelot. 'This is the time for blows!'

Then they put their spears in rest, drew apart, and came together as fast as their horses could gallop: and they smote one another in the midst of their shields so hard that both their horses' backs broke at the shock, and the two knights were flung to the ground, where they lay stunned for a little while. After that they fought for more than two hours with their swords, neither having the vantage, though both were bleeding from many wounds.

'You are the mightiest knight that ever I met!' gasped Sir Turquyn as they stood resting on their swords. 'I love a good fighter, and for love of you I'll set free all the knights in my dungeon – provided you are not that Launcelot who slew my brother Sir Carados of the Dolorous Tower: for him have I sworn to slay in revenge.'

'In that tower dwelt more evil than ever yet I have seen,' said Launcelot, 'and I slew Sir Carados the craven justly, whoever he was!'

'Ah!' cried Turquyn, 'then you *are* Launcelot! You are the most welcome knight of any ... Now we rest not until one of us is dead.'

To it again they went, and the end was that Launcelot smote off Sir Turquyn's head.

'Come now,' said Launcelot to Gaheris; and together these two wounded knights came to Turquyn's castle where hung the shields of Sir Hector and Sir Lionel, besides Sir Kay, Sir Marhaus and many others of the Round Table.

Then, while Launcelot washed his wounds at the ford, Gaheris went into the castle, flung down the porter and with his keys unlocked the dungeon doors and set free the prisoners.

Now, seeing that he was wounded, they all thought that he had fought and overcome Turquyn.

'Not so, noble sirs,' said Gaheris. 'It was Sir Launcelot of the Lake who set you free – for he fought and killed Sir Turquyn, whom no one else could conquer. Now he bids you hasten to the court of King Arthur, and he will meet you there next year at Pentecost, if you would speak with him. But he prays Sir Lionel and Sir Hector to meet him on that day, when King Arthur next holds his high feast.'

'That we will do,' said all the knights.

'But we will ride now to seek for him,' said Lionel and Hector.

'And I will ride with you,' said Sir Kay. 'I would ask his

pardon for the ill things I spoke of him on the day when our Lord Arthur made him a knight.'

Meanwhile Sir Launcelot had washed his wounds at the ford, and watered the horse which Gaheris had given to him; and, finding that the wounds were neither so deep nor so painful as he had thought, he did not come to the Castle of Turquyn, where the other knights were waiting for him, but rode on into the forest once more, to seek for further adventures.

On and on he went for many weeks after this, riding hither and thither in the forests which covered so much of Britain in those days: and many damsels he rescued from wicked men, many knights he fought with and overcame, even giants fell beneath his keen lance and the great sword wielded in his strong right hand.

Of all the adventures which he met with at that time we cannot speak here; but one of the strangest befell him not long before his return to Camelot before the Feast of Pentecost of the year after he had been made a knight.

He rode in a deep forest, more lonely and wild than any he had yet traversed, and suddenly in the shadowy undergrowth he saw a white brachet casting about as if following a trail; but the trail was plain upon the ground – great dark splashes of blood. Then Launcelot rode faster and faster, following the brachet, who kept looking behind her to see that he was still there: across a great marsh they went and came at length over a bridge to an old manor-house whose crumbling walls, half hidden by ivy, went down into a weed-grown moat.

Into the great hall ran the brachet, and there Launcelot saw a knight lying dead: and the brachet went and licked his wounds and howled dolorously. And then there came out a lady, weeping and wringing her hands, and said to Launcelot:

'Ah, to what sorrow have you brought me!'

'Lady,' he answered, 'I did never harm to this knight, for I but followed this brachet hither by the trail of blood. Therefore, be not displeased with me.'

'Truly, sir,' she answered, 'I do not think it is you who has slain my husband. But he that did the deed lies sore wounded

– of which wound he shall never be made whole, that I'll make certain!'

Then she fell to weeping, and to cursing the knight who had slain her husband, Sir Gilbert, with many terrible words.

'Now God send you better comfort,' said Launcelot, and rode sadly away. He had not gone far, however, when he met a damsel who knew him by the device on his shield, and cried at once:

'Well met, Sir Launcelot of the Lake, bravest of knights! I beg of your nobleness to help my brother who is wounded sorely with a wound that will not cease from bleeding. This day he fought with one Sir Gilbert and slew him in fair and open battle: but Sir Gilbert's lady is a wicked sorceress, and she brought it about by her magic that his wound shall never heal ... But I met the Lady Nimue wandering in the forest, and she told me that my brother's wound would close only if I could find a knight brave enough to go into the Chapel Perilous and bring thence a sword and a piece of cloth from a wounded knight who lies there.'

'This is a marvellous thing,' said Sir Launcelot. 'But tell me who your brother is.'

'Sir,' she answered, 'he is Sir Melyot, a true knight of Logres.'

'Then am I the more sorry,' said Launcelot, 'for he is my fellow of the Table Round, and to aid him I will certainly do all in my power.'

Then she said: 'Sir, follow this path and it will bring you to the Chapel Perilous; and I shall remain here until you return ... And if you do not return, then will there be no knight living who can achieve this adventure.'

Down the path went Launcelot, and came before long to a strange, lonely chapel in a little clearing. Then he tied his horse to a tree and went into the churchyard on foot. And on the end of the chapel he saw hanging many fair shields turned upside down: and suddenly thirty great knights dressed in black armour stood beneath the shields, taller by a foot and more than any mortal man: and they gnashed their teeth and glared horribly at Sir Launcelot.

Then, though he was much afraid, he drew his sword, put his shield before him, and charged into the midst of them. But they scattered on either side of him without speaking a word or striking a blow; and he grew bolder, and entered into the chapel. The interior was lit only by one dim lamp which cast weird shadows beneath the low stone arches; and he was ware of a corpse stretched upon a stone slab and covered with a silk cloth.

Stooping down reverently, Sir Launcelot cut a piece of the cloth away: and as he did so, the floor moved as if an earthquake had shaken the chapel, and the lamp swung, creaking dismally on its chain until the shadows seemed to writhe and clutch at him.

Sir Launcelot knelt awhile in fear; and then he saw a fair sword lying beside the dead knight and he took it quickly in his hand and came out into the churchyard once more. And then all the black knights spoke together in hollow tones, without moving their jaws:

'Knight, Sir Launcelot! Lay by that sword, or else thou shalt die horribly!'

'Whether I live or die,' cried Launcelot, 'I'll not yield it up for mere words: therefore, fight for it if you dare!'

But not a hand was raised against him, and he passed safely down the churchway path and came to the lych-gate. There a strange damsel stood waiting for him:

'Sir Launcelot!' she cried, 'leave that sword behind you, or you will die for it!'

'I leave it not,' he answered, 'whatever may be threatened me.'

'You speak wisely,' said the damsel, 'for if you left that sword, you would come never again to the court of King Arthur.'

'Then I would be a fool to give it up!' he answered.

'But, gentle sir knight,' said the damsel, 'you must kiss me once ere you pass.'

'Nay, not so,' answered Sir Launcelot, 'that were a sinful kiss.'

'Alas!' sobbed the damsel, 'I have lost all my labour. Had

you kissed me, you would have fallen to the earth a dead man. For I made this Chapel Perilous by magic, to entrap the three noblest knights of Logres – Sir Gawain, and you, and Sir Percivale who is not yet born. For I am Allewes the Sorceress, the companion of Morgana le Fay . . .'

'Now Jesu preserve me from your subtle crafts!' said Sir Launcelot, crossing himself. And when he looked up, Allewes the Sorceress had gone.

Then Launcelot untied his horse and rode back swiftly along the path until he found the damsel, Sir Melyot's sister, and when she saw him she clapped her hands and wept for joy.

Swiftly they went to the nearby castle where Sir Melyot lay, and they found him as pale as death, with the life-blood still flowing from his wound. Launcelot knelt down beside him, touched the wound with the sword and bound it about with the silk – and straightway Sir Melyot was made whole.

After this Launcelot abode with Sir Melyot and his sister, and rested in their castle for many days. But one morning he said: 'Now I must set out for the Court of King Arthur at Camelot, for the Feast of Pentecost draws near. There, by the grace of God, you may find me if you wish.'

Then he rode away swiftly into the forest, the spring sunlight flashing back from his burnished armour as it fell like golden rain between the fresh green leaves. But he did not come to Camelot without meeting with more adventures on the way.

Riding through pleasant country and open park-land as he drew nearer to Camelot, Launcelot chanced suddenly one day upon a lady who stood weeping beneath a great oak tree.

'Ah, Launcelot, flower of knighthood!' she cried. 'Help me now! Yonder in the tree-top is my lord's hawk caught by the golden lunes tied about its feet. As I held it, it slipped from me ; and my lord is a man of savage temper and will surely slay me for losing the hawk.'

'Well, fair lady,' said Launcelot, 'since you know my name and require me by my vows of knighthood to help you, I will do what I can. But the tree is passing high, and there are many dead boughs upon it.'

Therewith he loosed him of his armour, the lady helping him, and, clad only in shirt and breeches, he climbed into the tree and came at length to the hawk. Loosing it carefully, he tied the lunes to a rotten branch and threw it out from the tree, so that the hawk fluttered safely to the ground and was caught by the lady.

Then Launcelot began to climb down again: but before he reached the ground a great knight came striding out from a pavilion near by with a drawn sword in his hand.

'Ah-ha, Sir Launcelot!' he cried, 'now have I found you just as I would – and now will I slay you!'

'Ah lady,' said Launcelot, 'why have you betrayed me?'

'She did but as I told her,' said the knight. 'And this trap was laid for you by command of the Lady Allewes. Now come down and let me slay you!'

'It were evil shame to you,' said Launcelot, 'thus armed to slay a man who has neither armour nor weapons.'

'Such words will not save you,' growled the knight.

'At least give me my sword,' said Launcelot, 'that I may die with it in my hand.'

'Nay, I know better than to do that!' laughed the knight. 'No weapon shall you have if I can keep you from it!'

Then Sir Launcelot feared greatly that his hour had come; but nevertheless he would not let himself be slain tamely, nor would he attempt to leap out of the tree and run away, as he might have done without his armour. Presently as he looked about him he saw a thick, stumpy dead branch: this he broke off, jumped down suddenly, dodged the knight for a moment, and then stood up to him bravely. The knight lashed eagerly at Launcelot with his sword, but he turned the blow with his wooden club, and then whirling it round caught him such a bang on the side of the head that he cracked his skull. Then, seizing his sword he cut his head off at a blow.

'Alas!' cried the lady, 'why have you slain my husband?'

'It is no fault of mine,' said Launcelot grimly. 'You would, between you, have slain me by treason – and now your wickedness has returned on your own heads.'

Then he put on his armour and rode away; and a little

before nightfall he came to a castle where he found fair entertainment and a comfortable bed for the night. But before morning he was roused by a knocking at the gate, and looking out of the window he saw Sir Kay, who had been chased there by three knights.

'Truly,' said Launcelot to himself, 'I will go down and help Sir Kay, for those three knights will kill him otherwise!'

Then he put on his armour, and let himself down through the window on the end of a sheet.

'Turn!' he cried to the three knights as he rushed upon them: and in seven strokes he had laid out all of them on the ground.

'Sir knight!' they cried, 'we yield ourselves to you as to a matchless fighter!'

'Yield to Sir Kay,' said Launcelot, 'or I will kill you as you lie!' And when they had promised to do this, though grudgingly, for Kay was no fighter, he went on: 'Go now swiftly to Camelot, and give yourselves to King Arthur at the Feast of Pentecost, telling him that Sir Kay sent you!'

When they had gone he brought Sir Kay into the castle, and led him up to his bedroom: then Kay recognized him by the light of his candle, and knelt to thank him for saving his life.

'Nay,' said Launcelot, 'I did but my duty as a knight. Come now and rest, for you are wearied.'

So Kay ate and drank, and then fell sound asleep in Launcelot's bed. And when he woke, late in the morning, Launcelot had gone – but so had Sir Kay's armour!

'Ah-ha!' laughed Kay. 'Now there will be trouble for some of King Arthur's knights – for they will think it is I, and joust with him! But I myself will wear Launcelot's armour, and ride in peace!' For Sir Kay was not very popular among the Knights of the Round Table, and some of the younger ones took their revenge for the cruel things he was in the habit of saying about them by knocking him off his horse whenever they met him riding in quest of adventures – which Kay did not do more often than he could help!

This time he came back to Camelot without being challenged by a single knight: but Launcelot, wearing Kay's armour, but carrying his own spear, had a very brisk day of it.

'There goes the proud Sir Kay!' cried one of three fresh knights who had pitched their pavilion not far from the castle where Launcelot had lodged. 'He thinks that no knight is as good as he, however often we prove the contrary to him! But let us each joust with him in turn – he will not be so saucy at the feast to-morrow if we bruise him well to-day!'

Launcelot, however, knocked them off their horses one after the other like so many nine-pins, and as they sat upon

Launcelot knocked them off their horses ...

the ground, staring at him in wonder, he commanded them to yield themselves to Queen Guinevere next day, and say that Sir Kay had sent them.

Then he rode on again, and before long met his brother Sir Hector, with three of the best Knights of the Round Table, Sir Segramour, and Sir Uwaine, and Sir Gawain himself.

'Now, by my faith,' said Sir Segramour, 'I will prove Sir Kay's might of which he speaks so often!'

So he set his spear in rest and came against Launcelot, who did likewise: but Sir Launcelot smote Sir Segramour so sorely that horse and man rolled both on the ground.

'Look, friends!' exclaimed Sir Hector. 'There was a

mighty stroke indeed! ... Methinks that knight is much bigger than ever was Sir Kay ... Now we shall see what I can do to him!'

So Sir Hector set his spear in rest, and he and Launcelot came together like a clap of thunder: and Launcelot knocked him over his horse's tail and left him lying on the plain.

'By my faith,' said Sir Uwaine, 'yonder is a passing strong knight, and I am sure that he has slain Sir Kay and rides now in his armour. It will be hard to match him, but let us see what I can do!'

... like so many nine-pins

Together they came, galloping as if they were mad, but Launcelot sent Sir Uwaine flying out of his saddle; and he hit the ground so hard that he lay stunned for a long while.

'Now I see well,' said Sir Gawain, 'that I must encounter this knight!' And he raised his shield, took a good spear in his hand, and charged at Sir Launcelot with all his might; and each knight smote the other in the midst of his shield. But Sir Gawain's spear broke all to pieces, while Launcelot's struck him so hard that his horse could not keep its feet, but rolled over and over on the ground.

And Launcelot rode on his way, smiling to himself and saying: 'God give him joy that made this spear, for never came a better one into my hands.'

'I think that must be Sir Launcelot of the Lake,' said Gawain, rising slowly and helping the other knights to their feet. 'Let us hasten to Camelot, for then we shall know!'

Next day at the Feast of Pentecost all Arthur's knights were gathered together at the Round Table, and Sir Launcelot came in wearing Sir Kay's armour, but, of course, with no helmet: then Gawain, Uwaine, Hector, and Segramour knew for certain who it was that had overthrown them with one spear, and there was much laughing and joking among them.

Then Sir Kay told the king how Sir Launcelot had rescued him from the three knights who would have slain him. 'And he made the three knights yield to me instead of to him,' said Sir Kay – and there they were, all three, to bear witness. 'Then Sir Launcelot took my armour,' Kay went on, 'and left me his: and I rode home in peace, for no man dared joust with me!'

Then all those knights came in who had been held prisoner by Sir Turquyn, and told how Launcelot had saved them. And Sir Gaheris said: 'I saw all that battle from the beginning to the end, and that Turquyn was the strongest knight that ever I saw.'

There came also Sir Melyot to tell how Launcelot had saved him; and King Bagdemagus for whom he had fought, and many more, each with some story of mighty deeds and great daring.

And King Arthur was happy to have such a knight in his court, and Queen Guinevere loved him as she heard tell of all his mighty deeds; nor did any blame Arthur now for knighting an untried squire – for Sir Launcelot had in that year of adventures won the greatest name of any knight in the world, and the most honoured of high and low. Nor was there ever such another knight in the realm of Logres as Sir Launcelot of the Lake.

3

Sir Gareth, or The Knight of the Kitchen

'NOW my lord Arthur, you may sit down to the feast!' said Sir Gawain one Pentecost when all the Knights of the Round Table were gathered at Camelot, but could not sit down to dinner because no adventure had befallen, nor had anyone come with some strange tale or request for help. 'Let the feast begin – for here comes a young man in simple array, leaning upon the shoulders of two stalwart serving men – and he is a head taller than either of them!'

'Who think you it may be?' asked King Arthur, as he took his seat beside Queen Guinevere.

'I cannot tell,' answered Gawain, 'yet I love him even as I look, for a fairer man did I never see, nor one so likely to do honour to knighthood.'

A little while after this the stranger came into the hall: and when he reached King Arthur he drew himself up and cried:

'May God bless you, most noble King Arthur, and this your fellowship of the Round Table also! I come hither to ask you to grant me three gifts: and they shall not be unreasonable, nor any that you might fear to grant. And the first I will ask you now, and the others a twelve-month hence.'

'Now ask what you will, and you shall have it,' said King Arthur, for he also liked this tall young man with his fair hair and honest look, and trusted him on sight.

'I ask sir, that I may have meat and drink at your court for this first year.'

'Now I beg you to ask for something better than that!' said King Arthur.

'Sir, that is all I wish,' answered the stranger.

'Well, then,' said the King, 'you shall have meat and drink enough, for I never denied that to friend or foe. But tell me, I beg of you, what your name is.'

'That, sir, I would rather not reveal until the right time.'

'Then be it as you say,' King Arthur agreed. 'Yet I wonder greatly who you are, for you are one of the goodliest young men I have ever seen.' And after that he gave him into the charge of Sir Kay and bade him give as good food and drink as if he had been entertaining a great duke or baron.

'He's neither of those,' said Sir Kay contemptuously. 'If he were even a knight's son he would have asked for horse and armour, not food and drink. I'll wager he's only a vulgar peasant's son, and not fit to mix with us knights. Well, I'll give him a place in the kitchen, with as much food as he can eat – in a year's time he'll be as fat as a pork hog! And since he has no name, I'll call him Beaumains – Fair Hands – for I have never seen any so big, or so white – or so idle and lazy.'

So, for a whole year, Beaumains served in the kitchen; and Sir Kay laughed at him, said unkind things to him, made rude jokes about him, and generally did his best to make his life as unbearable as possible.

But Beaumains was always gentle and patient, never answering Sir Kay back, nor refusing to do whatever unworthy and lowly an office he commanded him – and Sir Kay, feeling that he might be in the wrong himself, jeered at him more and more unkindly.

Pentecost came once more, and the whole Round Table was met again at Camelot; nor would King Arthur sit down to the feast until a squire came to him and said:

'Sir, you may go to your meat; for here cometh a damsel with some strange adventures ...'

And in a few minutes the damsel came into the hall and knelt before King Arthur, begging him for help.

'For whom?' said the King. 'What is the adventure?'

'For my sister, the Lady Liones,' she answered, 'who is kept a prisoner in a castle by a wicked tyrant who has destroyed all her lands. And his name is The Red Knight of the Red Lawns.'

At these words Beaumains came suddenly before the King, and said:

'My lord, I thank you for that I have been these twelve months in your kitchen and have had my fill of meat and drink. And now I will ask for the other two gifts which you promised me: firstly, that you will grant me the adventure of this damsel, and secondly, that Sir Launcelot of the Lake shall ride with me until I have proved myself worthy of knighthood at his hands – for it is my desire to be made a knight by no one but Launcelot.'

'These things I will grant to you ...' began King Arthur; but the damsel, whose name was the Lady Linnet, broke in angrily:

'Fie upon you, King Arthur! What an insult is this, that you send a filthy scullion out of your kitchen to save my sister, when here at your Round Table sit Sir Launcelot and Sir Gawain, Sir Gaheris and Sir Bors – the best knights in the world – besides many others that are brave and noble also!'

Then in a great rage she mounted her white palfrey and rode away from Camelot. And as Beaumains made ready to follow her, there came a dwarf carrying a great sword for him, which he hung at his side; and outside the hall a mighty war horse was waiting, on which Beaumains mounted and rode away, Launcelot following a little behind.

Then in the hall Sir Kay sprang up angrily, exclaiming: 'I will ride after my kitchen-boy and thrash him soundly for setting himself up like this!'

'You had best abide at home!' said Sir Gawain. But Sir Kay would listen to no advice: away he went, fully armed, as fast as his horse would carry him, and before long he overtook Beaumains, who had just caught up with Lady Linnet.

'Hey, Beaumains!' shouted Sir Kay, 'what are you doing out of the kitchen? Where is your reverence for your betters? Do you not know who I am?'

'Right well I know you!' answered Beaumains, turning his horse. 'You are Sir Kay, the rudest and most ungentle Knight of the Court: therefore, beware of me!'

This made Sir Kay so furious that at once he set his spear in rest and charged at Beaumains, who, unarmed as he was, spurred to meet him, his drawn sword in his hand. And just as Sir Kay's spear seemed about to transfix Beaumains like a moth on a pin, he swerved his horse suddenly to one side, parried the spear with the back of his sword-blade, and caught Sir Kay deftly on the point of it. Then Sir Kay fell off his horse and lay there with a great wound; but Beaumains took his spear and shield and rode on after the Lady Linnet, while Launcelot, who was following close behind, flung Sir Kay across his horse and turned it loose to carry Kay back to Camelot as best it could.

Meanwhile Beaumains overtook Lady Linnet: but he met with no kind greeting.

'Fie upon you!' she cried. 'Why have you dared to follow me? You stink of the kitchen, and your clothes are mouldy with grease and tallow! As for that knight whom you have wounded or killed, you struck him a coward's blow ... Turn round, I tell you, and go back to your kitchen: for well I know that you are only the dirty scullion whom Sir Kay named Beaumains because of your big hands! Bah! Your hands are only fit for plucking fowls and turning the spigot in a beer-butt!'

'Damsel,' answered Beaumains politely, 'you may say to me what you wish, but never will I turn back. For I have promised King Arthur to undertake your adventure – and achieve it I will, or die in the attempt.'

'You'll achieve my adventure, will you!' jeered Linnet. 'Why, before long you will meet with such an adversary that you'll give all the broth in Camelot to be allowed to go back to your kitchen alive!'

'That we shall see,' answered Beaumains quietly, and they rode on in silence, the Lady Linnet a little way in front.

Before long they came to a great black hawthorn-tree by the side of a dark glade; and there hung a black banner and a black shield, and by it sat a knight all clad in black armour upon a black horse.

'Now flee away quickly,' said Lady Linnet to Beaumains. 'For this is the Black Knight of the Black Lawns!'

'I thank you for your words,' answered Beaumains. But he showed no sign of doing as she advised.

'Damsel!' cried the Black Knight. 'Have you brought this fellow from the Court of King Arthur to be your champion?'

'Heaven forbid!' said Linnet. 'This is only a scurvy scullion who follows me, whether I will or not. And I beg you, sir knight, to deliver me from him – for he wearies me greatly.'

'Why then,' said the Black Knight, taking up his black shield and his black spear, 'I'll knock him off his horse and let him walk back to Camelot ... It's a fine horse, and will be very useful to me!'

'You make passing free with my horse,' said Beaumains. 'Come now and take it if you can: and if you cannot, then stand aside and let me pass across these black lawns of yours.'

'Say you so!' cried the Black Knight. 'You speak saucily for a mere kitchen knave!'

'You lie!' shouted Beaumains. 'I am no scullion, but a gentleman born, and of nobler ancestry than you are!'

After this they set their spears in rest and came together like two mad bulls. The Black Knight's spear glanced off Beaumains' shield and did no harm; but Beaumains' pierced the Black Knight through shield and armour, so that he fell out of his saddle and died.

'Fie on you, cowardly scullion!' cried Linnet. 'You slew him by treachery!' And with that she rode away quickly.

But Beaumains got off his horse and clothed himself in the Black Knight's armour; but he kept his own sword and Sir Kay's shield and spear.

Now Sir Launcelot had seen all that passed, and coming up to Beaumains he said: 'Sir, you have done right valiantly, and I now will make you a knight with all my heart. But your name you must tell me first – though I will not speak it to others until you wish it.'

'My lord,' answered Beaumains, kneeling with bowed head, 'I am Gareth of Orkney, youngest son of King Lot and of

Arthur's sister Queen Morgawse. Sir Gawain is my brother and Gaheris and Agravaine also: but they knew me not, for none of them have seen me these last ten years.'

'Right glad am I this day!' said Launcelot. 'And herewith I make you a knight. Go forward as you have begun, and there will be a place waiting for you at the Round Table. And I hold that you will be one of the truest knights in all the Realm of Logres, and one of the gentlest and most valiant.'

Then Launcelot returned joyfully to Camelot, but Beaumains, whom we must now call Sir Gareth, sprang upon the Black Knight's horse and rode after the Lady Linnet.

'Away, kitchen knave!' she cried. 'Faugh, out of the wind – for the smell of stale grease makes me sick! ... Alas that so good a knight should be murdered by such as you! But there is one hereby who will make you pay dearly – therefore, run away while there is still time!'

'I may be beaten or slain,' said Gareth gently, 'but flee will I never, nor leave you until this adventure be accomplished.'

Before long they met suddenly a knight dressed all in green armour, with green spear and green shield.

'Greetings, damsel,' said the Green Knight of the Green Lawns. 'Is that my brother the Black Knight whom you have brought with you?'

'No, alas!' said Linnet. 'It's only a wretched kitchen knave who has slain him by treachery.'

'Traitor!' cried the Green Knight. 'You shall die for this!'

'I defy you,' answered Sir Gareth, 'for your brother died honourably and in fair fight. Indeed any unfairness lay on his side, for he was in full armour, while I had only a shield.'

Then the two knights jousted furiously – and broke their spears into little pieces. After this they fought with swords: on horseback until Gareth struck the Green Knight to the earth, and then on foot.

'Sir Knight!' cried Linnet presently. 'Why do you take such a time to dispatch a mere kitchen knave? Alas, it is a shame to let him live so long!'

Then, mad with rage, the Green Knight struck such a blow at Sir Gareth that he cut his shield into two pieces; but

Gareth dropped the broken half from his arm, took his sword in both hands, and gave the Green Knight such a buffet on the helm that he rolled over on the ground like a shot rabbit, and lay there asking for mercy.

'You plead in vain,' said Sir Gareth. 'For I will most certainly kill you unless this lady begs me for your life.'

'That I will never do!' cried Linnet. 'I would not be in debt to a mere scullion!'

'Then he must die,' said Gareth.

'Spare me, I beg of you,' gasped the Green Knight. 'I will forgive you for my brother's death, and serve you faithfully, with my fifty knights.'

'It is of no avail, unless she pleads for you,' said Gareth. 'You are about to die.'

'Do not kill him, you filthy scullion!' cried Linnet.

'Damsel,' said Gareth bowing to her, 'your command is my pleasure always: at your request I will spare this noble knight. Sir Knight of the Green Lawns, I release you herewith: get you to Camelot with your fifty men, do allegiance to King Arthur, and say that the Knight of the Kitchen sent you!'

That evening the Green Knight entertained Gareth and Linnet at his castle, and although she never ceased from railing and insulting words, Gareth received all honour from everyone else.

'Fie!' cried the Lady Linnet, 'it is shameful for you all to honour this man so!'

'Truly,' answered the Green Knight, 'it would be more shameful were I to do him any dishonour, who has proved himself a better knight than I am.'

'Lady,' said Sir Gareth as they rode through the forest next morning, 'you are uncourteous so to rebuke me and mock at me, for I think that I have done you good service so far, and overcome those knights who, you said, would beat me. Moreover, whatever you may say, I will in no wise depart from you until my quest is accomplished.'

'Well,' said she, 'very soon you will indeed meet your match. For now we draw near to the castle of the Blue

Knight of the Blue Lawns – and only Sir Launcelot, Sir Gawain, Sir Bors, or King Arthur himself, could vanquish him. And I doubt if even these could save my sister, the Lady Liones, for the Red Knight of the Red Lawns who holds her besieged is the mightiest man in the world, and the secret of his strength is that it comes of the magic of Queen Morgana le Fay.'

'The mightier mine enemies be, the greater my honour if I conquer them,' said Sir Gareth.

Then they came out of the forest into a great meadow carpeted with blue speedwell: and therein stood many pavilions of blue silk, and knights and ladies dressed all in blue moved amongst them. In the midst of the meadow grew a great mulberry tree on which hung many shields which had belonged to the knights whom the Blue Knight had slain: and from a low-sweeping bough hung a huge blue shield, with a blue spear struck into the ground beside it, and an iron-grey horse tied to the tree-trunk.

'Run away, you stinking scullion!' taunted the Lady Linnet. 'Hereby is the Blue Knight, and his hundred followers!'

'Then here shall I stay and fight,' said Gareth, 'and over-throw maybe a few of them – if they come at me in turns.'

'I marvel greatly who you are,' said the Lady Linnet, ceasing suddenly from her usual tone of mockery. 'Surely you must come of noble and gentle blood – for never did woman rail and insult a knight as I have done you, and still you answer me courteously and depart not from my service.'

'Lady,' said Sir Gareth gravely, 'a knight who could not put up with hard words from a woman would be of little worth. You anger me, certainly, by your cruel sayings – but then I fight all the more fiercely against your enemies. And as for my birth, I have served you as a gentleman should: if I be one or not, you shall know in time, for better service still I have to do before we part.'

'Alas, fair Beaumains,' sobbed Linnet, 'forgive me for all I have said against you – and fly before it really is too late.'

'I forgive you right joyously,' said Gareth. 'But fly I will not, rather fight the harder so that I may win from you fairer words still.'

At this moment the great Blue Knight saw Gareth, and sprang upon his horse, crying:

'You there! Knight in the black armour! Jump down from your horse and kiss my foot in surrender this instant, or I will kill you without mercy!'

'Nay, rather do you come to your knees,' answered Gareth, 'for I would need great mercifulness to spare the life of one who has slain so many good knights!'

Then the Blue Knight looked to his blue armour, closed the vizor of his blue helmet, set his blue spear in rest, and came thundering down on Sir Gareth, who met him in mid career – so hard that both spears were broken, and both horses rolled over on the ground. Then the two knights drew their swords, and began hacking and hewing until the sparks flew, striking such blows that sometimes they both fell grovelling on the ground.

And at last Sir Gareth struck off the Blue Knight's helmet and felled him to the ground, and made as though to slay him.

But the Lady Linnet begged for his life, and the Blue Knight yielded himself to Gareth.

'I will indeed grant you mercy,' Gareth said. 'For you are a mighty fighter, and it were a pity to slay such a one. Ride therefore to King Arthur's Court at Camelot with a hundred followers, and do homage to him, and say that the Knight of the Kitchen sent you.'

That night Sir Gareth and the Lady Linnet were entertained most hospitably by the Blue Knight, and next morning he rode with them for a little while to show them the way.

'Fair damsel,' he said, 'whitherward are you leading this knight?'

'Sir,' she answered, 'we are going to Castle Dangerous where my sister the Lady Liones is besieged.'

'Ah,' said the Blue Knight. 'Then you go against the Red Knight of the Red Lawns, which is the most perilous knight now living in the world, and a man without mercy: and by evil magic he has the strength of seven men. He has laid siege to that castle for long, and well might he have taken it many times: but he did not so, for the Queen Morgana le Fay made it by magic and gave him also his strength. And they hoped that Sir Launcelot or Sir Gawain would come on this quest, or King Arthur himself, and that the Red Knight would slay him, as I fear that he will slay you.'

'That shall fall out as God wills,' said Sir Gareth. 'And yet perchance He wills that the Red Knight shall fall by my hand, that I may bring honour to the realm of Logres ... And I will tell you now, but let it not come to the ears of any at Camelot until I desire it, that I am Gareth, brother of Gawain and Gaheris, youngest son of the King of Orkney and of Morgawse, King Arthur's sister.'

The Blue Knight left them before long, and they came through a thick wood and out on to an open plain, all red with poppies, and in the midst of it a castle built of red sandstone, and about the castle many tents and pavilions of red, where dwelt the followers of the Red Knight besieging the castle. Across the plain rode Gareth and the Lady Linnet, and before they reached the encampment they came to a great red Judas tree on which, half hidden by the scarlet blossoms, hung the decaying bodies of many goodly knights, each still in his armour with his golden spurs upon his heels.

'These are all those others who came before you to rescue my sister the Lady Liones,' said Linnet. 'The Red Knight of the Red Lawns overcame them one and all, and put them to this shameful death without mercy or pity.'

'Then it is time I came to blows with him!' said Gareth, angered at the sight of the slaughtered men. And he took a great horn made of an elephant's tusk which hung from a branch of the tree, and raised it to his lips.

'Stay!' cried the Lady Linnet. 'Blow not the horn until the noon be passed: for now it is still early in the morning, and it is said that the Red Knight's strength grows and grows until the middle of the day, and then wanes in the afternoon, until at sunset he is no stronger than other men – albeit he is always the strongest of any.'

'Ah, fie for shame, fair lady,' said Sir Gareth. 'I were

They came together with a noise like thunder

indeed unworthy if I should wait to fight with him when his strength had gone!'

With that he blew such a blast on the horn that the red walls of Castle Dangerous re-echoed it, and people came running out of all the tents and pavilions. And in the castle everyone came to the windows or looked down from the walls to see who it was that thus dared to challenge the terrible Red Knight of the Red Lawns.

'Look, Sir Gareth,' exclaimed Linnet suddenly, 'there is my sister the Lady Liones looking out of her window – and here comes the Red Knight himself!'

Then Gareth turned first towards the castle and bowed low to the lovely lady who was leaning out of the window and waving to him; and meanwhile the Red Knight, dressed all in red armour and riding a strawberry-roan war-horse, was riding towards him.

'Leave off looking at that lady – she's mine!' he roared. 'And look at me instead – for I'm the last thing you shall see before you die!'

So they set their spears in rest, and came together with a noise like thunder. Fair and square each hit the other in the centre of his shield – so mighty a stroke that the spears crumbled into sawdust, and the girths and bridles on their horses broke like cotton, and the two horses fell dead at the shock, and the two knights lay still and stunned on the red lawn so long that people began to murmur: 'They have broken their necks! A mighty man indeed is this stranger, for ere this none has even so much as thrown the Red Knight from his saddle!'

But presently they staggered to their feet, drew their swords, and rushed together like two fierce lions, lashing at one another until pieces of armour flew from them on every side, and the blood ran down, dyeing the lawn a darker, rustier red. Presently they rested, and fought again, and at the hour of noon the Red Knight struck Sir Gareth's sword out of his hand, and flung himself upon him to slay him. But Gareth wrestled with him, and at length threw him to the ground, tore off his helmet, and seized a sword to kill him.

'Noble sir!' cried the Red Knight, 'I yield myself to your mercy – therefore spare my life, I pray you.'

'It may not be,' answered Sir Gareth, 'for right shamefully have you dealt with many good knights, hanging them from the red tree – a churl's death.'

'Sir,' said the Red Knight, 'all that I have done I did for a lady's sake. She it was who made this Castle by her magic – and I loved her full well. Upon a time her brothers, so she told me, were slain by Knights of the Round Table: therefore had she great hatred towards King Arthur and all those who followed him. And she would have none of my love; howbeit, she swore to be mine when I had slain a hundred of King Arthur's knights and hung them from yonder red tree on the red lawn.'

Then came the Lady Linnet and begged Gareth to spare his life, saying:

'Know now, sir knight, that all this was done of Queen Morgana le Fay to bring sorrow and despite upon Logres. But, by your mighty deeds, greater glory than ever is come to Logres: for so always shall such as you bring good out of the workings of another's evil. Therefore spare this knight whose name is Sir Ironside, for in days to come he shall sit in an honourable siege at the Round Table.'

'Rise, Sir Ironside,' said Gareth. 'Your life I give you. But ride now to the Court of King Arthur, give yourself and all your followers into his service, and say that the Knight of the Kitchen sent you.'

After this Sir Gareth rested for ten days in Sir Ironside's pavilion; and when he was fully cured of his wound, he rode up to Castle Dangerous to meet the Lady Liones whom he had saved. But what was his surprise as he came over the drawbridge to see the door slammed shut in his face, and the portcullis come rattling down in front of him, while the Lady Liones leaned out of a window above the gate and cried to him:

'Go away, Beaumains! Go away, Knight of the Kitchen! When you are a noble knight of noble birth, you shall have my love – but not before!'

At this Gareth was so enraged that without a word he turned and rode away into the depths of the forest, followed only by his dwarf.

But the Lady Linnet came and rebuked her sister, saying:

'Fie upon you thus to treat the knight who has delivered you from your dangers! He is not what he seems, but of his name and birth I may not tell you as yet.'

Then Lady Liones called to her brother Sir Gringamour, and said to him:

'Go now and follow the knight who is called Beaumains; and when he lies asleep, steal away his dwarf and bring him here. For the dwarf will surely know his master's true name and lineage.'

'Sister,' said Sir Gringamour, 'all this shall be done as you wish.'

All day he rode, and that night he found Sir Gareth sleeping under a tree, with his head upon his shield. Then he seized the dwarf, who sat by the horse a little apart, and rode off with him at top speed.

But the dwarf cried out: 'Master! Master! Save me!' And Gareth woke at the cry and followed Gringamour in the darkness, through wood and marsh, to the Castle Dangerous, though he knew not whither he had come.

Gringamour was there before him, however, and the dwarf had told his tale by the time Gareth came riding into the courtyard shouting:

'Traitor knight! Give me back my dwarf, or by my faith as a knight, I will strike off your head.'

Then the Lady Liones came down to him and made him welcome:

'Fair greetings, Sir Gareth of Orkney,' she said. 'I am overjoyed to welcome you now into Castle Dangerous – my preserver and my love.'

'Lady,' said Sir Gareth, 'you spoke not such words to me a while gone, though for your sake I had fought and vanquished the Black Knight, the Green Knight, the Blue Knight, and the Red Knight. Wherefore, though right willingly will I lodge in your castle for this night, it shall be as your guest only, and not as your love.'

The Lady Liones was angered at this, but she still spoke to him fairly, and made a great feast in his honour.

But as he lay in bed that night she sent a servant with a great sword to slay him. Gareth woke, however, as the man bent over him, and guarded the blow so that it pierced only his thigh. Then he leapt up, took his sword, and slew the murderer, smiting him into many pieces in his rage.

In the morning the Lady Liones rode to Camelot and there told King Arthur of how Sir Gareth had saved her from the Red Knight. And she asked him to hold a great tournament in Gareth's honour – for full well she knew that he was either dead, or wounded with a sore wound that might not be healed.

But Linet had found Gareth as he lay groaning on his bed; and she had wept at the shame which her sister had wrought by the evil magic of Morgana le Fay. But she too had learnt of the magic arts that are known in Avalon where dwells Nimue, the Lady of the Lake; and she wrought so well that Gareth was quite cured of his wound by the day of the tournament. And then she gave him a magic ring of many colours: and to those who saw him it seemed at one minute that he was clad in yellow armour, and the next in brown, one minute in black and the next in red: and no one might know who he was.

And at that tournament he rode many courses, jousting in turn with the bravest Knights of the Round Table, and overthrowing them all. But with Sir Launcelot he would not joust, nor with Sir Gawain his brother, and Sir Tristram was not yet there. Howbeit, there was no other knight so great as Sir Gareth, until the later days when Sir Galahad and Sir Percivale came also to Camelot.

When the tournament was ended King Arthur held his feast in the great hall, and Sir Gareth set the ring upon Linnet's finger – and straightway was known by all.

Then the Green Knight, the Blue Knight, and the Red Knight came with their followers to do homage to King Arthur and to tell how the 'Knight of the Kitchen' had overcome them in fair fight. And King Arthur rejoiced in the glory which his nephew Sir Gareth had won, and set him in an honourable siege at the Round Table. And Gareth wedded the Lady Linnet with much joy, and they lived happily ever afterwards.

But the Lady Liones departed from Camelot, sad and ashamed. And she forswore all the evil magic which she had followed for so long; and in after years Sir Gaheris, Gareth's brother, won her to be his wife.

4

Sir Tristram and the Fair Iseult

FOR many years after the founding of the Round Table two sieges remained empty, besides the Siege Perilous. The other places might sometimes lack a name for a little while as one knight or another was killed in some desperate battle or dangerous quest; but always there was another to take his place. But King Arthur knew that the two places by the Siege Perilous could not be filled so easily: these two places, the Siege Perilous, and one on either side of them were for the five best knights in Logres, and for these alone; Gawain sat in one and Launcelot in another to right and left of the Siege Perilous – but not even Sir Gareth or Sir Bors might sit in the two empty seats.

Now upon a certain Feast of Pentecost when all the knights were gathered in Camelot, King Arthur spoke with Launcelot and Gawain concerning these two sieges.

'There is one knight whose name I have heard tell of as the greatest of any,' said Gawain. 'But to your court he has never been. He is a Cornish knight, nephew to Mark, who is King of Cornwall under your overlordship, and his name is Tristram of Lyonesse.'

'I met him once,' said Launcelot. 'He jousted with certain knights of the Round Table, Sir Lamorak and Sir Segramour, and overthrew them. Then he and I broke a lance together – and I will here avow him to be the best knight with whom I ever yet have jousted.'

'We will send into Cornwall,' said King Arthur, 'and bid him come to our Court. For sure am I that it is of him that Merlin spoke, saying that for a little space he should sit at our

board, and bring great glory to Logres. ... But here, methinks, begins the adventure of this day, without which we
may not turn to the feast.'

For suddenly, as he spoke, they heard in the distance outside the hall the sad, sweet notes of a harp; and as they
listened the music drew nearer to them – music so sad and
sweet that no man there had ever heard the like, nor might
many restrain the tears from running down their cheeks.

And then the minstrel came into the hall: a fine man, tall,
broad and very noble to look upon; dark hair, dark eyes, and
a dignity about him that might well have become a king. Yet
he was poorly clad in such humble garments as a wandering
minstrel wore, and when he had bowed to King Arthur, he
took his seat on a stool near the door.

'Come hither, good minstrel,' said Arthur, when the magic
of the music had a little faded from his heart, 'and play to us
once more, and sing of brave deeds, of noble knights and
lovely ladies, for in them our heart delights. Whence come
you?'

'From Cornwall, noble King,' answered the minstrel.

'Have you heard tell of Sir Tristram of Lyonesse?'

'Yea, noble Arthur, and him have I seen full often,' said
the minstrel. 'And his story will I sing to you: a sad tale and
a true one, as ye shall hear.' He took the wine that was offered
him in a great horn cup, drank to King Arthur, and sitting
on a stool beside a great pillar, he began his lay, sometimes
telling it as a story, and sometimes singing it to the sad, sweet
music of the harp.

'The tale tells that in Lyonesse a king lived and a queen;
very happily they dwelt together, until upon a day an enemy
came into the land of Rivalin that king to lay it waste with fire
and sword. Rivalin went against him with all his men, but
he was slain in battle, and Morgan the wicked ruled his land.
And at that time Morgan made search for the queen, but she
had fled into the forest with one faithful follower named
Rual. And there in the forest a child was born to the queen,
and there she died and was buried. But before she died she
gave the child to Rual: "Faith-keeper," she said, "keep faith

'Have you heard tell of Sir Tristram of Lyonesse?'

now to your dead lord and to your lady who will soon be dead. Take my child, and call him Tristram, for he was born in sorrow; tend him carefully and guard him as your own son, that in a day to come he may avenge our deaths and rule once more in Lyonesse. And when he is a man, let him seek help of my brother, King Mark of Cornwall."

'Rual took the boy, and never was child more kindly and lovingly fostered by his own parents than was Tristram by Rual and Rual's wife. And when he grew older Kurwenal the wise taught him many things: to play upon the harp and to play at chess; to use a sword and a spear, and to ride a horse: and he took him through many foreign lands so that he might learn to speak their languages.

'When Tristram was a tall youth, it chanced that a ship of Norway came to Lyonesse to trade; and the merchant spoke well with Rual, and was kindly entertained. But ever he looked upon Tristram. And at the last he invited Tristram to come aboard his ship and play at chess with him; and Tristram came, and he beat the merchant at every game. But while they played, the sailors drew up the anchor silently, hoisted the great white sails, and slipped out to sea, meaning to sell Tristram as a slave for much money.

'A great storm arose, however, and for nine nights and days the ship drove before it, and all aboard feared greatly for their lives. Then the sailors clamoured, saying that a curse was upon them for stealing Tristram, and the merchant hearkened to them and set Tristram ashore upon the nearest land they chanced to see: and it happened that this was Cornwall. And when Tristram was come to shore, the storm ceased and the sun smiled out again.

'In Cornwall, he came soon to King Mark's Court at Tintagel, knowing not yet that Mark was his uncle – for still he believed that Rual was his real father. King Mark entertained the wanderer kindly, and Tristram served him so well that before long he rose to be the King's nearest and most trusted councillor. Then Rual came, seeking the wide world over for his lost fosterling, and he found Tristram with King Mark, and he saw that God had been working in these things.

'When Mark knew that Tristram was his own nephew, he made much of him, and the two dwelt there in happiness. For Mark sent his armies under Tristram's charge into Lyonesse, and Morgan the wicked was slain: but Tristram set Rual to reign in Lyonesse, though he made it a part of Mark's kingdom, and himself he dwelt still at Tintagel.

'On a day Tristram came into the court and found there great sorrow and lamentation: and in the seat of honour sat a great, dark man with a fierce face and mighty hands. And this was Sir Marhault of Ireland, who came from Gurman, Ireland's King, to demand tribute from Mark whom once he had overcome in battle. And the tribute was that thirty lads of noble birth be sent into Ireland to become servants at the Court: or else that a knight should do battle with Marhault and slay him. But no one would do battle, for never was there a stronger knight in the world than Marhault.

'"Shame be to you all," cried Tristram. "Call you yourselves men, that you sell your own sons into slavery?"

'"But nephew, we may not do otherwise! " said King Mark.

'"You can fight!" cried Tristram. "Refuse to pay the tribute: do battle with Gurman the Irish tyrant – or let a knight of yours fight and slay this boastful braggart Sir Marhault!"

'But none dared to fight, and Marhault laughed in scorn.

'"I will fight with you, wild hound of Ireland!" cried Tristram, and he struck Sir Marhault across the face with his glove so that there might be no drawing back with honour.

'The duel was to be upon a little island off the coast of Cornwall: with swords only were they to fight, and alone, with none to watch. Marhault came first in a little boat, and moored it to the shore; but Tristram pushed out his own boat so that it drifted away.

'"What do you, insolent child?" growled Marhault. "You will need your boat when you want to run away from me!"

'"Two men came living to this island," Tristram said simply. "One living man only shall depart!"

'Then Marhault laughed and drew his sword: Tristram drew his also, and they fought all day, giving each other many sore blows. And Marhault wounded Tristram once, a deep gash in the thigh. "That shall be your death!" he laughed, "for upon my sword is a magic ointment, and there are few indeed who can heal the wound into which it comes!"

'Then in a fury Tristram rushed upon him, shouting: "Treacherous and ungentle knight, thus do I answer you." And he clave through Marhault's helmet and deep into Marhault's skull, and his sword chipped, leaving a little piece in the wound. But Marhault fell to the ground, stricken to death, and yielded himself to Tristram. And that evening the men of Ireland set him upon a ship and sailed sadly home to Dublin; and there Marhault died, for all that his sister Queen Isaud could do – and she was skilled above all other women in the healing of wounds – but she drew out the broken chip of steel and kept it in a casket, swearing vengeance upon the striker of that blow.

'Tristram lay sick in Tintagel, and none might cure his wound. And at length the wise men told him that in Ireland lay the cure, for thence the poison came, and only Queen Isaud might be able to heal it.

'Tristram went to Ireland in disguise: he called himself the minstrel Tramtris, and sang so well that those who found him brought him to the court. Now Gurman and Isaud had one child only, the loveliest damsel in the world, whose name was Iseult: all men speak of her the world over as Iseult the Fair – and surely there is none fairer: these eyes have seen her, and they have seen the beauties of many lands. King Gurman wished greatly that his daughter should learn to play upon the harp; yet there was no man in Ireland skilled enough to teach her. He heard of the minstrel Tramtris, whose harping all men praised, and he sent for him. Tramtris came, borne in a litter: "This wound I got of pirates as I voyaged to Ireland," he told the King. "I travelled with a merchant in a ship of rich merchandise, and the sea-robbers took us after a fierce fight: they slew all on the ship, but me they spared because of my harping, and they set me in a little boat, with food and water, and therein your people found me when I drifted at length near to the Irish coast."

'Then the Queen Isaud tended Tramtris the minstrel, so that his wound closed up and grew better day by day, until he was whole again. And day by day he taught the Fair Iseult to play upon the harp, and to sing; and his heart was stirred by her beauty – yet still he set fame and deeds of arms before love, so that he wooed her not.

'For a year dwelt Tristram unknown in Ireland, and at the end of that time he sailed back to Lyonesse, into Cornwall, and came to King Mark at Tintagel. But King Mark had heard tell of Iseult the Fair, and when Tristram spoke of her, his royal heart was stirred: and he held council with his lords, saying to them: "King Gurman of Ireland has no other child: would it not be well for both our lands if we made a firm peace together, and I took the Fair Iseult to wife?"

'The nobles thought that this was indeed wise: "But how may it be brought about?" they asked. "Gurman of Ireland and Isaud his queen hate us for the slaying of Marhault, hate us also for the ceasing of our tribute. How then shall you win the hand of the Princess Iseult?"

'Then answered Mark: "On this thing have I set my heart: some means must be found." He looked towards Tristram, and the lords murmured among themselves, for they grew jealous of Tristram, fearing that he would be next King of

Cornwall if Mark had no children. Now Tristram knew of this, and wishing to prove to them that he had no ambitions towards the Kingship of Cornwall, he arose and said: "My uncle, and you, lords of Cornwall, this is a dangerous venture indeed – yet I will undertake it. For I have been once into Ireland, and there Queen Isaud cured me of my wound – though against Tristram of Lyonesse she had vowed eternal hatred and vengeance."

'Tristram set sail in one small ship with scarcely thirty men, and he came to Ireland at dead of night, and anchored his ship in a quiet haven. "If any question you," he said to his faithful friend Kurwenal, who had accompanied him, "say that we are merchants, and that I your captain have gone into the land to make bargains with the merchants of Ireland."

'Now at that time there was a dragon in Ireland, a fearful monster which devoured the people and laid waste the land; and King Gurman had promised that whoever should slay the dragon might have to wife his daughter the Fair Iseult. This Tristram had heard, and he went on shore that night fully armed and sought out the dragon's lair high up among the burnt rocks above a fire-scorched valley. Early in the morning, when the red rays of the rising sun slanted down the valley like blood dripping between the rocks, Tristram saw three knights, and one following them, ride over the pass and down towards the lair of the dragon. And anon he heard the dragon roar, and there came cries as of men in mortal anguish, and a cruel smoke curled up among the rocks; then the one man who had followed the knights at a distance came galloping back the way he had come, and spurring his horse to make it go yet faster. Now this was the Seneschal of King Gurman, a cowardly knight and a braggart, who dared never face the dragon, yet who boasted often that full many times he had ridden in quest of it.

'Tristram rode quietly down the valley, and at length he saw the dragon standing over one of the knights whom it had slain. A terrible monster it was, with great shining claws, scales of blue and green, and jaws breathing fire and smoke between sharp white teeth. Tristram set his spear in rest and charged the dragon suddenly, his shield held well before him; and the monster turned at the sound of hooves, and made ready to seize him with open jaws. Right well aimed Sir Tristram, so that the spear entered at the dragon's mouth and pierced deep towards its heart. Tristram leaped forward over the dragon's head; and the monster, screaming with rage and pain, slew the horse in a blast of fire and began quickly to devour it. But the spear, though the wooden handle charred swiftly away, left its sharp point deep in the creature's vitals, and it went screaming away into a rocky ravine, leaving the horse half-eaten.

'Tristram followed swiftly on foot, and met the dragon at the valley's head. There for an hour the battle raged, Tristram sheltering behind rocks lest the scorching flame should destroy him. Many times he wounded it, yet might not slay it, but the spear-point drew nearer to its heart, so that at last it rolled over in agony. Then Tristram rushed forward and drove in his sword right to the hilt; and so the dragon died; but in its dying it breathed such a blast of flame and poison upon Tristram that his shield melted and dripped from his arm, and he fell to the ground half poisoned by its breath.

'Presently, however, he crept to the dead dragon and cut out its tongue, placing it in the pouch at his side. Then he began seeking for the way out of the valley, but ere long the poison overcame him, and he fell down in a deep swoon, and lay like one dead.

'Then the false Seneschal came silently into the valley, and he saw the dragon lie dead, and Tristram dead also, or so it seemed. Laughing to himself that cowardly knight cut off the dragon's head, bound it upon his horse and went with all speed to the Court of King Gurman. "Lord King!" he cried, "See, I have slain the dragon! Fulfil now your promise and give me in marriage your daughter the Fair Iseult."

'Then was Gurman much distressed, feeling full sure that the cowardly Seneschal could never have slain the dragon. Yet there was the head, and he knew not how to question the deed.

'But Iseult the Fair came in tears to her mother, Queen

Isaud: "Rather than marry him, I will slay myself!" she cried.

'"Things have not come yet to such a pass," answered Isaud the Queen. "For sure am I that the Seneschal slew not the dragon!"

'That night the two of them went secretly to the place and found there the dead dragon, headless and terrible in the moonlight. And there also they found Tristram lying in a sore swoon.

'Then Iseult cried out in surprise: "Lo, here lies Tramtris the minstrel, whether alive or dead I know not. He is clad in knightly armour, his shield is melted and his sword stained to the hilt with the dark blood of the dragon ..."

'Then they had Tristram carried secretly to the palace, and the Queen Isaud worked so well with her skill in medicine that in a little while Tristram came out of the swoon and told them how he had slain the dragon, showing as further proof the tongue which he had placed in his pouch.

'Then Queen Isaud said: "Tell me, Tramtris, wherefore came you into Ireland, and why did you go up against the dragon?"

'"I came as merchant," Tristram answered, "and, feeling that we of Cornwall were not well loved of the Irish, I thought to find favour and peace in the sight of this folk by slaying the dragon."

'"Favour and peace shall be yours to your dying day," said Isaud the Queen, and she swore it with a great oath.

'The day came when King Gurman must redeem his pledge to the dragon-slayer, and the Seneschal came proudly before the Court, vaunting his courage and boasting that Iseult the Fair was his already. But Queen Isaud arose and defied him, and there came Tristram and called him coward and cheat.

'"I slew the dragon!" cried the Seneschal. "Behold its head which I cut off before the beast was well dead!"

'"Look within the dragon's mouth." commanded the Queen. And when they found that its tongue was gone, and that Tristram had it in his pouch, all men rejoiced at the proof, and mocked the Seneschal. But he grew mad with rage, called Tristram a liar and a thief, and challenged him to the ordeal by battle.

'"On the third day shall the battle be," said Gurman the King.

'When the day was come, Iseult the Fair looked well to Tristram's armour and her heart was heavy as she thought of what might chance that day. She drew Tristram's sword out of its scabbard and gazed earnestly upon it; and as she did so, she saw that a chip was wanting from the blade. With a great fear at her heart she brought the piece of steel which had been drawn from the head of her uncle Sir Marhault – and it fitted exactly. Then she went swiftly to her mother and said:

'"Lo! This minstrel Tramtris whom we have saved is none other than Tristram of Lyonesse who slew Marhault! Here you may see the proof by the sword which struck the blow – and with this sword will I now slay him!"

'But the Queen held her back, and together they went to Tristram and spoke with him. Then he told them all, hiding not even the reason of his second coming to Ireland.

'"Then let us swear peace with Sir Tristram," said Isaud the Queen. "For King Mark is a noble match for you, and a brave man. But if Tristram does not help us, then the Seneschal must become your husband."

'So the oath was sworn, and Tristram went forth to do battle with the Seneschal: and he fought so well that day that the Seneschal died beneath his sword, and Iseult the Fair was won as wife to King Mark.

'Tristram's ship put into Dublin with all honour, and the cabin was made ready to receive Iseult, who came aboard, the loveliest damsel in the world, followed only by Brangwain her faithful friend and attendant.

'Now before the ship set sail, Queen Isaud by her arts brewed a strange potion. She set it in a wine-flask and brought it to the Lady Brangwain, saying to her:

'"Lo, now I give into your keeping my daughter's happiness. Guard you this potion with your life, and see to it that on her wedding-day the Princess Iseult drinks of it, and King

Mark also, and none else besides. For it is a love potion, so strong that nothing in the world may undo its effects – so strong that once a man and a maiden have drunk of it together, they shall love one another even unto the world's end with a love greater than any in the world."

'Tristram set sail from Dublin, and the ship was many days on the high seas, sailing merrily through the joyous spring-tide, leaping like a white bird of love from the curling waves. All day Iseult the Fair sat in the cabin, and there Tristram tended her, singing brave lays of great lovers and mighty deeds, telling her tales of old Cornwall – of Ygerne the Queen, and how Merlin brought Uther Pendragon to dark Tintagel – telling in song and in story of Arthur the good King and his knights, the flower of chivalry, and of the wondrous realm of Logres which they were building up like the clear light of God in the dark land of Britain. But Lady Brangwain took no joy in the dancing waves, but lay sick in a cabin far apart.

'On a day when song and tale were ended and Iseult sat with Tristram playing at chess with pieces wrought cunningly in red and in white ivory upon a chess-board of carved cedar, they grew thirsty. Then Tristram espied the flask of wine which stood in a casket in the great cabin, and Iseult said, laughing:

'"Brangwain has brought it with her to drink when the sickness of the sea departs from her! Let us drink it now, and when she rises from her bed she will find but an empty bottle!"

'They poured the wine into golden cups, knowing not that it was the love potion brewed by Isaud the wise queen, knowing not that they held fate in their hands and gave themselves to much joy and a deeper sorrow. Then, laughing still, they pledged one another, draining the sweet wine to the very dregs.

'Straightway strong love awoke in their hearts, and the world grew dim because of the light which now shone about each of them to the other's eyes. As they drained the flask, Brangwain entered the cabin and saw what had chanced. She spoke no word of it to them for many a year thereafter, but,

It was the love potion brewed by Isaud

cold at heart, she flung the wine-flask far into the deep sea,
lamenting that she had ever come upon that voyage, lamenting that drink which should be the death of Tristram and
Iseult.

'Fair was that voyage through the sunny seas, more bright
the sunshine than ever it might be again. For Tristram and
Iseult spoke together soon of their great love, and were happy
for the brief hours of their youth – more happy than any
lovers since this world began. Speeding over the blue sea they
forgot the sorrow that awaited them in Cornwall, forgot the
struggle betwixt love and honour, and remembered only that
spring was short, and that love held them as one in the joyous
sunlight.

'All too soon came the tall ship to the dark crags of Tintagel: and there Iseult the Fair was wedded to Mark the King
of Cornwall. For that way it seemed that honour called her,

and for honour Tristram must let go his love and leave his youth behind him. Moreover, had he sailed away with Iseult, such war would have been 'twixt Cornwall and Ireland that might not have ended without the slaying of many men and the keen sorrow of two kingdoms.

'Little else is there to tell. Tristram in Lyonesse wrought many deeds, till his fame was carried far through the world. But ever he loved Iseult the Queen of Cornwall, and ever she loved him and hated Mark.

'Then one spring love triumphed over honour, and Mark's wife sought Tristram in the greenwood. She went a-hunting with Brangwain her maid, and Mark, suspecting nought, set Tristram his nephew in command of her huntsmen and attendants. But right soon the hunt was left behind them and the lovers sat alone together by a clear stream where the white daisies dew the new grass like tears.

'They met again – many and many a time: love was turned into fear and grew dark and wild: for so love must that is lawless and dishonourable. Yet blame them not over-much, for the love-charm was upon them always. ... For them surely there is much excuse, where none could be for others who thus break their vows.

'Ere long the nobles, who still hated Tristram, grew to suspect his love, and whispered of it to Mark. The king for long would not believe it, for well he loved and trusted both wife and nephew. But on a day Marjodo, a jealous knight, brought Mark where he might see Tristram and Iseult seated under a tree together, close by the murmuring stream: after that there was no longer room for doubt.

'King Mark called together his council and sought to have Tristram condemned to death. But this, though they hated him, his nobles and his knights would not permit: for none there was so mighty as Tristram, and no man so fit to save Cornwall in times of need. Moreover the people loved him, and had he been put to death civil war might have broken out.

'So King Mark banished Sir Tristram, sent him out of Cornwall and far from Lyonesse – so far from Iseult the Fair

that hardly might he see her ever again. And he wanders now
through all the land of Britain, seeking for the comfort that
he cannot find, wandering in minstrel's garb and singing, ever
singing the song of his love.

> "Iseult of the emerald isle,
>   Still I seek you, mile on mile
>   Through the wide world following
>   Love – a white bird on the wing.
>   Iseult, though the world wax old,
>   Never shall our love grow cold:
>   Still while youth and Spring are sure
>   Lives our love and shall endure.
>   Iseult, in the after-time
>   Poets still shall fit their rhyme,
>   Tell of love beyond compare:
>   Tristram and Iseult the Fair."'

The Minstrel ceased from his tale, and a great silence was
over all who sat in the great hall at Camelot. Only Launcelot
bowed his head in his hands, and the tears ran between his
fingers as he thought of his own love for Guinevere – for
King Arthur's queen.

'Minstrel,' said King Arthur presently. 'How comes it that
you know so well all things that have befallen Sir Tristram of
Lyonesse?'

The Minstrel smiled sadly as he rose from the stool and
stood, tall and noble to behold, before King Arthur.

'I knew it well,' he said. 'Right well indeed – even as a man
knows his own sorrow ... For I am Tristram of Lyonesse!'

There was a little murmur through the hall at this, of
wonder and of pity. But King Arthur rose from his seat and
came down to Tristram and greeted him.

'Right welcome are you to Camelot,' he cried. 'Welcome
indeed to me and to all this fellowship of the Round Table.
Your name was spoken to us by Merlin the wise enchanter on
the day of the making of the Table – and see! There is a seat
at it for you. Yonder siege beside Launcelot, where your name
grows even now in letters of gold. Welcome, true knight of
Logres!'

And so Sir Tristram became a Knight of the Round Table, and, after Launcelot and Gawain, there was no knight so worthy to sit there as he. For many years he came on every Feast of Pentecost to take his place at the board; and many were the mighty deeds which he wrought for Logres. But always he sorrowed for the love of Iseult the Fair, with a love and with a sorrow that no time might heal.

After some years he was married to another Iseult, daughter of Jovelin the Duke of Arundel, who was called Iseult of the White Hands; and she brought him much comfort, and he was a true and noble husband to her. Yet ever his heart turned towards Iseult the Queen of Cornwall; wherefore Iseult of the White Hands was jealous at heart.

At the last Tristram was wounded with a poisoned spear as he fought to save Kahedin, his wife's brother; and the wound festered and might not be cured.

Then Tristram said: 'My death is upon me, unless Iseult of Cornwall comes to my aid: for she alone has all the skill which was her mother's.'

So he bade the faithful Kurwenal take ship and sail to Tintagel to beg Iseult to come and cure him. And if she would come, Kurwenal was to hoist a white sail on his ship as he returned: but a black sail if she would not come.

Iseult of Cornwall came with all the speed she might, and Kurwenal hoisted the white sail. But Tristram lay upon his bed, so weak that he could not rise and look out from his window. Then he said to his wife:

'Go now and look out to sea: Kurwenal's ship will soon be nearing the land, with Iseult the Fair aboard, should the sail be white. But there will be a black sail if she will not come.'

Then Iseult of the White Hands looked out over the sea, and she saw the ship of Kurwenal flying over the waves with all its white sails set. But in her jealousy and her hatred for Iseult of Cornwall, she said to Tristram:

'Lo now, I see Kurwenal's ship sailing heavily through the waves. And the sails are all black . . .'

Then Tristram turned his face to the wall: 'God keep you, my love Iseult the Fair,' he said, 'for I shall not look upon your face again.' Then he ceased to struggle for his life, and in a few minutes Tristram of Lyonesse was dead.

And when Iseult the Fair, Queen of Cornwall, found him dead she knelt at his side until her heart broke for very sorrow, and she died also. And they were buried in one grave, for Iseult of the White Hands repented of her jealousy when it was too late.

And over the grave she planted two rose trees, one red and one white; and as they grew the two trees leant over the grave towards one another, and their branches twined together, and they grew into one tree bearing roses both red and white. For never in all the world have there been two such faithful lovers as Sir Tristram of Lyonesse and Iseult the Fair.

5

Geraint and Enid

ALTHOUGH the high Feast of Pentecost was held ever by King Arthur at Camelot where the great Round Table stood in the castle hall, he would often hold court upon other feast days in other places, with as many of his knights as chanced to be in the neighbourhood. Sometimes he held it at Cardiff and sometimes at Colchester or Carlisle, once even it was at Chester and once at Cardigan; but the most usual place was at Caerleon in South Wales, in the castle from which he had first come forth as the true King of the Realm of Logres.

King Arthur did not wait for an adventure to come before he began every feast, but none the less he was always happy if such a thing should happen; therefore he was particularly pleased one Easter Day as he sat feasting at Caerleon to see a tall, handsome youth dressed in green and white, with a great golden-hilted sword at his waist, come striding suddenly into the hall.

'Greetings, noble King Arthur!' said the youth, bowing low before the king.

'I give you welcome, fair sir,' answered King Arthur. 'Come you to tell of some adventure? Methinks I have seen you before this day – and yet your name I know not.'

'I am Geraint, the son of Erbin,' was the answer. 'And I dwell in the Forest of Dean not far from here. This day as I wandered down a leafy glade, I beheld a strange and won-drous stag: pure white it was, with antlers of clear gold, and it stepped delicately over the grass and leaves, not herding with any of the other deer in your forest. Then I sought out your royal huntsmen and bade them mark where the white stag went: and I came in haste to tell you.'

'You did well, young sir!' said Arthur. 'To-morrow we will rise early and go forth with many of our knights to hunt this stag.'

'Let me come after you, to watch the hunting,' begged Queen Guinevere. 'This young squire Geraint shall accompany me.'

'Be it as you say,' answered Arthur. 'And whosoever slays the stag, Geraint shall have the head of it, on this condition: that he shall give it to the lady of his heart.'

'Alas, I have no lady,' sighed Geraint.

'Then we will find you one!' laughed Guinevere. And so the matter was arranged.

On the morrow King Arthur, with Gawain and Kay, and many another knight, rose early and went forth into the forest in search of the white stag. But Guinevere followed later in the day, accompanied by one maiden only, and by Geraint, who rode still in his tunic of white and his green cloak, with only the golden-hilted sword at his side.

Presently they came to the edge of the forest, and they heard the horns blowing in the distance, but could not tell in which direction the hunt was going. And as they sat waiting there on the green verge of the forest, they saw a little cavalcade come by upon the road. First of all came a misshapen dwarf riding upon a prancing horse, and carrying a long, cruel whip of leather thongs; and behind him rode a proud lady on a beautiful white horse; her garments were of gold brocade, and she was followed by a knight in shining armour who rode upon a great black war-horse – a giant of a man upon a monstrous horse.

'Geraint,' said Guinevere, 'know you the name of yonder knight?'

'I know him not,' answered Geraint, 'and I cannot see his face, for he rides with his vizor down.'

'Go you and ask,' said Guinevere to her damsel, who rode at once towards the dwarf and asked him the knight's name.

'I will not tell you!' snapped the dwarf.

'As you are so rude, I'll ask the knight himself,' said the damsel.

'That shall you not, by my faith!' said the dwarf.

'Wherefore not?' asked the damsel.

'Because you are not fit to speak to such a one as my lord!' answered the dwarf. But the damsel turned her horse nevertheless, and was about to ride towards the knight when the dwarf struck her a savage blow with his whip so that the blood ran from her face.

Sobbing bitterly, the damsel returned to Queen Guinevere, and told her what had happened.

She asked the dwarf the name of his lord

'A vile churl this dwarf is!' cried Geraint. 'I'll ride and speak with him myself!'

'Go!' said Guinevere, and Geraint went up to the dwarf.

'Who is yonder knight?' he asked.

'I will not tell you!' snapped the dwarf.

'As you are so rude, I will e'en ask the knight himself,' said Geraint.

'That you shall not, by my faith!' cried the dwarf.

'Wherefore not?' asked Geraint.

'Because you are not fit to speak with such a one as my lord!' answered the dwarf.

'I've spoken with greater than he!' said Geraint angrily, and turning his horse, he was about to ride after the knight, when the dwarf struck him a savage blow with his whip, so that the blood ran down his face and stained the whiteness of his tunic.

Geraint's hand flew to the golden sword-hilt, but then he thought: 'It will be no vengeance if I slay the dwarf and am myself slain unarmed by this knight.' So he returned to Queen Guinevere, and told her what had chanced.

'I will ride after them,' he said, 'and when we come where I may borrow some armour and a spear and shield, I will do battle with this proud knight.'

'Go then,' said the Queen, 'and, if you prove yourself worthy, you shall be a Knight of the Round Table.'

'Ere long you shall hear of me,' said Geraint; and with that he departed.

All day Geraint followed the knight, the lady and the dwarf through the edge of the forest, down by deep valleys, and then upwards into the hills of South Wales; and in the evening he came to a strange town with a castle towering in the midst of it. As the knight rode up the steep street towards the castle, people came to their doors and bowed low to him; and everywhere there was bustle and the jingle of steel as men-at-arms and knights strode up and down. But there was no friendly smile for Geraint as he rode slowly through the town and out at the further side once he had seen the knight his enemy enter into the frowning castle.

The shadows were growing long and dark as Geraint came once more to the edge of the forest and saw among the trees the ruins of a mighty mansion, a fortified house almost like a castle, with a moat and tall towers, thick walls and narrow windows. But the moat was grown with weeds, the towers were split and broken with their staircases curling up into nowhere, the walls in many places were mere heaps of rubble, and only the windows of one room showed any light.

On the stone parapet of a bridge leading across the moat sat an old man in tattered garments which had once been fine, and he greeted Geraint kindly:

'Young sir, wherefore do you ride pensively, with bowed head?'

'I am thoughtful,' answered Geraint, 'because I know not where to rest this night. For I am in a strange land, and all whom I meet greet me with hostile looks.'

'Come hither with me,' said the old man, 'and I will give you such welcome as I may. Once you might have feasted splendidly in my halls – but much evil and sorrow has befallen me since that time.'

Geraint rode over the bridge into the ruined manor, tied up his horse in a roofless stall, and followed his host up a stone stairway into a fine room where a fire was burning, and a table was set for a frugal dinner. Beside the fire sat an ancient lady in a high-backed chair of carved oak, and on a footstool at her side the loveliest maiden that ever Geraint had seen.

'Surely,' said Geraint to his host as they sat down to supper, 'you did not always dwell thus in a ruined manor with none to tend upon you?'

'Oh no, young sir, once it was far otherwise,' said the old man. 'I am Liconal, by right the Duke of this town and of all the wide domains hereby. But in the pride of my heart I withheld from Yder my nephew his dukedom which I ruled for him until he came of age. And the end of it was that he took both his own dukedom and mine, driving me out from the castle, so that I and my wife and our daughter Enid, then but a child, were forced to dwell in the one place which remained to us – this ancient manor that for long had been the home only of rooks and daws.'

'Then it was Duke Yder who came riding into the town this day and was saluted by all?' said Geraint. 'I desire greatly to break a lance with him, for he is a proud and ungentle knight: his dwarf raised the lash of his whip to a damsel of Queen Guinevere – and me also he smote across the face. But I had no armour nor spear – for I am not yet a knight – so that I could not defy Duke Yder. Therefore I rode after him to discover where he dwelt – and to see if any there were who would lend me arms.'

'That will I right willingly,' cried Duke Liconal. 'And to-morrow you may ride against Yder. For he holds then his yearly tournament, and thinks to bear away the Sparrow Hawk.'

'Tell me of this Sparrow Hawk,' said Geraint. 'I know not the custom.'

'It is wrought all of pure silver,' answered Liconal, 'and each year come knights with their ladies to joust for it. He who wins it for three years is called the Knight of the Sparrow Hawk – and that will Duke Yder be if he win it to-morrow: and he will give the Sparrow Hawk to his lady, and she shall be held to be the fairest lady in the world.'

'To-morrow I will fight him for that Sparrow Hawk,' said Geraint quietly.

'You may not enter the lists to fight for it,' said Liconal, 'unless your lady-love rides with you, and you proclaim her the fairest lady in the world.'

'I have no lady,' said Geraint. 'And yet ... there is none fairer that ever I have seen than this damsel your daughter, the lady Enid ... If she will ride with me, she shall be my lady as long as I live – and if I die to-morrow she is no worse off than she was this morning.'

Then the lady Enid blushed sweetly, and said that she would indeed ride to the tournament with Geraint: but of what should chance thereafter she would say nothing.

That night Geraint slept in the ruined manor, and early the next day Duke Liconal armed him in ancient armour, set a great spear in his hand, and with Enid and his wife, led him to the great meadow below the castle. There many people were gathered together in bright array, and many knights in shining armour.

Then Duke Yder rode down the field on his great black horse to where his lady sat beneath a canopy.

'Lady,' he cried, 'see yonder at the meadow's end the silver Sparrow Hawk awaits you. For you are the fairest of women – and that have I proved these two years, and will prove it again this day if any dare doubt my words ... Rise now and fetch the Sparrow Hawk, for there is no man so hardy as to do battle with me for it!'

'Tarry a little!' cried Geraint, riding forward suddenly. 'Fetch it not, fair lady, for there is here a lady fairer even than you – and I will prove her right to the silver Sparrow Hawk upon any who dares deny it!'

Then Duke Yder laughed: 'Here comes a churl who has found a suit of armour, old and red with rust, lying in some ditch!' he said. 'Now it were good sport to chastise his insolence: but first I will knock him off his horse!'

Then the two drew apart, and came together down the length of the field so hard that both their spears were shivered into pieces. Three times they jousted, and each time their spears were broken to fragments; but for the fourth encounter Duke Liconal gave a mighty lance to Geraint, saying: 'This spear was set in my hand on the day when I was made a knight, and from that day to this have I jousted with it and broken it not. Moreover the point is yet sharp.'

Geraint thanked him, set the spear in rest, and thundered down once more upon Duke Yder. And this time he smote him so hard that his girths broke, and over his horse's tail went Yder, with his saddle still under him.

Geraint sprang down to the ground, drew his golden-hilted sword, and they fought up and down the meadow, dealing mighty strokes, until the grass was all tramped and blood-stained. Moreover pieces of Liconal's ancient armour lay scattered on every side like rusty-red petals of fallen poppies.

Duke Yder struck mightily, and Geraint staggered beneath his blows. 'Remember the insults done to you and to Queen Guinevere!' cried Liconal. 'Think upon the beauty of my daughter Enid!'

Then Geraint felt new strength come to him: whirling up his sword he rushed upon Duke Yder and smote him to the earth, splitting the helmet and wounding the head beneath.

'Have mercy upon me now,' cried Yder. 'I yield me to you, noble knight. Moreover, the Sparrow Hawk shall be yours to give to whom you will.'

'Go then to the Court of King Arthur at Caerleon,' said

Geraint, 'you, your lady, and your dwarf. Ask pardon there of Queen Guinevere for the insult which your dwarf did to her, and say that Geraint the son of Erbin sent you. Moreover the old Duke Liconal shall ride with you, and you shall lay your dispute before King Arthur – for long enough have you kept him from his dukedom, and long enough has he dwelt in the ruined manor.'

'All these things will I do,' said Duke Yder. 'But come you now to my castle, and my uncle Liconal also. There we shall feast, and there our ancient hatred shall be ended.'

Great was the feast that night in the castle of Yder; and on the morrow they made ready to ride to Caerleon.

'Come you with us also, brave sir knight,' said Yder to Geraint.

'Not so,' answered Geraint. 'For knight am I not yet. Therefore I will ride further into the woods and valleys, seeking adventures: and so perchance I may show myself worthy to be made a knight. And thus too, fair lady Enid, may I prove myself worthy of your love.'

Then Enid was angered with Geraint, for she had thought that he was a knight already, and that he would have come that day to Caerleon with her and wedded her on the morrow: and in her anger she spoke to him foolishly:

'You are indeed not worthy to be made a knight!' she cried. 'For now you ride away in fear. That you go forth to seek for adventures I may not believe – and if you go now, be sure I will seek at Caerleon for a braver and a nobler man to be my lord.'

White to the lips between anger and dismay spoke Geraint: 'Lady, you do me a passing great wrong. For mine honour, I cannot now ride to Caerleon with you: but if it pleases you, ride now before me on the road that I must follow, and then you shall see what may chance. Ride far ahead, looking not behind: and see that you speak to me no word, whatever may happen!'

'I will do this indeed,' said Enid, sorry already for her rash and cruel words. And therewith she bade farewell to her father, turned her horse, and rode away into the deep mountain valleys, with Geraint, silent and angry, riding a little behind her.

Before long, as they came down a steep hill-path into the forest, three armed robbers met them, and one said to the others:

'Here is a fine chance truly! We will capture this lady and the two horses – for yonder knight who hangs his head so pensively can do naught against us!'

Then Enid turned and rode swiftly back to Geraint: 'I will warn him,' she thought, 'though he bade me not to speak to him!'

But Geraint merely said: 'You may wish to see me dead at these men's hands, but it shall not fall out so. Therefore I command you to keep silence!'

He set his spear in rest and rode suddenly at the first robber, catching him in the throat and laying him dead on the plain. The second he pierced through shield and armour; and the third he overtook and slew from behind as he turned to run away.

Then Geraint stripped off their armour, tied it upon the horses, and said to Enid:

'Ride ahead once more, driving these three horses before you. But say never a word to me, unless I speak first to you.'

Forward they went through a deep wood, and in the midst of it six more armed robbers met them:

'Here is a fine chance, truly!' they cried. 'We will capture this lady and these five horses – for yonder knight who hangs his head so pensively can do naught against us!'

'I will warn him this time!' thought Enid, 'though he bade me not speak to him!'

'Did I not command you to keep silence?' said Geraint. 'Much though you may wish me dead at these men's hands, I do not fear them.'

He set his spear in rest, and with it smote down the six robbers, one after the other, transfixing each like moths on a pin. Then he stripped off their armour, tied each suit upon its wearer's horse, and said to Enid:

'Ride ahead once more, driving these nine horses before you. But say never a word to me, unless I speak first to you.'

Forward they went through the wood and out into a desolate great valley of bare stones. And there Enid spied nine armed robbers coming towards her; and the leader of them cried:

'Here is a fine chance, truly! We shall have no difficulty in capturing all these horses and suits of armour – and the lady also: for yonder knight who hangs his head so pensively can do naught against us!'

'This time he will surely perish, unless I warn him!' thought Enid.

But Geraint only answered as before: 'I do not fear these men, though you may desire my death at their hands. Moreover, methought I bade you to keep silence!'

Then he set his spear in rest, and came charging upon the robbers, piercing the leader through shield and armour so that he fell dead. Geraint turned then and charged the band of robbers from the other side, laying another dead on the ground as he passed through them. And so he rode backwards and forwards until all lay dead. Then he bound each suit of armour upon the several horses, and said to Enid:

'Ride ahead still further, driving these eighteen horses before you. But say never a word to me, unless I speak to you first.'

Night fell not long after this, and they came to a castle at the head of the valley where Geraint asked for lodging.

'Right welcome shall you be,' said the lord of the castle, whose name was Sir Oringle of Limors, 'and your fair lady also: there was surely never a fairer seen than she.'

After the banquet Geraint sat moodily apart, for his heart was still sore on account of Enid's cruel and thoughtless words. She sat alone also, not knowing how to win back Geraint's love, for she feared greatly that she had lost it for ever by her folly. And as she sat thus, Sir Oringle came and sat beside her:

'Fair damsel,' he said, 'surely the journey with yonder dolorous knight is none of your seeking?'

'I would rather journey with him than with any other,' answered Enid.

'Be counselled by me,' went on Sir Oringle. 'Leave this man and dwell always with me. All my earldom shall be yours, and all the good things that you shall wish for – the jewels, the fair robes, servants and handmaidens.'

'That will I not, by Heaven!' cried Enid. 'My faith is pledged to yonder man, and never shall I prove inconstant to him.'

'If I were to slay him,' said Sir Oringle, frowning, 'I could keep you with me as long as I choose, and then turn you out as soon as I grew tired of you. But if you come to me of your own free will, then you shall be my wife and the lady of all these wide lands.'

'Be it as you wish,' said Enid. 'To-morrow I shall ride on my way as before. But I shall turn aside from the road and lie hidden until you come by. Be sure that you follow swiftly behind us.'

'It shall be done,' answered Sir Oringle. 'Nor will I work any mischief upon this man with whom you ride.'

That night they slept in peace at the castle, and set forth once more on the morrow, Enid riding before and driving with her the eighteen horses with their loads of armour. But as soon as they were out of sight of the castle, she turned hastily back and said to Geraint:

'My lord, forgive me that I speak to you against your wish, but we are in mortal danger from Sir Oringle, the evil knight of the castle.' Then she told him all that had been spoken on the previous evening, and of how she had seemed to agree to Sir Oringle's wicked suggestions, knowing that if she did not he would have murdered Geraint there and then, and taken her by force. 'He will be here soon with many men whom you cannot withstand. Let us turn aside and fly into the depths of the forest before he overtakes us.'

'I thank you for this timely warning,' said Geraint. 'But run away I will not. Here will I remain and meet this evil knight and his men. But for you: my counsel is that you ride with all haste to Caerleon, to the Court of King Arthur.'

'Never will I leave you, my lord Geraint –' began Enid. And then suddenly she paused, listening. 'I hear the jingle of harness!' she exclaimed, 'the clash of armour, and the sound of horses' hooves!'

They had paused in an open space on the skirts of the forest where the road came up out of the valley which lay between them and the castle of Sir Oringle which they could still see behind them, glowing in the morning sun and rising above the sea of white mist which filled the valley. Out of this mist came the sounds of many men in armour riding fast, and Geraint draw back his horse, set his spear in rest, and made ready for battle.

'I see the silver glint of armour in the mist!' cried Enid. 'Just there where the mist lies on the ground in the sunlight!'

'The mist is red in the beams of the morning,' said Geraint grimly. 'Yonder knights ride to the girths in a sea of blood!'

Out of the valley into the sunlight came Sir Oringle fully armed and four-score knights riding in solid ranks behind him.

'Now yield you!' cried Sir Oringle. 'We be eighty to one – and if you yield not the lady Enid to me, you shall die at our hands. But if you give her to me – and I warrant she'll come willingly enough! – you may go your ways unharmed!'

But Geraint only set spurs to his horse and smote Sir Oringle in the midst of his shield so hard that horse and man rolled on the ground. Then he charged into the midst of the riders, and a fearful battle began in which Geraint slew many and overthrew others, fighting so mightily that oft they drew back in fear, saying 'This is a magician and no ordinary man!'

The end of it was, however, that at length they overcame Geraint, and he fell to the ground bleeding from many wounds, and lay still in the dust.

'Alas!' cried Enid, bending over him. 'Now the only man I have loved or ever shall love, lies slain. And it was I who, in my folly, brought him to his end!'

'Right soon will we cure your sorrow!' said Sir Oringle; and he bade his men lead Enid back to his castle, and bear thither also the bodies of those who were slain or wounded.

In the hall, when the feast was set that night, Sir Oringle caused Geraint to be carried on a stretcher and set down upon the stone floor.

'Lady,' said he to Enid, 'be not sorrowful for this matter. Yonder knight is dead indeed – but here am I to be thy lord: therefore be joyful.'

'I shall never again be joyful while I live,' said Enid sadly.

'*I will not drink until Geraint drink also*'

'Come at least and eat,' said Sir Oringle. 'Here, see, is your place beside me.' He led her to the table against her will – but eat she would not.

'I call Heaven to witness,' she cried, 'that I will not eat until the man that is upon yonder bier shall eat likewise.'

'That oath you cannot fulfil,' scoffed Sir Oringle. 'For yonder man is dead already.'

'Then,' said she, 'I shall not eat again.'

'Drink then from this goblet,' urged Sir Oringle. 'The strong wine will cause you to change your mind!'

'May evil befall me if I drink aught until Geraint drink also,' said Enid.

Then Sir Oringle swore an evil oath: 'Since gentleness is of no avail with you,' he shouted, 'I will see what harsh words and blows will do!' And with that he struck her in the face until she cried aloud.

And at the sound of her cry Geraint awoke from the deep swoon which held him and sprang up suddenly, his golden-hilted sword still in his hand. Then, while all men stood amazed, thinking that they saw a ghost, he leapt upon Sir Oringle without a word and smote off his head at a single blow so that it fell upon the table, bounced thence on to the floor, and went rolling away into the darkness, right horrible to see.

Then everyone rose up and fled in terror from the hall, not so much through fear of the living as in the dread they felt at seeing what they took to be a dead man rise up to slay them.

'Come, my Lady Enid,' said Geraint. 'Show me where the horses are, and we will ride away speedily before these men return: for I am so weak with loss of blood and the pain of my wounds that I may not fight for long.'

Mounting their horses, they rode away swiftly into the night: side by side now, and at length hand in hand.

Meanwhile King Arthur hunted the White Stag through the Forest of Dean, and on into the forest-clad hills and valleys above the Usk and the Wye, deep into South Wales. For two days and nights the hunt continued: Queen Guinevere had long turned back to Caerleon, and many knights had been left behind so far that they also gave up the hunt and returned home. But on the morning of the third day they came up with the White Stag; and Cavell, Arthur's favourite hound, pulled it down, and Arthur himself came up with it first and smote its head off with his sword Excalibur.

Then they dismounted and made their camp, and rested there. But Sir Gawain and Sir Kay remained upon horseback, carrying shield and spear, to guard against a sudden attack by robbers in that wild place. As they rode up and down upon the road at a little distance, suddenly Geraint and Enid appeared riding towards them.

'Lo!' said Sir Kay. 'Here comes a stranger knight! I will

joust with him!' And away he rode before Gawain could stop him.

'Ho! You knight there!' shouted Sir Kay. 'Who are you, and what are you doing?'

'I seek adventures, and my name is my own concern,' answered Geraint, recognizing Sir Kay.

'Well, stop seeking adventures, and come with me to see King Arthur who is camped hard by!' said Sir Kay insolently.

'That will I not, by Heaven!' answered Geraint angrily.

'Come swiftly before I make you come!' taunted Sir Kay.

Then, in a rage, Geraint rode up suddenly to Sir Kay and struck him so hard with the butt-end of his spear that he fell from his saddle and rolled in the dust.

'You are well answered, Sir Kay,' said Gawain gravely, as he rode up. 'And now, noble Geraint, son of Erbin, and your lady also, come I beg of you to our lord King Arthur.'

'Right gladly will we,' replied Geraint, 'for we are well weary after many adventures, and sore wounded am I by many desperate fights.'

So they came to King Arthur, and he was right glad to see Geraint and to hear of his adventures. Glad also was he to welcome the Lady Enid, and he bade them both ride back with him to Caerleon.

When they were come there, and the feast was set, King Arthur handed the head of the White Stag to Geraint; and Geraint gave it to Enid, saying: 'Lady, this head was to be given to the fairest lady in the Court of King Arthur; but I give it to you as to the fairest lady in all the land.'

Then came Duke Liconal and Duke Yder and told of all that Geraint had done; and the followers of Sir Oringle came also to swear allegiance to King Arthur, telling him of how Geraint had done battle with them and slain Sir Oringle himself. And they brought with them the eighteen horses loaded each with the robbers' armour: and of these Enid told the tale to all in the court.

Then King Arthur made Geraint a knight; and when he was healed of his wounds he was wedded to the Lady Enid.

And at the Feast of Pentecost when all the Knights of the Round Table were met in Camelot, Geraint was there also, and his name was written in letters of gold upon one of the sieges.

6

▚▚

Sir Gawain and the
Lady Ragnell

ONE of the strangest adventures of any that befell during the reign of King Arthur began on the Christmas Day when the King and a number of his knights were holding their feast in the Castle of Carlisle. Not long before this Arthur and his knights had fought a great battle against the Saxons far up in the north-east of Scotland, and driven them out of the whole Island of Britain: and it seemed at last that the Realm of Logres was firmly established throughout all the country.

Southwards marched the armies once more, King Arthur and a chosen band of his best knights following more slowly: and Christmas overtook them before they were well out of Scotland.

So to Carlisle they came and the great feast was set: but the banquet had scarcely begun when there came into the hall a fair damsel weeping and wringing her hands:

'King Arthur!' she cried. 'My lord, King Arthur! Grant me a boon, I beg of you! The brave knight my husband has been overcome and carried away by the wicked master of Hewin Castle! It is a terrible place, that castle, rising darkly on a black rock high over the deep lake of Tarn Wathelyne: and there the dreadful master of the castle lies in wait for unwary travellers, carries them off to his stronghold, robs them, holds them to ransom, or casts them from the walls into the deep waters of the lake. It was but yesterday that, as my lord and I rode deep in the Forest of Inglewood, the dread Knight of Tarn Wathelyne came suddenly upon us: my husband he smote from his horse and carried him away bound, after he had sorely misused me. You may all see the cruel marks of his whip-lash across my face! ... As the Knight of Tarn Wathelyne rode away I cried after him that good King Arthur would come swiftly and avenge the wrong that had been done me: but he laughed evilly, and shouted: "Tell yonder cowardly king that he may find me when he will at Tarn Wathelyne – but indeed I know well that he will never dare to stand against me!" So I have come swiftly to you, most noble King Arthur – for if any man in this world dare stand against him, it is you!'

'Now, by my faith as a knight!' cried King Arthur, 'this adventure will I dare myself! It is long since I rode out alone in quest of adventures: but this Knight of Tarn Wathelyne shall fall beneath no spear but mine!'

'Let me go rather, my lord,' said Sir Gawain. 'Maybe some evil shall befall whoever rides to the haunted Castle of Tarn Wathelyne ... and without you the realm of Logres cannot endure.'

'I thank you, good nephew, for your love,' said King Arthur gently – for he loved Gawain better than any of his knights. 'But this time I will not be turned from following a quest myself. Bring me now my sword Excalibur and my spear Ron: and bid my squires saddle my horse with all the speed they may!'

Then, though Gawain and Launcelot, Geraint and Gareth sought to persuade him to let one of them undertake the adventure – even Sir Kay offering himself as a champion – King Arthur rode away from Carlisle with the damsel, and was soon lost to sight in the dark Forest of Inglewood.

Many and many a mile they went until, just as the sun began to sink towards the great hills and mountains of Cumberland, they came out of the forest on to the shores of a dark lake with black, angry rocks going sheer down into it on every side, and saw a grim, forbidding castle set on an island a little way from the shore.

'This is the Tarn Wathelyne!' said the damsel. 'And see! Here comes the loathly knight himself!'

King Arthur looked where she pointed, and saw the great

drawbridge of the castle sink slowly until it rested on a rim of rock where the road ended on the shore. And sitting on a great horse in the castle entrance was the most terrible man he had ever seen, and the largest: almost a giant he seemed, with his long arms and his huge fierce face.

'Ah-ha!' roared the Knight of Tarn Wathelyne. 'Is that Arthur, the muling monarch of miserable Logres? Long have I wished to meet you: welcome to the Castle of Tarn Wathelyne! I am Gromer Somer Joure – and I defy you, coward king!'

Then Arthur was so angry that he waited for nothing, nor did he pause to think how strange were all things that were happening that day, nor to see the wicked smile which came suddenly to the lips of the damsel. He set his spear in rest – the mighty spear which none might withstand – and rode at the knight as hard as he could go. Down the road he went, over the ledge of rock and on to the long drawbridge ... and then suddenly his horse stopped dead, neighing in terror, and his own arms sank powerless to his sides, while a fear came over him so great that it was not of this world.

'Gromer Somer Joure!' shouted the knight, and he laughed until the hills echoed his voice and the carrion crows flew screeching from the towers of the Castle of Tarn Wathelyne. 'Gromer Somer Joure has conquered! No man may withstand the terror of him.'

'This is devil's work!' gasped Arthur, the very hair of his head rising with the fear that he could not understand.

'It is the castle of my mistress, the Queen Morgana le Fay!' said the damsel riding up and mocking at Arthur with cruel, hard words.

'Have pity!' said Arthur, 'I will grant whatsoever you may desire!'

'Pity will I have!' boomed Gromer Somer Joure the Knight of Tarn Wathelyne. 'Go hence now for a year and a day; but first give me your royal word as a King and a Knight of the Round Table that you will return – and return alone. And I will set you this quest: Go where you will and ask of

all you meet what thing it is that women most desire in this
world. What it is I know well, and if you can tell me truly a
year hence, you shall go free, I swear it – and I am a true
knight, whoever I may serve at this time. But if you find not
the true answer, then I will slay you here upon this magic

He did not see the damsel's wicked smile

bridge and cast your body into the dark waters of Tarn
Wathelyne! Go!'

He waved his arms as he spoke, uttering the last word in
a great roar; and the King's horse spun round almost on its
hind legs and bolted up the rocky road into the forest in a
mad gallop of terror – nor could King Arthur rein it in for
many a long mile.

Before the moon rose he came to Carlisle, and there Sir
Gawain met him and heard all the adventure.

'I scarcely know what to do,' said King Arthur. 'My sister plots my death with a new and terrible power – and I know not how to withstand it.'

'Surely this is the last stroke against the might of Logres,' said Gawain. 'If we can defeat the evil this once more it shall not again come against us clothed in evil magic.'

'One thing I know,' said King Arthur. 'I must keep mine oath and return to this Knight of Tarn Wathelyne a year hence. And in the meantime I will seek for an answer to his riddle.'

'And I will seek also,' said Sir Gawain.

A year had gone by when King Arthur and Sir Gawain rode once more through the Forest of Inglewood to speak with Sir Gromer Somer Joure. Sadly they went on their way, for though Arthur carried with him two books filled with the answers which he and Gawain had collected from all over the country, he felt sure that none of them would satisfy the Knight of Tarn Wathelyne.

Not far from the end of their journey they came out of the thick woodland across a bare upland of moor and marsh, and there they met suddenly with a lady dressed in fine clothes and riding a great white horse. Her garments were of the richest and many a jewel sparkled and shone about her: but as Gawain looked at her he turned pale, and King Arthur crossed himself as if in the presence of something uncanny.

For she was the loathliest lady that ever the eye of man rested upon: her face was as red as the sinking sun, and long yellow teeth showed between wide, weak lips; her head was set upon a great, thick neck, and she herself was fat and unshapely as a barrel. Yet the horror of her seemed to lie in something more than the hideousness of her looks, for in her great, squinting, red-rimmed eyes there lurked a strange and terrifying shadow of fear and suffering.

'All hail, King Arthur!' she cried in a shrill, cracked voice. 'Speak to me nicely now! For your very life depends on it!'

'Lady,' said King Arthur gravely, 'I give you greetings; nor should my greetings change were you the greatest lady or the meanest lass in the land.'

'I thank you,' the lady replied. 'Now listen well: I know upon what errand you ride, and of the riddle that you must answer this day, or die – and the answers you have already found are not worth a louse!' She laughed her cackling screech at this, and then, suddenly serious, she went on: 'The true answer I can tell you, and tell you I will upon one condition.'

'What is your will, lady?' asked King Arthur as she paused.

'Your word as a King and a Knight of Logres that a knight of yours, as nobly born as you, shall be my husband this day!'

'That can I not promise,' said Arthur looking her in the face, and turning aside, sick with horror, try though he might to keep his face composed.

'Then you ride to your death!' chuckled the loathly lady, her eyes a little darker with pain than before.

'Stay!' cried Sir Gawain suddenly, 'I am King Arthur's nephew and a Knight of the Round Table: if I take you as my wife, will you tell the answer to Sir Gromer Somer Joure's riddle?'

'Oh yes, indeed Sir Gawain, surely and indeed I will!' she made answer eagerly.

'Bethink you what you do –' exclaimed King Arthur. 'This is too great a sacrifice to make –'

'Yet will I make it, lord King of Logres,' said Sir Gawain quietly. 'Lady, I pledge you my knightly word to take you in lawful marriage if you will save the life of my uncle King Arthur!'

'Ride on then to Tarn Wathelyne,' said the lady, 'and when you return I shall be waiting for you here, and we will return together to Carlisle.'

Then she came beside King Arthur and told him the answer to the riddle.

A little while after this Arthur came once more to the dark Tarn of Wathelyne and the evil castle of the knight; but Sir Gawain tarried on the edge of the forest. And there, sitting his great horse as before, was Sir Gromer Somer Joure.

'Greetings, King Arthur!' he cried. 'You are a brave man to keep your tryst so well. Come now, tell me the answer to

my question: "What do women desire most in the world?"
For if you reply rightly I swear that you shall suffer no harm
from me.'

Then King Arthur opened the two books and read from
them the many answers he had collected ... But at the end
Sir Gromer Somer Joure laughed till the hills echoed round
the dark Tarn:

'You are but a dead man, King Arthur!' he cried. 'Pomp,
state, fine clothes, mirth, love, luxury, idleness, and the rest
of the nonsense you have been reading me – none is the true
answer. Come now, bow down your head that I may strike it
from your shoulders and carry it to my lady, Queen Morgana
le Fay!'

'Tarry a little,' said King Arthur. 'As I came on my way I
met a loathly lady on the moor, and she told me that what
women most desire is to rule over men – yea, even over the
greatest ...'

Then the Knight of Tarn Wathelyne swore a terrible oath:
'It is that accursed witch the lady Ragnell!' he cried. 'She
has betrayed us, thinking to escape – but escape she never
shall. ... Go your ways, King Arthur, for you are safe from
me; and if I ever may free myself from the rule of Queen
Morgana le Fay maybe you will find a place for me at your
court. I am a rough fellow and rude of speech: but true to
mine oaths, faithful to my lords, and a mighty fighter.'

'Come when you will,' said King Arthur. 'The realm of
Logres is wide enough for any who would serve it truly and
with a pure heart ...'

But Sir Gromer Somer Joure had swung round his horse,
and, with a cry as of one in pain, he galloped across the drawbridge and into Hewin Castle by the dark waves of Tarn
Wathelyne. And behind him the portcullis clanged down and
the drawbridge swung screeching to its place like a tomb
closing upon some evil ghost of the night.

Slowly King Arthur rode back the way he had come, and
found Sir Gawain waiting for him at the edge of the forest,
rejoicing to see him return safely from his terrible adventure.

'To me the joy of one freed from death,' said King Arthur

sadly, 'but to you, I fear, the sorrow of an evil that only death can cure ...'

Back they rode through the forest, and upon the bleak moorland found the loathly lady Ragnell waiting them.

'I have saved you, King Arthur!' she cried in her shrill, cracked voice. 'And now the gallant Gawain shall be my husband. ... Ride before us to Carlisle, lord King, so that you may bid welcome with due honour to the bravest Knight of Logres and his bride!'

Sadly King Arthur set spurs to his horse and hastened through the Forest of Inglewood till he came to Carlisle. There he gathered the knights and ladies of his court together, told them something of his adventures, and bade them prepare for a great wedding.

That evening he and Queen Guinevere rode through the streets to the city gate with a noble following of knights and ladies, while all the people of Carlisle lined the way ready to cheer the bride and bridegroom. They came to the gate and waited there awhile until they saw Sir Gawain come riding slowly along the high-road from the forest with a lady upon a white horse beside him. They could see that she was clad in rich garments, and that the setting sun flashed and reflected from many jewels: and all those who were gathered to meet them began to cheer ...

But suddenly a hush fell upon them and the cheers faded into groans and murmured into silence when they saw the hideous twisted face of the lady Ragnell, the horror of her great squinting eyes, and how she sat hunched on her horse like a great bale of straw.

Sir Gawain presented her to the king and queen as if she had been the fairest lady in all the world, and she grinned and chuckled as Sir Launcelot and Sir Tristram, Sir Gareth and Sir Geraint, and many another noble knight came in turn to kiss her hand. But the words stuck in their throats when they would have wished Sir Gawain joy, and in silence that gay cavalcade rode up the street to the great minster, the same silence falling suddenly upon the watching crowds as the bride and bridegroom rode by.

Without a falter in his voice Sir Gawain took to wife the lady Ragnell in the presence of all people before the high altar, and led her then to the place of honour in the hall of the castle where a great feast was made ready.

But the mirth and gaiety were forced at that feast, all looked with loathing and horror upon the lady Ragnell as she sat by Gawain guzzling and slobbering over her food and wine, and not one of them but pitied Sir Gawain and marvelled over this strange wedding.

Early the feast broke up, and Gawain, his face pale and drawn with suffering, led his bride to the great, shadowy chamber in the castle keep where the candles flickered on the embroidered hangings and the shadows fell darkly among the rushes on the stone floor.

When they were alone beside the great bedstead, carved and curtained and spread with fine linen, the lady Ragnell said, her voice more hateful now that it was thick with drink as well as harsh and cracked:

'Dear husband, beloved lord Gawain – kiss me now, as a bridegroom should his bride. For now indeed we are husband and wife until death shall part us!' She laughed a cackling laugh that choked into wheezy silence.

Gawain drew near to her, his face paler still and his eyes glazed with agony: but he caught the deep agony behind her eyes, and the repulsive horror of her face grew pale and indistinct as he bent down and kissed her on the lips. Then he turned away with a cry of anguish and leant against the wall with his face hidden in his arms and his shoulders shaking with sobs that he could not keep down.

'Gawain! My dear lord Gawain!' said a voice behind him, a low sweet voice tremulous with love.

Slowly he turned as if in a dream, and where the loathly lady Ragnell had stood a moment before he beheld the loveliest maid that ever his eyes had seen. Tall and slim she stood there, her white arms held out towards him, the sweet face and the lovely eyes alight and shining with love for him ...

'Lady!' he gasped in wonder and bewilderment. 'Lady! Who are you? Where is my wife Ragnell?'

'I am the lady Ragnell – and your wife, if you will have me,' came the answer in the low sweet voice that fell like a gentle wind of the deep night on his tortured mind. 'By your great love and your noble sacrifice you have loosed me from the evil enchantment that the wicked Queen Morgana le Fay had laid upon me and upon my brother the brave knight Sir Gromer Somer Joure ... But still I am not altogether free, for only during twelve hours out of each twenty-four shall I

He turned away with a cry of anguish

be as you see me now: for during the other half of each day I must wear again the hideous form to which you were wedded. Choose now whether by day or by night I shall be fair – whether by night or by day I shall be foul!'

Gawain stood as one bewildered and amazed, and Ragnell went on:

'Bethink you now, my lord! If I am foul by day, what you must endure when I come into the Court as your wife and am seen by all the knights and ladies of Logres ... Bethink you also what you must endure if I am foul by night – when you and I are alone together, when you come home weary after the long day and find the shrill-mouthed horror waiting to disturb your rest ... Choose now which it shall be!'

'Lady,' said Sir Gawain presently, standing before her with bowed head. 'In this matter the word rests not with me ... Bethink you what you must endure by day when the knights and ladies eye you with loathing, draw away in horror, fall silent when you speak ... Bethink you also what you must endure by night when I who have seen you lovely by day, cannot overcome the loathing that will fill me when you draw near to me in that form of horror ... With you is the greatest suffering, and you alone must choose which you are most able to bear.'

'Oh Gawain, Gawain!' cried Ragnell, and a moment later she was weeping in his arms. 'There was never knight in all this world so noble and so unselfish as you! By this your choice – to leave the choice to me – you have undone the enchantment for ever: in the fair form in which you now see me shall I be yours by both day and night, until the fated hour comes wherein I must leave you ... But we have many years of happiness before that parting – and well you deserve all the happiness this world can give you!'

On the morrow there was such joy in King Arthur's Court as had never been seen there before, nor was any honour too great that could be done to Sir Gawain and his lovely bride the lady Ragnell.

For seven years they lived happily together – no couple more happily in all the wide realm of Logres; and then, on the appointed day, Ragnell went from Sir Gawain for ever. Some say that she died, but others that she fled away into the deep forests of Wales and there bore a son to Sir Gawain who in time became one of the noblest of all the Knights of the Round Table: but whether that son's name was Percivale the old tales do not tell us. Some call him simply 'The Fair Unknown' – but his adventures were so like those of Percivale that we may well believe that in a tale now lost this was indeed the name of the son of Sir Gawain and the lady Ragnell.

▨▧▨▧▨▧▨▧▨▧▨▧▨▧▨▧▨▧▨▧▨▧▨▧▨▧▨▧▨▧

7

Sir Percivale of Wales

IN the wild forests of Wales there lived once a boy called Percivale, with his mother. Never another living soul did he meet for the first fifteen years of his life, nor did he learn anything of the ways of men and women in the world. But Percivale grew strong and hardy in the wild wood, of deadly aim with the dart, and simple of heart, honest and upright.

Now, one day as he wandered alone, discontented suddenly and longing for he knew not what, a new sound fell upon his ears – not the voice of any bird, nor the music of wind or water, yet music it was, of a kind that set his heart leaping, he knew not why. He paused listening in a leafy glade, and as he waited there five knights came riding towards him, their armour jingling and the bridles of their horses ringing like silver bells.

'Greetings, fair youth!' cried the first knight, reining in his steed and smiling down at Percivale. 'Nay, look not so stricken with wonder: surely you have seen our like before?'

'Indeed not,' said Percivale. 'And, truth to tell, I know not what you are, unless you be angels straight out of Heaven, such as those of whom my mother teaches me. Come tell me, noble sirs, do you not serve the King of Heaven?'

'Him do we serve indeed,' said the knight, crossing himself reverently. 'And so also do all men who live truly in this the realm of Logres. But on earth we serve His appointed Emperor – the noble King Arthur, at whose Round Table we sit. It is he who made us knights – for that is all we are: and you too he will make a knight if you but prove yourself worthy of that great honour.'

'How may I do that?' asked Percivale.

'Come to King Arthur at Caerleon'

'Come to King Arthur at Caerleon,' answered the knight.
'Tell him that I sent you thither – I, Sir Launcelot of the
Lake who, under King Arthur, rule this land of Pant, which
is also called North Wales. Then he will set you such deeds
to do, such quests to accomplish, as we of his Court follow
after all our days: and, if you prove worthy, he will make you
a knight. But not in great deeds of arms lies the true worth of
knighthood – rather in the heart of the doer of such deeds:
if he be pure and humble, doing all things to the glory of God
and to bring that glory and that peace throughout all our holy
kingdom of Logres.'

Then Sir Launcelot bowed his head to Percivale, and rode
on his way, followed by the four other knights, leaving him
wrapped in wonder – but with a great longing and a great
humility stirring dimly within him.

'Mother!' cried Percivale excitedly as he came striding up the path to the little cave where they lived. 'Mother, oh mother – I have indeed met with wonders this day! They said they were not angels, but knights – yet to me they seemed fairer than all the hosts of Heaven! And one of them – the leader – Sir Launcelot was his name – said that I too could be a knight ... Mother, I shall set out to-morrow morning and seek for King Arthur who dwells in Caerleon!'

Then Percivale's mother sighed deeply, and she wept for a little while, knowing that the appointed time had come when she must lose her son. Indeed, at first she tried to persuade Percivale to remain with her in the peace and safety of the forest, telling him of the dangers and sufferings that a knight must undergo. But all that she said only made Percivale the more eager to set out on his quest; and at length she bowed her head quietly and gave him his way.

Early on the following morning Percivale clad himself in his simple garment of skins, took a long sharp dart in his hand, and prepared to bid his mother good-bye.

'Go bravely forward, my son,' she said as she kissed and blessed him. 'Your father was the bravest and best of knights: be worthy of him and of me. And if you live all your days in honour and purity, you too shall be numbered among the chosen few whose names will live for ever among the true Knights of Logres. ... Go on your way now, and remember that if dame or damsel ask your aid, give it freely and before all else, seeking no reward. Yet you may kiss the maiden who is willing, but take no more than a kiss, unless it be a ring – but be that only when you place your own ring upon her finger. Beware in whose company you travel on your quest, and see to it that only worthy men come near to your heart: but above all, pray to God each day that He may be with you in all your deeds – and pass not by church nor chapel without pausing awhile in His honour.'

Very gravely Percivale kissed his mother good-bye, and set out through the forest, walking swiftly, yet with his head bowed as he thought of the solemn things which she had said to him. But in a little while the spring came back into his step and he went on his way singing joyfully and tossing his long dart up into the air until the keen blade flashed like silver in the sunlight as he caught it and whirled it up again and again.

The shadows were falling in long black folds between the trees and the sun drew near to the western hills when Percivale came suddenly to an open glade in the forest where the daisies clustered the green grass like snowflakes, and saw a pavilion of silk pitched beside a tinkling stream.

'Be this church or chapel,' thought Percivale, 'it is wondrous fair – and I will go into it!'

Stepping softly over the threshold, he passed into the shadowy bower, and there stood in wonder looking down upon a damsel who lay sleeping on a couch of rich silk and samite, with one arm stretched out, more white than the coverlet, and her hair lighting up the pillow like sunshine. Very gently Percivale bent down over her and took from her finger the one ring that she wore – a plain gold band set with a single red ruby: in its place he put his own gold ring from which shone one white diamond, and the maiden's ring he set on his own finger. Then, still without waking her, he kissed her gently on the lips and stole once more from the tent, his heart singing with a new wonder and a new longing.

Deep into the forest went Percivale, slept, when darkness fell, among the roots of a great oak tree, and with the first light was on his way again, striding through the wood until he came to the wide road which led to Caerleon.

At noon he reached the city gates, passed them without stopping, and in time found himself within the very castle.

King Arthur with many of his knights sat feasting there that day, for the time was Easter and they had ceased from their labours for a little while. Percivale stood by the door, marvelling at all he saw and envying even the serving-men who waited upon the King and his company.

And suddenly as he stood there unobserved, all eyes turned towards the door as a great man in golden-red armour strode unannounced into the hall. Now at that moment Sir

Kay was standing beside the King holding in his hands the golden goblet from which it was Arthur's custom to pledge all his company ere the cup was passed round from hand to hand that each might drink to him and to the glory of the realm of Logres.

'Stay, you pack of wine-bibbing hinds!' roared the great red stranger. 'Here is a better than all of you!' And with that he snatched the goblet from Sir Kay, drained it at a draught, and, with a great roar of laughter, strode from the hall with it still in his hand, leapt upon his horse and galloped swiftly away.

'Now, by my faith!' cried King Arthur springing to his feet, 'this insult shall not go unpunished. Who will bring me back my cup?'

Then every knight rose as one man and cried: 'Let this quest be mine!'

'Not so,' said King Arthur, motioning them to sit once more. 'Yonder red braggart is not worthy to fall at a knight's hands. Let some humble squire follow and overthrow him – one who seeks to be made a knight. Such a one who returns to my Court wearing the Red Knight's armour and carrying my golden goblet, will I knight forthwith!'

Then Percivale sprang forward from his place by the doorway and stood in the midst, clad as he was in the skins of wild goats and with the long dart held in his hand:

'King Arthur!' he cried, 'I'll fetch your cup! I want some armour, and that golden suit will do me very well!'

'Bah!' exclaimed Sir Kay rudely. 'What can this miserable goat-herd do against so great a knight?'

'Who are you, fair sir?' asked King Arthur, courteous as always to all men.

'My name is Percivale,' was the answer. 'I do not know who my father was, for I never saw him nor heard my mother speak of him. But she has brought me up in the forests of Wales – and I come now to ask you to make me a knight!'

'Make you a knight, indeed!' scoffed Sir Kay. 'Go and tend sheep on the mountains before yonder ram in the golden armour makes you run away in terror!'

'A knight shall you be,' said King Arthur, 'if you bring back my cup and return wearing the armour of the robber who has taken it. Lo now, this quest is yours! Follow it only and no other!'

'I have no horse,' said Percivale.

'One shall be ready for you at the door,' answered Arthur. 'Eat now swiftly, and get you gone ... But you need arms and weapons ...'

'I have my dart,' interrupted Percivale. 'As for armour, I'll wait until I can put on that golden suit which you all saw not long ago!'

When he had eaten Percival rose to go: but as he passed down the hall, a damsel stood before him and cried aloud: 'The King of Heaven bless you, Sir Percivale, the best of knights!'

'Be silent, witless wench!' cried Sir Kay angrily, and he struck the damsel across the face.

'Beware of me when I return in my golden armour!' said Percivale looking scornfully at Sir Kay. 'That unknightly stroke will I revenge with a blow that you will not lightly forget!'

Then he hastened from the hall, sprang upon the waiting horse, and rode away into the forest.

Percivale went much faster than the Red Knight so that before sunset he overtook him as he rode quietly up a mountain path towards a lone grey tower outlined against the pale pink of the clouds.

'Turn, thief!' shouted Percivale as soon as he was near enough. 'Turn and defend yourself!'

A little way behind him three of King Arthur's knights reined in their horses to watch: they had followed all the way from Caerleon to see what should befall – Gawain, Ywain, and Gareth – but not even now did Percivale know that they were there.

'Ha!' cried the Red Knight, wheeling his steed. 'What insolent boy are you? And why do you bid me stand?'

'I come from King Arthur,' answered Percivale. 'Give me back the golden goblet which you stole this day at his feast!

Moreover, you must go yourself to the Court and do homage there – but first of all you must yield to me and give me that fine suit of armour which you wear so proudly!'

'And if I do not?' asked the Red Knight, speaking quietly but his eyes flashing with fury like the lightning in the quiet sky before a mighty storm.

'Why then I will kill you – and help myself to cup and armour!' exclaimed Percivale.

'Insolent child!' roared the Red Knight in a voice of thunder. 'You have asked for death – now take it!'

With that he set his spear in rest and came down the hillside like a mighty avalanche, expecting to transfix his enemy as if he were a butterfly on a pin. But Percivale leapt suddenly from his horse so that the spear passed harmlessly over its head, and stood in the middle of the path, shouting taunts:

'You great coward!' he jeered. 'First you try to spear an unarmed man, and then you run away down the hillside!'

With horrible oaths the Red Knight wheeled his horse once more and came charging up the path, his spear aimed at Percivale. But this time Percivale drew back his dart and threw it suddenly – so suddenly that it sped like a flash of light over the Red Knight's shield and caught him in the throat just above the rim of his armour, so that he fell backwards from his horse and lay there dead.

Percivale knelt down triumphantly beside his fallen foe and drew out King Arthur's golden cup from the wallet at his waist. But when he tried to loosen the golden armour from the body he found himself defeated: for he did not know how it was fastened on, and thought indeed that it was all made in one piece.

After many vain attempts to pull the Red Knight through the gorget or neck-piece of the armour, Percivale changed his tactics. Swiftly he gathered together a pile of dry wood, and was busily striking a flint from the road against the point of his dart when suddenly he heard the sound of a horse's hooves, and looking up saw an old man on horseback dressed in dark armour, whose helmet hung at his saddle-bow, and whose grey hair fell to his shoulders.

'Greetings, young sir,' said the old knight smiling kindly upon Percivale. 'What do you with this dead robber whom you have slain so valiantly?'

'Out of the iron burn the tree,' said Percivale, quoting a woodman's saying which his mother had taught him. 'I want to get this man out of the armour and wear it myself!'

The old knight's smile grew broader still, but he dismounted from his horse and showed Percivale how to unlace the armour and draw it off and on piece by piece.

'My name is Gonemans,' said the knight presently, 'and I dwell near by in an ancient manor-house. Come you thither with me, young sir, and I will teach you all things that you should know before you can become a worthy knight, for not alone by such a deed as this may you win to the true honour.'

So Percivale went with Sir Gonemans and dwelt all that summer in his house, learning to fight with sword and spear, to wear his armour and sit his horse as a knight should. And he learnt also of the high order of knighthood which was so much more noble than the mere doing of mighty deeds: he learnt of right and wrong, of a knight's duty ever to defend the weak and punish the cruel and evil.

And at last he rode forth on his way once more, clad in shining armour, with a tall spear in his hand, after bidding a courteous farewell to Sir Gonemans. It was late autumn by now, and as he rode beneath the trees in the deep woods and forests the leaves gleamed red and gold like his armour which seemed almost to be part of the foliage and bracken through which he passed.

Many days rode Percivale in quest of adventure, and often as he went his eyes fell upon the ruby ring on his finger, and he thought more and more of the lovely damsel whom he had found sleeping in the pavilion.

At length on a dark, sombre evening when the clouds lowered threateningly above him, he came by a winding way among great bare rocks through a sad and desolate land, until suddenly he saw a dark castle in front of him.

The walls were shattered and overthrown, the towers were cracked down the sides as if by lightning: yet no weeds grew among the stones or even between the cobbles under the yawning gateway; and in the centre stood the great keep firm and solid in the midst of that desolation.

Beneath the sharp teeth of the portcullis rode Percivale, his horse's hooves ringing hollowly on the stone and on through dark arches and deserted courtyards until he came to the entrance of the great hall. Here he could see a light burning and so, having tied his horse to a ring in the wall, he walked up the steps and into a mighty room with a high roof of black beams. There was no one to be seen, and yet a fire burned merrily in the great fireplace, torches shone brightly from rings in the walls, and dinner was set at a table on the dais. Percivale walked slowly up the hall and stood looking about him: on a little table not far from the fire he saw laid out a set of great ivory chessmen, with a chair drawn up on one side as if ready for a game. While still wondering what all this might mean, Percivale sat down in the chair, and presently he reached out idly and moved a white pawn forward two squares on the board. At once a red pawn moved forward by itself: Percivale was alert in an instant, but all was quiet, there was not even the sound of any breath but his own. So he moved another piece, and immediately a red piece was moved also. Percivale moved again as if playing – and behold! the red pieces moved in turn, so cunningly that in a very few minutes he saw that he was checkmated.

Swiftly he re-arranged the pieces, and this time the red moved first and a second game was played, which Percivale lost also. A third time this happened, and Percivale rose in a sudden fury, drawing his sword to crush the pieces and hack the board.

But as he did so a damsel ran suddenly into the room: 'Hold your hand, sir knight!' she cried. 'If you strike at these magic chesspieces a terrible evil will befall you!'

'Who are you, lady?' asked Percivale.

'I am Blanchefleur,' she answered, and as she spoke she came forward into the light of the candles which stood near to the chess-table, and with a sudden gasp of wonder and joy Percivale knew her for the maiden in the pavilion. And even as he recognized her he saw his diamond ring shining on her finger.

He held out his hand to her, and saw her suddenly pause as she recognized her own ring which he still wore.

'Lady Blanchefleur,' he said gently, 'I have sought for you long. My name is Percivale – and I beg you to pardon me for the wrong I did you, meaning no wrong, when I took this ring from you as you slept, and took also one kiss from your lips.'

Percivale knew her for the maiden in the pavilion

'Percivale,' she answered gently, 'I have seen you only in dreams: each night you have come to me, wearing my ring, and have kissed me once on the lips – and my heart has gone out to you across the darkness ... But in this magic castle I have waited for you: the time to speak of love is not yet. Come sit down to supper, for you shall see a more wondrous thing than yonder enchanted chess-board.'

They took their places at the table: but there was no food nor wine upon it, nor did any man or woman come to wait upon them.

Yet Percivale sat silent, looking at Blanchefleur.

'Lady,' he said at length, 'all times are the true time for such a love as mine: lady, will you be my wife? I swear to you that no other in all the world shall come near me, nor shall my lips touch those of any save you alone.'

Blanchefleur laid her hand in his with never a word, and as she touched him suddenly a roar of thunder shook the castle, the great door of the hall flew open, and a strange damsel, dressed and veiled in white, walked slowly into the hall, holding aloft a great goblet or grail covered in a cloth. A light shone from within the Grail, so bright that no man might look upon it: yet it was with another and a holy awe that Percivale sank to his knees and bowed his head in his hands.

A second veiled woman followed the first, bearing a golden platter, and a third followed her, carrying a spear with a point of white light from which dripped blood that vanished ere it touched the floor. As they passed up the hall and round the table where Percivale and Blanchefleur knelt, the whole room seemed to be filled with sweet scents as of roses and spices, and when the Procession of the Grail had passed down the hall once more and out of the door, which closed again behind them, there fell upon Percivale a peace of heart that passed all understanding, and a great joy.

'The Holy Grail draws near to Logres,' said Blanchefleur. 'Ask me no more concerning what you have seen, for the time has not yet come. One other must enter this castle and see it – and that is Sir Launcelot of the Lake. But, Percivale, you are more blessed than he: for through him shall come the ending of the glory of Logres, though in Logres there has so far been none so glorious as he, save only Gawain. Go you now to Camelot and wait for the coming of Galahad: on the day when he sits in the Siege Perilous you shall see the Holy Grail once more.'

'Lady,' said Percivale, rising to his feet, but standing with bowed head, 'I would seek for it now! It seems to me that there is no quest in all the world so worthy.'

'No quest indeed,' answered Blanchefleur, 'but not yet

may you seek it. On the day when the glory of Logres is at its full, the Grail shall come to Camelot: then all shall seek, but only the most worthy shall find it.'

'I would be one of those!' cried Percivale. 'None but I shall achieve the Quest of the Grail!' And forgetting all else he ran down the hall, never heeding Blanchefleur's cry, leapt upon his horse and galloped away into the forest.

When morning came the madness seemed to leave him suddenly, and turning round, he tried to ride back in search of Blanchefleur. But though he wandered for many, many days he could never again find any trace of the desolate land or of the mysterious Castle of Carbonek.

Sad and wretched, Percivale turned at length and rode towards Caerleon. It was winter by now and the snow lay thick on the high road as Percivale came out from the mountains and forests of Central Wales and drew near to the city. One night he slept at Tintern on the Wye, and early next day rode slowly and sadly down the valley by the bright river.

Suddenly as he went he saw a hawk swoop from above like a shining bolt of brown and strike a dove. For a moment the two birds fluttered together in mid-air, and then the hawk flew triumphant up once more bearing his victim in his claws. But from the dove's breast fell three drops of blood which lay and glistened in the white snow at Percivale's feet. As he looked he thought of the blood that fell from the spear at Castle Carbonek; he thought of the ruby ring on his finger; but most of all he thought of Blanchefleur, of her red lips, red as blood, and of her skin like the white snow.

As he sat there on his horse four knights came riding towards him: and these were Sir Kay, Sir Ywain, Sir Gawain and King Arthur himself.

'Ride forward now,' said King Arthur to Sir Kay, 'and ask yonder knight his name, whither he journeys and why he sits thus lost in thought.'

'Ho, sir knight!' shouted Kay as he drew near. 'Tell me your name and business!'

But Percivale was lost so deeply in his thoughts that he neither saw nor heard.

'Answer, if you be not a dumb man!' shouted Kay, and then, losing his temper somewhat, he struck at Percivale with his iron gauntlet.

Then Percivale sat upright on his horse, reined backwards a little way, set his spear in rest, and cried:

'No man shall strike me thus and go unpunished! Defend yourself, you cowardly, craven knight!'

Sir Kay drew back also, levelled his spear, and they galloped together with all their strength. Sir Kay's spear struck Percivale's shield and broke into pieces; but Percivale smote so hard and truly that he pierced Kay's shield, wounding him deeply in the side and hurling him to the ground.

Then he sat with his spear ready, in case one of the other knights should attack him.

'I will joust with all or any of you!' he cried, 'I will defend my right to sit my horse by the roadside without having to suffer the blows and insults of such a shameful knight as this!'

'It is Percivale!' exclaimed Sir Gawain suddenly. 'He who slew the Red Knight – whose armour now he wears! Truly he must have been lost in deep thoughts of love to sit as he did while Sir Kay struck him!'

'Ask him to speak with us, fair nephew,' said King Arthur, and Gawain rode forward towards Percivale.

'Gentle sir,' said he with all courtesy, 'yonder is King Arthur, our sovereign lord, and he desires you to speak with him. As for Sir Kay, whom you have smitten down, well he deserves this punishment for his lack of knightly gentleness!'

When Percivale heard this he was glad.

'Then are both mine oaths fulfilled,' he cried. 'I have punished Sir Kay for the evil blow he gave the damsel on the day when I came first to Caerleon; and I come before King Arthur wearing the armour of the Red Knight whom I have slain and carrying in my wallet the golden goblet which was stolen from his board!'

Percivale rode forward, dismounted from his horse, and knelt before King Arthur.

'Lord King,' he said, 'make me a knight, I pray you. And

here I swear to spend all my days in your service, striving to bring glory to the realm of Logres.'

'Arise, Sir Percivale of Wales,' said King Arthur. 'Your place awaits you at the Round Table – between Sir Gawain and the Siege Perilous. In the days long past Merlin the good enchanter told me that you would come when the highest moment of the realm of Logres drew near.'

Then Sir Percivale rode to Caerleon between King Arthur and Sir Gawain, while Sir Ywain followed after them, leading Sir Kay's horse while Sir Kay lay groaning across its saddle.

Many deeds did Sir Percivale after this, but there is no space to tell of his adventures with Rosette the Loathly Damsel, how he fought with the Knight of the Tomb who lived in a great cromlech on a mountain in Wales, how he overcame Partiniaus and Arides, King Margon and the Witch of the Waste City. But always he sought for the Lady Blanchefleur, always he was true to her alone: but he could not find her – until the years were accomplished, and he found his way once more to the Castle of Carbonek not long after the Holy Grail came to Camelot.

8

The Story of Launcelot
and Elaine

FOR many years King Arthur and his knights fought against the Saxons at different places all over the land of Britain, but when the great Battle of Mount Badon had been fought – one of the greatest battles ever fought on British soil – there followed long years of peace when the realm of Logres seemed to smile in a long divine summer between the clouds that were gathering thickly over all the rest of the world.

At first there were many robbers and evil men, giants too and wizards, against whom the knights must be ready to fight at any moment; and it was not only at the great feasts of Easter and Pentecost, Michaelmas and Christmas that damsels came riding to King Arthur's Court to seek redress for the wrongs that had been done them. But as the years rolled by fewer and fewer needed help, the peace of a true and holy state settled more and more surely upon Logres, and King Arthur's knights spent more and more of their time holding great tournaments at Camelot or Caerleon – growing more and more skilled in arms, it is true, but finding less and less cause to prove their prowess.

Most of the younger knights rode about all over the country in quest of adventures; but the older ones waited more and more for some great thing to befall: and foremost amongst these was Launcelot.

For long years he had been supreme, no knight equalling him in strength and valour, in courtesy and nobleness of mind – not even Tristram or Gareth, Geraint or the young knight Percivale: only Gawain might compare with him, and they were friends so true that no rivalry ever sprang up between them.

Now from the very first day when he came to court Launcelot had loved Queen Guinevere and her alone of all ladies in the world. Faithfully and truly he served her for many years as a knight should, and King Arthur felt no jealousy, for he trusted the high honour of both Launcelot and the Queen. And for a long time Launcelot served Guinevere as a true knight and a true subject, seeking only to bring her honour by his mighty deeds. But in the long years of peace when he was so seldom called away from Camelot on a quest, and when King Arthur needed no longer to lead his hosts forth to battle, both Launcelot and Guinevere began to spend more and more of their time together – more and more often without King Arthur's knowledge.

In this way the first shadow of a great evil crept into Logres, so silently and so innocent in seeming that no one observed it, nor did either Launcelot or Guinevere dream whither it would lead. But the powers of evil, seeking now more and more desperately to find some tiny loophole through which to climb into the stronghold of good, saw it, and set a cunning snare for Launcelot.

One blithe spring day at the Feast of Easter which King Arthur held at Camelot there came a hermit into the great hall and greeted those who sat there at meat.

'May God's blessing fall upon all this company!' he cried. 'Surely a fairer gathering of knights the world shall never see! But there is yet one place empty: tell me of that seat, I pray you, my lord King.' And he pointed with his staff to the empty place between Sir Launcelot and Sir Percivale.

'Reverend father,' answered King Arthur, 'that is the Siege Perilous, and therein one knight only shall sit, for so Merlin foretold on the day of the making of this table. But if another man sit there he shall die swiftly by the magic of that siege.'

'Know you who shall sit therein?' asked the hermit.

'Nay,' said King Arthur and all his knights, 'we know not who it is that shall sit there.'

'He is not yet born,' said the hermit. 'But this same year he shall see the light. And he it is who shall win the Quest of the Holy Grail . . . But of that I came not hither to speak, rather of another quest and the saving of a lady who is the victim of wicked enchantments in the Dolorous Tower. Only the best knight amongst you can win her freedom, and that is Sir Launcelot of the Lake: therefore I beg you to send him with all speed . . .'

Far and far Sir Launcelot rode with the hermit until on a day he came to a city upon a dark hillside with narrow streets and a great black tower at the top. Then all the people cried out as he rode amongst them:

'Welcome, Sir Launcelot, the flower of knighthood! By your aid shall our lady be saved!'

Up to the tower went Launcelot, the hermit still guiding him; into the tower and up a great staircase until they came to a mighty door of iron.

'Within this place,' said the hermit, 'has lain the fairest lady in the land for five long years. By enchantment Queen Morgana le Fay has imprisoned her, out of evil jealousy, and none may free her save the best of knights.'

Then Launcelot set his hand to the door and at once the great bolts and bars fell into pieces, the hinges screamed shrilly, and pressing into the room he found the Dolorous Lady lying in a bath of scalding hot water where she had been bound by her wicked enemy. But the enchantment ended when Launcelot broke through the door, and the Dolorous Lady came back to her people.

'Sir knight,' said the hermit, 'since you have delivered this lady you must deliver us also from a serpent which dwells near by in an ancient tomb.'

Then Sir Launcelot took up his shield and said:

'What I may do to save you from evil that will I attempt with the help of God. Therefore bring me thither.'

When he came up to the mountain top there stood a great stone cromlech of three upright stones and a fourth laid over them. And out of this dark abode came a mighty wingless dragon, breathing fire and hissing horribly. All through the long day the battle lasted, and in the evening Launcelot smote off the dragon's head. Then he mounted his horse once more and rode down beyond the hill and deep into the lonely passes of Wales until he came through the Waste Lands to where a mighty castle stood, half ruined and half whole, the great keep rising high above rent walls and fallen towers. Round the castle rode Launcelot, marvelling to see the desolation of it, and how no weeds nor creepers grew even over the fallen stones; and he came in time to a part of the building which still stood unharmed.

Here two squires met him and led him into the great hall where Pelles the Maimed King, whom Balyn had smitten long years before when he struck the Dolorous Stroke, sat amongst his knights and ladies at the high table on its dais above the body of the hall.

'Welcome, fair knight,' said King Pelles, raising one wasted arm where he lay unable to move on a golden couch. 'Sit you down at my table! It is long since any knight came to this haunted Castle of Carbonek, and I fear that many years still must pass before one comes who may heal me of my grievous wound ... But tell me your name: I require you, by your knightly honour, tell me truly.'

'Sir,' said Launcelot, bowing gravely, 'I hold it great honour that you should welcome me thus. And as for my name, it is Launcelot of the Lake.'

'And I,' answered his host, 'am Pelles, King of the Waste Lands and of Haunted Carbonek. But I hold a sacred trust, for Joseph of Arimathea was my ancestor – and anon you shall see a wonder ...'

Launcelot seated himself at the table, and he noticed that there was no food nor wine set before anyone there, and that a great silence had fallen upon them all.

Then suddenly there was a peal of thunder, the door flew open and into the hall came three women dressed all in white and veiled, moving so silently that he thought they must be spirits and not women. The first bore in her hand a spear with a point of light from which dripped blood that vanished ere it touched the floor; the second held a golden platter covered with a cloth, and the third a golden cup covered also, but seeming to be filled with a light so pure and bright that no man might look at it: but it was with a deeper awe and reverence that Launcelot hid his face in prayer as the procession passed round the table and out of the hall once more. When it was gone a great peace and well-being fell upon all present, and it seemed to Launcelot that he had eaten and drunk of more than mortal food.

'My lord,' he said in a hushed voice, 'what may this mean?'

'Sir,' answered King Pelles, 'you have seen the most precious tokens in the world, and I, the descendant of Joseph of Arimathea, am their guardian. From that Cup and Platter Our Lord Jesus Christ ate and drank at the Last Supper; with that Spear Longinus the Roman centurion pierced His side as He hung upon the Cross, and in that same Cup, which is called the Holy Grail, Joseph of Arimathea caught His most precious blood as it ran from the wound ... Know, I say, that the Holy Grail has passed by you beneath that cloth: when it passes amongst you all as you sit at Camelot, the Round Table shall be broken for a season as you all ride forth in quest of it ...'

When the wonder of what he had seen had passed from Launcelot a little, he spoke to his host of other matters, and many days he remained at Castle Carbonek – but never again did he see the Procession of the Holy Grail.

But King Pelles had a daughter called Elaine, one of the fairest damsels in the world, and she loved Launcelot the moment that she saw him. All the time he was at Castle Carbonek Elaine tended on him, served him in all things, and tried her hardest to win his love; but though Launcelot treated her with all courtesy, rode hunting with her, listened to her singing, played at chess with her, yet still his heart was unstirred and he remained faithful to Queen Guinevere – though unfaithful in thought at least to his honour as a Knight of Logres and to his king.

Then Elaine spoke with her father, King Pelles, and he, who could see a little of the future as through a glass darkly, made answer:

'Do not weep and lament, my daughter, Launcelot shall indeed be your lord, and you shall bear him a son, which shall be called Galahad, who shall bring the Waste Lands from under the shadow of the curse, and heal me of my wound. ... I know not how this may come to pass, but that it will be so, have no fear.'

The days went by while Launcelot dwelt in peace at Carbonek, but Elaine prospered not at all in her love. At length, in despair, she turned aside to seek the aid of enchantments, and there came to her a damsel named Brysen who was skilled in all the arts of which Morgana le Fay was queen.

'Ah lady,' said the damsel, 'know well that Sir Launcelot loves only Queen Guinevere, and no other woman in all the world. Therefore we must work by guile if you would have him.'

After this they spoke together for a long time, and the end of it was that Elaine went secretly from Carbonek. Then there came a man to Launcelot bearing a ring, which seemed to him one that he knew well which Queen Guinevere always wore.

'Where is your lady the queen?' asked Launcelot.

'Sir,' answered the man, 'she is at Case Castle not many miles from here, and she bids you come to her as soon as may be.'

Then Launcelot bade a hasty farewell to King Pelles, mounted his horse, and rode swiftly through the Waste Lands until Carbonek was lost behind him, and he came at sundown to the little Castle of Case on the skirts of the great forest. And there he found Queen Guinevere, or so it seemed to him, waiting for him with her eyes full of love: but really it was Elaine who, by the arts of Brysen, had taken the form of Guinevere for a little while in the dim glow of evening.

When Launcelot saw her alone thus he quite forgot his honour and his oath, the glory of Logres and his faith to King Arthur: all his thoughts were on Guinevere – and when she spoke to him of marriage he forgot even that she was King Arthur's wife: and indeed Brysen the enchantress had made all things ready at the Castle of Case ...

The morning dawned grey and ominous, and Launcelot awoke to find the lady Elaine sleeping by his side. Then he remembered all, and how he was shamed for ever, even though Elaine and not Guinevere was beside him.

'Alas!' he cried, 'I have lived too long, for now I am dishonoured!' Then Elaine woke and knelt before him, confessing all and praying for his forgiveness.

'Ah, noble Sir Launcelot!' she cried. 'I did all these things only for love of you!'

But Launcelot cried aloud in his agony of mind, and the world seemed to spin round him. Flinging open the window, he leapt out of it, clad only in his shirt, fell into a bed of roses, sprang to his feet all scratched and bleeding from the thorns and rushed away still crying aloud, until he was lost in the forest. And there he wan-

And there he wandered, his wits quite gone from him

dered, and upon the desolate hills of Wales, his wits quite gone from him.

The months sped by, and at Camelot men began to ask what had become of Sir Launcelot that no one had seen him for so long. Christmas came, and still he did not return – nor had he graced the feast at Pentecost or Michaelmas.

When the new year was in, Launcelot's cousin, Sir Bors de Gannis, went quietly away from Camelot in search of him. In time he came to the Waste Lands and then to the mysterious Castle of Carbonek which so few men could ever find. Here he found King Pelles and the lady Elaine – and Elaine carried in her arms a new-born babe.

'Lo! sir knight,' said Elaine, 'this is my son, and his father is Sir Launcelot of the Lake. To-day shall this boy be christened, and his name is Galahad.'

Then Elaine told Sir Bors all the story of Launcelot's visit to Carbonek and Case, and of how he had run mad with shame and sorrow, and had wandered away into the hills of Wales.

At supper that night the Grail Procession passed once more through the hall: but in place of the Bleeding Lance the second ghostly maiden carried a golden candlestick with seven branches.

'You have seen a great wonder,' said King Pelles, 'nor has this procession passed before the eyes of any save Sir Percivale and Sir Launcelot. High up in a room above the keep those candles burn ever upon an altar in a little chapel, and the Grail rests there, and the Bleeding Lance wherewith Longinus pierced Our Lord. I, the Grail-Keeper, have entered that room, and my father before me, and his father, and so back to Joseph of Arimathea who built this castle. But no other man has entered that room, save only the good knight Sir Gawain: once another knight came there and laid impious hands upon the Lance – that was Sir Balyn who smote the Dolorous Stroke, and perished sadly for his sin ... Go now in search of Sir Launcelot: you will come here once more, but he, by reason of his sin, is not worthy to touch the Grail – though in earthly matters he is the best knight in the world.'

Sir Bors rode away next morning, and when he had come out of the Waste Lands he met Sir Gawain and Sir Percivale, Sir Ywain and Sir Segramour, and many other knights who were also seeking for Sir Launcelot. East and west and south and north they went, but never a trace of Launcelot did they find: many adventures befell them on their quest, and many strange things did they see, but no one whom they met had seen a mad knight running through the land without armour or weapons.

On a day, however, Sir Percivale and Sir Bors drew near to the Castle of Case, and there Elaine met them and greeted them joyfully, for she had come away with Galahad from Carbonek, and now not even she could find it again.

She entertained them well in her castle, but grieved sorely when she heard that Launcelot was still lost. For many days they remained at Case, hoping that Launcelot might come there in his wanderings – and at last he came . . .

Elaine walked in the garden one day, and her little son Galahad came running to her suddenly, crying:

'Mother, come and look! I've found a goodly man who lies sleeping by the well!'

And when Elaine beheld him she knew that it was Launcelot, and weeping sorely she hastened to Percivale and Bors and told them.

'Do not wake him,' they said, 'for perchance he is still mad and will slay you in his fury, or run wild once more.'

Then there came a hermit who dwelt in a little chapel near by, and he counselled that Launcelot should be carried from the castle while still sleeping and laid therein.

'All night I will pray before the altar,' said the hermit. 'It cannot be that the good knight Sir Launcelot shall pass all his days as a madman wandering naked in the wilderness . . .'

Early next morning Percivale and Bors stood bareheaded in the doorway of the little chapel and saw the hermit kneeling before the altar, while Launcelot lay like a dead man on a black bier in the little chancel. For long they stood there in the quiet shadow, with bowed heads, praying also for Launcelot: and then quite suddenly the Holy Grail was in the place, hanging in a great halo of light above the altar, shining so brightly that both the watchers sank on their knees and buried their faces in their hands. When they looked up again Launcelot was kneeling too – but of the Holy Grail there was no sign, only the light of the rising sun shining down upon him through the little round rose-window above the altar.

When they had thanked the hermit, Sir Bors and Sir Percivale led Launcelot back to Castle Case, he walking like a man asleep; and he was laid in a bed and tended well by Elaine and her maid Brysen. But Sir Bors and Sir Percivale rode back to Camelot and told King Arthur all that they had seen.

At length Sir Launcelot woke from his long sleep, his mind whole and untroubled once more, and found Elaine bending over him.

'Ah me!' he exclaimed, 'tell me, for God's sake, where I am and how I came hither!'

'Sir,' answered Elaine, 'into this country you came as a madman, wandering naked and without knowledge. In my garden were you found, and the madness was raised from you by the good offices of Naciens the Divine Hermit, and by the coming of the Holy Grail.'

For many days after this Launcelot remained at Case, and Elaine tended him until he was strong and well again. But then, in spite of her tears and entreaties, he bade farewell to her, mounted his horse, and rode on his way towards Camelot. For still his heart turned only towards Queen Guinevere, and he loved her now with a greater, fiercer passion, even though Elaine had tricked him, wearing her form, and had wedded him when he thought that she was Guinevere.

What became of Elaine after Launcelot had left her the old tales do not tell, or tell confusedly. When Launcelot came again to Carbonek, Elaine was there no longer, and Galahad, almost from the day when Launcelot rode away from Case Castle, was entrusted to the care of certain holy monks and nuns who dwelt not far from Camelot.

The old tales tell, however, of another Elaine who loved Launcelot and from whom he rode away, refusing her love by reason of the faith unfaithful that kept him falsely true to Guinevere, King Arthur's queen. This Elaine pined away when Launcelot left her, and died of a broken heart; and when she was dead her attendants laid her, richly clad, in a barge on the broad river that flows down to Camelot, and they placed a letter in her hand and let the barge drift with the stream – for such had been her dying wish.

Floating on the river that flows down to Camelot

'Sir,' said Kay coming into the hall where King Arthur sat with many of his knights some days later: 'Here is a great marvel! Out yonder upon the river floats a black barge, and dead within it lies a lovely damsel clad in rich robes and jewels.'

Then King Arthur, with Queen Guinevere and many of his knights, went down to the river side and beheld how the barge floated quietly down the stream, and lodged at length against the bank. And now all might see the letter which the dead maiden held in her hand, and bending down King Arthur took it gently from her, broke the seals, and read:

'Most noble knight, my lord Sir Launcelot, now has death won me from your love. For I loved you truly, and my name was Elaine of Astolat. Therefore I beg all ladies to pity me, and for my soul that they shall pray, and for my body that they give it honourable burial ... And pray you for my soul, most peerless Sir Launcelot.'

When Launcelot heard this he covered his face with his hands and wept. 'Ah, my lord Arthur,' he said, 'know that I am sad indeed, and filled with pity for the death of this lady. But I call God to witness that I was not willingly the cause of her death ... Truly she loved me, and longed above all things to be my wife: but it might not be, for love cannot be commanded, and I would think it foul shame and dishonour to wed one whom I did not love.'

'That is truth indeed,' said King Arthur. 'Love comes as a gift divine, and must be treated with all honour and reverence: he is no true knight who would do aught to bring a stain upon it.'

Then each of them passed by the lady Elaine with bowed head, and thereafter she was buried solemnly in the great minster. But it was some while before the shadow passed wholly from the Court of Camelot where was the heart of the high realm of Logres. And it never quite passed from Sir Launcelot, for he knew that in one thing he was unworthy of his high place: yet for all that, he ceased not to love Queen Guinevere, nor she him – and from their love came at length the passing of the glory of Logres.

BOOK THREE

The Quest of the Holy Grail

I

︿︿︿︿︿︿︿︿︿︿︿︿︿︿︿︿︿︿︿︿︿︿︿︿︿︿

How the Holy Grail came
to Camelot

IT was the day before the Feast of Pentecost, and the
knights were riding in to Camelot from every direction to
take their places at the Round Table on the next day. Nearly
all of them had arrived in time for the evening service in the
great minster, and thereafter they were gathered together for
supper in the hall of the castle.

On a sudden there came a fair lady riding fast on a white
horse, and she came before the King and did reverence to
him, crying:

'Sire, for God's sake tell me where is Sir Launcelot!'

'He is yonder,' answered King Arthur. 'Look, you can see
him!' Then she went to Sir Launcelot and said:

'Good sir knight, I require you to come with me into the
forest near by.'

'What will you with me?' asked Sir Launcelot.

'That you shall know when you come thither.'

'Well, I will gladly go with you.'

And so saying, Sir Launcelot turned to bid farewell to the
king and queen.

'What!' cried Guinevere, 'will you leave us now, the night
before Pentecost?'

'Madam,' said the lady, 'he shall be with you again by
dinner time to-morrow, that I promise you.'

Then they rode away into the forest, and came before long
to an abbey; and there Launcelot was welcomed by the
monks and nuns, and led into a fair guest chamber where he
was unarmed. There he found his two cousins Sir Bors and
Sir Lionel who were spending the night there on their way to
Camelot, and they rejoiced to be together again.

While they were talking there came in twelve nuns leading Galahad with them, the fairest, finest youth in all the world.

'Sir,' said the lady abbess to Launcelot, 'this boy is of royal lineage, and him we have tended since he was a child; Naciens the hermit of Carbonek has instructed him, and of the use of arms he has learnt also. Now we pray you to make him a knight, for there are no man's hands more worthy than yours wherefrom he may receive the high Order of Knighthood.'

'That will I do,' said Sir Launcelot, for he knew now that Galahad was his own son, born in the mysterious Castle of Carbonek.

All that night Galahad kept his vigil kneeling before the altar in the chapel of the monastery, and in the morning after the early service Launcelot blessed him and made him a knight.

'God make you a good man,' he said, 'even as there is none more fair to see in this world than you are. And now, fair Sir Galahad, will you come with me to the Court of King Arthur?'

'Not yet,' he answered, 'but soon shall you see me there.'

So Launcelot rode back to Camelot with Bors and Lionel, and found the whole company gathered about the Round Table in the great hall: and in letters of gold upon each siege was written the name of him who should sit there; and that morning every seat was full except for the Siege Perilous, wherein none might sit and arise from it living save he for whom it was made.

As Launcelot went to take his place at one side of it, and Percivale on the other, they saw suddenly a new writing grow in letters of gold upon the Siege Perilous:

'FOUR HUNDRED AND FIFTY AND FOUR YEARS AFTER THE DEATH OF OUR LORD JESUS CHRIST THIS SIEGE SHOULD BE FILLED.'

'It seems to me,' said Sir Launcelot, after they had all gazed for a little while in silence, 'that this siege ought to be filled upon this very day. For to-day is the first Pentecost after the four hundred and fifty-four years! But let us cover the Siege Perilous with a silken cloth until he comes whose place it is.'

When this was done King Arthur bade them all sit down to dinner; but Sir Kay the steward exclaimed:

'Sir, if you go now to your meat you break the old custom of your court, for never before on this day have you sat down to dinner until you have seen some strange adventure.'

'You speak truth,' said King Arthur, 'but I marvelled so at the words written upon the Siege Perilous that I did not for the moment think of the old custom.'

Even while they stood speaking in came a squire and said to the king:

'Sir, I bring you news of a wonder!'

'What is it?' asked the king.

'Sir,' answered the squire, 'there is a great square stone floating upon the river, and in it I saw sticking a bright sword with a handle of gold shaped like a cross.'

Then the king said: 'I will see this marvel.'

So all the knights went with him, and they came across the great meadow beside the castle and found the stone floating by the river bank with the sunlight flashing from the jewels in the hilt of the sword until it circled the cross like a halo. And upon the sword were written these words:

'NEVER SHALL MAN TAKE ME HENCE BUT ONLY HE BY WHOSE SIDE I OUGHT TO HANG, AND HE SHALL BE THE BEST KNIGHT IN THE WORLD.'

When the king read these words he said to Sir Launcelot:

'Fair sir, this sword ought to be yours, for I am sure that you are the best knight in the world.'

But Sir Launcelot thought upon Queen Guinevere and the shameful love that was between them, and he said quietly:

'Sir, this is not my sword, nor am I worthy to wear it at my side. Evil shall come to any who seeks to draw it knowing that he is not worthy ...'

'Now, fair nephew,' said King Arthur to Sir Gawain, 'do you try to draw it.'

'Sir,' answered Gawain, 'that have I no wish to do.'

'Try to draw it, nevertheless,' said King Arthur. 'I command you.'

'Sir, your command I will obey,' said Gawain. So saying, he took the sword by the handle, but he could not stir it.

Then Sir Percivale tried also at King Arthur's wish, but he might not stir it either: and there was no other knight who dared set his hand to it.

'Now may we go to our dinner,' said Sir Kay, 'for you have indeed seen a marvellous adventure.'

So they returned to the hall and sat themselves down, every seat being filled save only the Siege Perilous which was covered with the silken cloth. But they had not put forth their hands to the meal when there came a mighty blast of wind which seemed to shake all the castle, and after it a great stillness.

'Before God, fair friends,' said King Arthur in a hushed voice, 'this is a day of marvels: what else we shall see before night, I wonder greatly!'

Even as he spoke there appeared in the doorway an ancient man with a long white beard leading by the hand a tall young knight, the fairest that any had seen, who was clad all in dark red armour. He had no sword or shield, but an empty scabbard hung at his side: and Launcelot knew that it was his son Sir Galahad and Naciens the ancient hermit of Carbonek.

'Peace be with you all, fair lords,' cried Naciens; and then to King Arthur he said:

'My lord king, I bring you hither a young knight of royal lineage, the descendant of Joseph of Arimathea. And by this knight the marvels of your court and of the strong realm of Logres shall be fully accomplished.'

'Right welcome are you to my court,' said King Arthur.

Then Naciens the hermit led Galahad straight up the hall to the Siege Perilous between Sir Launcelot and Sir Percivale, and drew away the silk cloth. And now all might see that the letters of the morning were there no longer, but in their stead a new inscription:

'THIS IS THE SIEGE OF SIR GALAHAD THE HIGH PRINCE.'

'Sir,' said Naciens, 'you perceive that this place is yours.'

Then Galahad sat down in the Siege Perilous, and said: 'Now, reverend sir, you may go, for your commands have been done. But know that I shall come again to Carbonek, and that before long.'

So Naciens the hermit departed from amongst them, and all the knights of the Round Table wondered greatly that Sir

The hermit led Galahad to the Siege Perilous

Galahad sat there unharmed. But Launcelot looked upon his son and smiled proudly.

'Upon pain of my life, this young knight shall achieve great things!' exclaimed Sir Bors de Gannis.

When dinner was ended King Arthur led Galahad down to the riverside and showed him the sword in the floating stone. 'Here is as great a marvel as ever I saw,' said the king. 'Two of the best knights in the world have tried in vain to draw it forth.'

'Sir,' said Galahad, 'that is not strange, for this adventure is not theirs, but mine. See you, I wear a scabbard, but no sword, for I knew that I should find this waiting for me.'

So saying he put out his hand, drew the sword easily from the stone, and slid it into the sheath at his side, saying as he did so:

'Now have I the sword that struck the Dolorous Stroke. Once it hung at Sir Balyn's side, and with it he slew his brother Balan. But Merlin set it thus in the stone that it might come to my hand on the day appointed, and shine there to the glory of God.'

After that armour and horses were brought, and the knights jousted in the meadow by the river:

'Fair sir,' said King Arthur to Galahad, 'let me now give you a shield.'

'Not so,' answered Sir Galahad, 'for God will send me a shield at the time appointed.'

Then he took a spear and jousted with all who came, striking such mighty blows and riding so well and so furiously that none might stand against him, shieldless though he was – no, not even Sir Tristram or Sir Gareth. But with Sir Launcelot, Sir Gawain, Sir Percivale, and Sir Bors he did not joust.

In the evening King Arthur and his knights rode back towards the castle; and as they went a damsel on a white palfrey came riding towards them. She greeted King Arthur, and asked if Sir Launcelot was there: and he answered himself:

'I am here, fair lady!'

Then she said, weeping sorely, 'Ah, Sir Launcelot! You know not how great a change has come upon you this day!'

'Damsel, why say you so?' he asked.

'Sir,' she answered, sobbing bitterly, 'I speak the truth. In the morning of this day you were the best knight in the world. But now a better than you has come into the realm of Logres, and has drawn forth the sword out of the floating stone, as Merlin knew it should be.'

'I knew well that I was never the best,' said Sir Launcelot.

'Of sinful men you are still the best,' cried the damsel, 'but now a better than you is here. Ah, King Arthur, a greater glory shall be yours this day than any king's ever in the land of Britain. But weep, Sir Launcelot, weep for that which you have lost!'

So crying, she rode away and was lost in the gathering gloom.

Silently they went into the great hall and sat down in their places at the Round Table. Then King Arthur looked about him and saw that all the sieges were full, and he remembered the words of Merlin the wise enchanter.

'Lo! now,' said King Arthur, 'there sits about this board the fairest company that ever the world shall see. This is the highest hour of this our holy realm of Logres, the hour of the Glory of Logres.'

Even as he said these words there blew a great wind about the castle and a mighty crash of thunder shook the place; then on a sudden a sunbeam cut through the gloom from end to end of the great hall, seven times more clear than ever man saw on the brightest day of summer; and the glory of God was upon them all. Each knight looked upon one another, and each saw the other fairer than he had ever seemed before: yet none could speak a word, and they sat there at the Round Table as if they had been stricken dumb.

Then the Holy Grail entered into the hall covered in a cloth of white samite, so filled with glorious light that none might behold it. Nor could they see who carried the Holy Grail, for it seemed to glide upon the sunbeam, passing through the midst of them and filling them with the joy and peace of the fullness of God. Then on a sudden it departed from among them, and none might see where it went: but the sunbeam faded also, and they sat in silence, filled with a great peace. Only Sir Mordred hid his face in his hands, and the hot tears of shame trickled between his fingers.

Presently King Arthur said, in a hushed voice:

'Surely we ought to thank Our Lord Jesus Christ that He has sent His blessing upon us on this the high Feast of Pentecost.'

'Truly we are blessed above all men,' said Sir Gawain. 'Yet surely this day has but shown us that there are greater glories yet to seek after. Even now when the Holy Grail came amongst us, it was so veiled from our sight that we might not see it nor draw near to it. Wherefore I make here a vow that to-morrow morning, without any delay, I shall go forth in quest of the Holy Grail, and never cease until I have achieved that quest – or learnt that I am not worthy to achieve it.'

When the other knights of the Round Table heard Sir Gawain say this, nearly all of them rose up also and made the same vow.

'Alas,' cried King Arthur, 'fair nephew, you have well nigh slain me with that vow: for now you have taken from me the fairest and the truest knighthood that ever was seen together in any realm of the world. For when you all depart from hence, I am sure that never again will this full company be met together here about the Table Round – for many shall die upon that quest. And thinking that, I am sorely grieved, for I have loved you all as well as my life. Moreover I know that hereafter shall come the passing of the realm of Logres, and that the time draws near of that last battle whereof Merlin warned me.'

In the morning all those knights who were sworn to the great adventure met in the minster and made anew their vows of knighthood. Then in ones and twos they rode away from Camelot, some this way, and some that, in quest of the Holy Grail.

2

The First Adventures of Sir Galahad

BY hill and dale, forest and plain, rode Sir Galahad on his way without meeting with any adventure, and on the evening of the fourth day he came to a great abbey. Here he was received kindly by the monks, who unarmed him and led him into the guest-chamber, where he found two other Knights of the Round Table already sitting at supper, King Bagdemagus and Sir Ywain.

'Sirs,' said Galahad, when he had greeted them, 'what adventure brought you hither?'

'Sir,' they answered, 'we heard tell of a wondrous shield that is kept in this abbey, and that no man may bear it on his arm without meeting with ill-fortune within three days. Yet it is also said that whosoever can bear this shield shall achieve the quest of the Holy Grail.'

'To-morrow,' said King Bagdemagus, 'I shall take the shield and try the adventure of it. Wherefore I beg you to remain here three days: for if I be not he who may wear it, the shield shall be returned to this abbey before that time is passed. And I think that if I be not the man, then surely Sir Galahad will not fail.'

'Surely I will wait,' said Galahad, 'for indeed I require a shield.'

Next morning they heard mass together, and then King Bagdemagus asked the abbot concerning the shield.

'It is for the best knight only,' said the abbot, 'wherefore I counsel you not to touch it.' Yet he led them behind the altar and showed them the shield, which was polished until it seemed as white as snow all over except for a cross painted red in the middle of it.

'I know well that I am not the best of all knights,' said King Bagdemagus, 'but nevertheless I will try to wear it!' With that he set it on his arm, mounted his horse and rode away into the forest, with his squire following a little way behind him. They had not gone two miles when they came to a fair open valley with a stone hermitage built at one side of it, and King Bagdemagus had scarcely left the cover of the trees when he saw a strange knight clad all in shining white armour come riding out of the forest at the further end with his spear in rest. Then Bagdemagus set his spear in rest also, and the two of them came together like a whirlwind. Straight though Bagdemagus aimed, his spear seemed to hit nothing at all; but the White Knight's spear struck him through the shoulder where the shield did not cover him, and laid him senseless on the ground.

'This man has done great folly to wear the shield,' said the White Knight to Bagdemagus's squire. 'But take him up gently and return whence you came. Take the shield also, for it belongs to Sir Galahad the good knight, and to him alone.'

'Sir,' said the squire, 'what knight are you, that I may tell Sir Galahad?'

'Take no heed for my name,' said the White Knight. 'It is not for you, nor for any man on earth to know it.'

Then the squire set King Bagdemagus on his horse, hung the shield at the saddle-bow, and led him slowly back to the abbey where he was put to bed and tended long before his wound was healed.

'Sir,' said the squire to Galahad, 'the White Knight who overthrew King Bagdemagus sends you greeting, and bade me say that this shield is yours alone and that, wearing it, you shall meet with great adventures.'

'Now blessed be the good fortune that brings this shield to me,' cried Sir Galahad; and, setting it on his arm, he rode away into the forest.

Before long he came to the glade by the stone hermitage, and there the White Knight met him suddenly, coming out of the forest like a sunbeam which is not there until the moment it is seen.

'I greet you, sir, in the name of God,' cried Galahad. 'Tell me, I pray you, the marvels of this shield I bear.'

'For long has it hung in yonder abbey,' said the White Knight, 'waiting there until the holy knight of Logres should come for it: and you are that man. More than four centuries ago that shield was fashioned in the city of Sarras in the Holy Land, and Joseph of Arimathea brought it with him to Britain upon the Enchanted Ship. When he lay dying he drew the cross upon it with his own blood and caused it to be hung behind the altar where you found it this day. Go forward now, Galahad, true Knight of God, for your quest shall prosper!'

When the White Knight had spoken all these words he turned and rode swiftly away: yet before ever he reached the forest edge he was gone from sight as a sunbeam fades when a cloud passes over the sun.

Galahad sat there, lost in wonder, and while he did so, the squire, who had followed him from the abbey and heard what the White Knight had said, came and knelt at his feet, crying:

'Grant me one boon, noble Sir Galahad! Make me a knight and let me ride with you on your quest! My name is Melyas, and my father is the King of Denmark.'

'Fair sir,' answered Galahad, 'since you come of a race of kings, look to it that you set a good example to knighthood, for you ought to be a mirror to all chivalry. And therefore will I make you a knight forthwith, and you shall ride with me until some adventure parts us.'

So Galahad rode on his way with Sir Melyas: but before long they came to a parting of the ways, and there a pilgrim met them and said:

'Sirs, you must choose now which road you will take. He who goes to the right comes easily to his journey's end, but by no prowess of his own. But he who rides down the left hand road must win through, if he can, by showing his own strength and prowess.'

'I'll take the left-hand way!' cried Sir Melyas, who was longing to show off his worth as a knight; and away he rode before Galahad could stop him. Deep into the forest he went, and before long he found a rich pavilion standing empty, and in it a golden crown hanging on a splendid throne, and a banquet set out upon a table. Melyas dismounted and helped himself to the meal; then he took the golden crown, and was about to ride off again when a knight came suddenly into view shouting:

'Put down that golden circlet which is none of yours, and defend yourself!'

'Lord of Heaven, help now Thy new-made knight,' prayed Melyas. Then he set his spear in rest and rode against the stranger. But the other knight smote him from his horse, took up the crown and rode away leaving him nearly dead with a great wound in his side.

Galahad had taken the other road, but it merely wound through the forest and joined on to that which Melyas had followed; and now he came to the open space by the pavilion in time to see the strange knight smite down Sir Melyas and ride away.

'Turn, coward!' cried Galahad, and the knight wheeled round and jousted with him furiously. Galahad struck so well that the knight was flung on to the ground, but his spear broke into little pieces with the force of his blow.

'You fight well,' said the stranger knight rising slowly to his feet, 'and I yield me to you. Have no fear for this man whom I have overcome, for I will tend him here and cure the wound which I have given him. I am a hermit, though now I ride in armour and am skilled in such arts. For his pride in choosing the left-hand road and for his greed in taking the golden crown which he did not need, Sir Melyas has received this overthrow. But go you forward, noble Sir Galahad, and trust ever in God and not in your own earthly prowess.'

Then Galahad knelt to receive this strange hermit's blessing, and rode on his way through forest and cities, through fields and moorlands, for many, many days, meeting with more adventures than there is space to tell of, until on a day a fair damsel came riding towards him and cried:

'Sir Galahad! Come you swiftly with me! Near at hand lies the Enchanted Ship which you must enter. Therein are Sir Percivale my brother and the strong knight Sir Bors de Gannis, and they lack only you before the ship can sail. For your quest draws near to its close, and you three knights shall come together to the castle where lies the Holy Grail.'

'Lead on, fair maiden,' said Sir Galahad; and together they rode forward by many steep paths among the rocks until they came to the secret bay where the Enchanted Ship awaited them.

3

The Adventures of Sir Percivale

WHEN Percivale set out from Camelot in quest of the Holy Grail he rode for many weeks without meeting with any unusual adventures. One day he met suddenly with Galahad, and they jousted together, neither knowing the other, and Sir Galahad struck him from his horse and rode away.

'I must find this knight who carries a white shield with a red cross upon it,' thought Percivale as he got slowly to his feet and remounted his horse. 'Until this day no knight in the world has been able to overthrow me except Sir Launcelot: and that, I am sure, is not he!'

Percivale rode deep into the forests after this, anger and envy growing in his heart against the unknown knight with the red cross on the white shield. But at length he came to a little hermitage where dwelt a recluse, a holy woman who spent her days in tending all those who came to her for aid, and in praying for their souls and for her own.

She made Percivale welcome, and by degrees he told her many things, both of his past life and of his present quest.

'Noble sir,' said she when he had spoken concerning the knight who had overthrown him, 'if you seek to be revenged, you run into great sin: for it is pride, and pride only, that prompts you to it. Know, moreover, that he who smote you from your horse was Galahad, the holy knight of Logres, who sat in the Siege Perilous. You knew him not because of the shield he bore: yet that shield is the divine token of his mission, and is marked with the blood of Joseph of Arimathea.'

'Now madam,' said Sir Percivale, 'having learnt these things from you, I give you my word that never again will I feel envy towards Sir Galahad: rather will I seek him and be his fellow on this quest, if I am worthy.'

'Worthy indeed you may be,' answered the Recluse, 'if you beware of all temptations. The powers of evil will lie in wait for you, armed with many enchantments: if you win through them in all pureness of heart and come to Castle Carbonek in the Waste Lands, there you shall find the Holy Grail; and there also shall you find the Lady Blanchefleur whom you have sought these many years, and she shall be your wife. But these things shall come to pass only if you are worthy of them: go forth, Sir Percivale, in pureness of heart and in obedience to the law of Heaven, and win your kingdom!'

Then the Recluse blessed Sir Percivale, laced his armour upon him, and sent him on his way, his heart singing with joy at the thought of his quest. So he rode all the morning, and in the middle of the day came suddenly upon about twenty armed men who were carrying a dead knight on a litter, all pierced and cut with many wounds of spears and swords. When they saw Sir Percivale they asked him whence he came, and he answered:

'From the Court of King Arthur.'

Then they all cried at once 'Slay him! Slay him!' and set upon him from every side. Percivale fought bravely, striking more than one of them dead to the earth; but seven of them smote him at the same time while others killed his horse under him so that he fell to the ground and would have been slain by them there and then. But on a sudden there came out of the forest a knight in red armour bearing a white shield with a red cross on it: like a thunderbolt he came, and men fell right and left beneath his spear and sword. Before long those who were left alive turned and fled away, crying with terror, and the knight rode after them and away into the distance.

'Fair knight, abide and suffer me to thank you!' cried Percivale, for he realized that it was Sir Galahad; and he ran after him on foot as fast as he could, begging him to stop. But Galahad was too far away, and in a very few minutes Percivale could not even hear the sound of his horse's hooves.

Sad and weary he wandered on through the forest, and when night fell lay down under an oak tree and was soon asleep. But at midnight he woke suddenly to find a strange woman standing beside him, her eyes flashing in the moonlight.

'Sir Percivale, what do you here?' she asked.

'My horse is slain,' he answered, 'and I have followed on foot after Sir Galahad until weariness overtook me.'

'If you will promise to help me in the thing I shall ask you,' said the Strange Damsel, 'I will lend you my own horse, and it shall carry you wherever you wish to go.'

'That will I surely promise!' exclaimed Sir Percivale eagerly.

'Wait for me here, and I will fetch the horse,' said the Strange Damsel. In a few minutes' time she returned leading a great black horse, and Percivale was amazed when he saw it, for never before had he seen a horse so large and strong and fierce. But nevertheless he took the bridle in his hand, leapt upon the creature's back and set spurs to its sides. Away went the horse into the forest, by mountain pass and rugged hillside, on and on through the cold, clear moonlight, rushing through the air so fast that Percivale seemed to have gone four days' journey in an hour.

At last they came down a hillside to a wide river which rushed roaring between its banks, and it seemed as if the horse was going to carry him right into the midst of the flood. Percivale tugged at the bridle, but the horse would neither stop nor turn: to the very edge they came, and Percivale saw the dark, foaming water roaring in front of him. Then he made the sign of the cross, and the horse reared up suddenly, neighing wildly, and shook him from its back; then it plunged into the river, screaming terribly, and was gone from sight: only it seemed that the water burnt after it.

Percivale knelt on the bank and prayed to God, for he knew that it was a fiend who had sought to carry him to Hell. For the rest of the night he knelt there praying, and in the morning he saw another strange thing. A great lion came down to the riverside to drink, and as it bent over the stream, suddenly a dreadful serpent fell from an overhanging rock and twined about the lion's neck and body, seeking to strangle it. Then a terrible fight began between the two: only it seemed that the serpent would soon gain the victory over the lion. Presently the lion roared, as if asking for help, and Percivale drew his sword and attacked the serpent, and in a little while cut off its head and flung it into the dark river.

Then Sir Percivale turned to see if the lion would attack him also; but, instead, it came and rubbed its head against him, and fawned upon him like a great cat. Percivale cast down his shield and rested after the fight, and the lion stood and guarded him.

'Fierce and mighty though the lion was,' thought Percivale, 'he was taken unaware by the serpent, and could not prevail against it, but must needs call upon me for aid ... Even in such case was I, when the fiend tempted me, and strong though I am, I would have perished miserably had I not called to God for help.'

After this he wandered for many days through a wild and desolate country, and the lion went with him, protecting him by day and night from all the dangers of the way. But at last he came to the sea-coast and the lion left him on the edge of the forest, while Percivale sat down to rest by the shore, wondering which way to go.

'Noble sir,' said a gentle voice behind him suddenly, 'surely you are the good knight Sir Percivale of Wales who seek for the wonders of Castle Carbonek?'

Turning round, Percivale saw a lovely maiden dressed in black standing beside him with her hands clasped. Then he rose and greeted her courteously, but he said:

'Lady, how know you my name and of the quest which I follow?'

'But a little while ago,' she answered, 'as I came through the Waste Lands I met with a knight who rides in red armour, bearing a red cross upon a white shield ...'

'Ah, fair damsel,' interrupted Percival eagerly, 'that is Sir Galahad the good knight who I have been seeking these many weary days. Tell me where he is, I pray you!'

'I saw him in the Waste Forest,' she answered, 'chasing two wicked knights into the Dead Waters; and there he slew them, but there his horse was drowned and he hardly escaped with his life. Now he rests at a hermitage near by, and to-morrow I will lead you to him. But come now to my pavilion and rest, for I do not think that you have been well entertained these many days.'

'Who are you,' asked Percivale, 'that offer me so much kindness ?'

'A poor disinherited lady who was once the richest in the world,' she answered. 'Wicked men drove me from my castle, taking the most part of my goods; and I journey now to King Arthur's Court that he may send knights and men-at-arms to overcome the robbers.'

While they talked the Disinherited Damsel led Percivale along the sea-shore until they came to a little glade carpeted with grass and flowers where a silken pavilion was pitched.

'Here, noble sir, you may rest during the heat of the day,' she said; and Percivale thanked her and took off his armour which he placed beneath a tree, leaning his sword against the trunk. Then he lay down on a couch spread with silk and sweet linen, and slept all the day through.

In the evening he awoke, and found the damsel awaiting him beside a richly covered table on which was set the finest meal that ever he had seen. When they had eaten she led him back into the pavilion and brought him wine in a great golden bowl, red wine, sweet and strong, and she pledged him in it, and handed it to Percivale; and he drank of it, the strongest wine that ever he had tasted. Once more she filled the bowl, but she did not give it to him for a little while: instead, she sang to him, a slow mysterious song, and drew nearer and nearer to him all the while, until her arms were about him.

'Lady,' he said in a broken voice, 'you are passing fair!'

'Sir,' she murmured, 'noble Percivale, I am yours for ever and ever: of all men in the world I love only you. So kiss me now: pledge me in this bowl of wine, and swear that from henceforth you will be mine alone, and do all things that I command you.'

A great wind tore the pavilion away and her also

Then Percivale pledged her in the strong wine, and bent forward to kiss her on the lips. But as he did so he thought suddenly of Blanchefleur his own true lady and how he had sworn to love her alone of all women in the world; and he saw his sword which leant against the tree with the hilt uppermost flashing in the evening light like a great shining crucifix. Then he cried to God for help, and made the sign of the cross upon his forehead.

Immediately a great wind tore the pavilion away so that it floated in the air like a cloud of black smoke and was gone:

'Fair sweet Lord Jesus Christ, let me not be shamed!' prayed Percivale. And the damsel screamed aloud:

'Alas, Sir Percivale, you have betrayed me!'

Then the great, pure wind took her also, and she went with it across the sea, shrieking horribly, and it seemed that all the water burnt after her.

Once more Percivale knelt alone, praying by the sea-shore when the fiend had gone from him. Then he slept beneath the tree and woke in the morning to find a ship moored by the shore and a woman dressed in the white robes of a nun, with an ivory crucifix hanging at her neck, bending over him.

'Awake, Sir Percivale!' she cried. 'Wake and put your armour on! You have overcome the temptations of this world, and now you may enter the Enchanted Ship and sail with me towards Carbonek. Soon shall Sir Galahad be with you on the ship, and Sir Bors also who must bear witness to the wonders that shall be. Do not fear, but come with me: I am your sister, though you know me not, and Naciens the holy hermit of Carbonek has been my instructor.'

Then Percivale was filled with joy, and he did on his armour and went down with his sister to where the Enchanted Ship was awaiting them.

4

▰▰▰▰▰▰▰▰▰▰▰▰▰▰▰▰▰▰▰▰▰▰▰▰▰▰▰▰▰▰

The Adventures of Sir Bors
de Gannis

SIR BORS DE GANNIS, who was a cousin of Sir
Launcelot, rode quietly away from Camelot in quest of
the Holy Grail; and before he had gone very far he met with
a hermit riding upon an ass.

'Greeting, sir knight,' said the old hermit, 'what manner of
man are you?'

'Good father,' answered Sir Bors, 'I am a simple Knight of
King Arthur's Court, and my great desire is to learn how best
to seek for the Holy Grail, for in quest of it am I bound.'

'Come with me,' said the hermit, 'and I will instruct you.
For not by earthly strength may you reach the Grail, but only
by purity of heart.'

For many days Sir Bors remained at the hermitage learning
many things; and all that time he ate nothing but bread and
water as the hermit did.

At length the day came when he must ride on his way once
more.

'Gentle sir,' said the hermit, 'see to it that you eat bread
only and drink water until you are fed at the table of the Holy
Grail.'

'Good father,' answered Sir Bors, 'that I promise. But how
do you know that I shall ever come to the table of the Holy
Grail?'

'There are but few of you who shall come to it,' said the
hermit, 'and you, Sir Bors, are one of them, though you have
done no great deeds nor won undying fame in Logres. For in
purity of life and not in pride of deeds dwells that which makes
a man worthy to achieve this quest. Go forward in the fear

'Go forward in the fear of God'

of God, and live to tell of the ending of the quest of the Holy Grail ... My words you may believe, for I am Naciens the Hermit of Carbonek.'

Bors rode forward after this for many days, meeting with some few adventures by the way, but nothing very unusual. But at last it chanced as he passed through a forest and came to a parting of two roads that a great adventure befell him. On one side he saw suddenly two knights leading a horse on which was bound a naked man, and the two knights were beating him with thorns until the blood ran down to the ground. As Sir Bors came into sight the wounded man raised his head and Bors saw to his horror that it was his brother Sir Lionel. Full of fury, Sir Bors made ready to attack the two cowardly knights; but just as he was about to set spurs to his horse a cry rang out from the other road:

'Help me, for the love of Maiden Mary!' Wheeling round, Sir Bors saw a lovely damsel struggling with an armed knight who was dragging her towards his horse to carry her away.

'Help me, noble knight!' cried the maiden. 'For King Arthur's sake, who surely made you knight – help a damsel in distress, and suffer me not to be shamed by this wicked man!'

When Sir Bors heard this he knew not what to do. 'If I let those two carry my brother away,' he thought, 'he will probably be dead before I can come to his rescue. But if I leave this maiden then she will suffer black shame and maybe death also – and by mine oaths of knighthood I may not leave any woman who is in need of my help.' Then Bors prayed: 'Fair Lord, whose creature I am, preserve my brother Lionel and let not these knights slay him – for I must succour this maid first.'

Then he turned to the knight who had the maiden across his horse's neck by now and was riding away with her held in front of him.

'Sir knight!' cried Bors, 'loose that maiden this instant, or I will smite you dead from behind!'

Then the knight tried to escape by riding away swiftly, but finding in a little while that Sir Bors drew nearer and nearer to him, he let the maiden slip to the ground, wheeled his horse and with spear in rest came galloping to meet him. Then Sir Bors couched his spear also, and the two met with a crash that broke both spears. They drew their swords after this and lashed together until the sparks flew; but in a little while Sir Bors struck the knight a mortal blow so that he fell to the ground and lay still.

'Fair damsel,' said Sir Bors, 'now you may go free of this evil knight.'

'I thank you, noble sir,' said the maiden. 'But lead me back to my home I pray you, for I am afraid lest I should meet others such as him in the dark forest.'

'Right gladly will I,' answered Sir Bors; and he rode with her until the evening when they came to a high tower set upon a hill. There the damsel made Bors welcome, and he sat down to a fine dinner beside her, while ten other maidens waited on them or sang and played sweetly.

'I pray you,' said Sir Bors, 'let plain bread be brought for me to eat, and a goblet of pure water – for nothing else may I eat until my quest is accomplished.'

And though the damsel and the other maidens strove to persuade him, Bors would touch none of the feast. And when he had eaten his bread and water he would not even rest upon the soft bed which had been prepared for him, but lay down on the hard stone floor among the rushes, and there was soon asleep.

In the middle of the night the damsel came to Sir Bors and tempted him in many ways; but he answered her courteously, yet would do none of the evil things to which she tried to persuade him. Then she led him up to the top of the tower in the bright moonlight, and there all the other maidens were standing.

'Ah, Sir Bors, gentle knight,' they all cried, 'have mercy on us and suffer our lady to have her will; for if you do not she will cast herself from this tower, and we must do the same and die with her. Save all our lives, for if we die now surely you are shamed for ever!'

Then Sir Bors trembled, not knowing whether to commit deadly sin or save the damsels from death; and in his doubt he prayed for guidance, and made the sign of the cross upon his forehead.

As he did this the moon seemed to go out like a candle; there was a rushing of wind, and a crying as of all the fiends of Hell. Then the moon came out again – and Sir Bors found himself alone on the bare hillside, with no sign of any tower nor any damsels.

In the morning Sir Bors continued on his way, and before very long as he rode through the forest he heard the sound of sweet bells on the breeze. Turning aside from the high road he followed a path which led him to an abbey built in a beautiful clearing where a few mighty cedar trees grew upon great open lawns. Up to the abbey he rode, and what was his surprise and joy to see his brother Sir Lionel, fully armed, sitting his horse in the gateway. To earth he sprang and went towards him crying:

'Fair, sweet brother, how glad I am to see you alive and well!'

But Sir Lionel scowled fiercely upon him and exclaimed: 'Ah, Sir Bors, you who wished me dead have been disappointed! You went off to help a damsel, leaving those two knights to torture and kill me ... Never come near me again, for if you do I will fight with you and slay you!'

When Sir Bors realized how angry his brother was, he knelt down before him and asked his forgiveness.

'Keep away, Sir Bors,' was all that Lionel would say, however. 'Keep away: for if you do not, I shall treat you as a felon and a traitor, and hew you in pieces where you kneel. ... Evil coward, you are not worthy to be called the son of good King Bohort de Gannis who was our father! But get you quickly upon your horse and either flee away or else turn and fight with me as a knight should.'

When Sir Bors realized that he must fight with his brother, or else die, he did not know what to do. But he would not fight, for it was an unholy combat; moreover he remembered that Lionel was his elder brother to whom he must show all reverence and obedience. So he knelt still on the ground and said:

'Fair sweet brother, have mercy upon me and slay me not: but remember the great love which there has always been between us.'

But Lionel seemed like one possessed of a devil, so filled with evil hate and madness was he. Crying aloud, he set spurs to his horse and rode over Sir Bors, so that his horse's hooves struck him to the earth, wounding him so grievously that he fainted with the pain.

Lionel leapt to the ground, drew his sword and was preparing to cut off his brother's head, when a monk came out from the abbey and ran between them, flinging himself upon Sir Bors and crying:

'Ah, gentle knight! Have mercy upon me and upon your brother! For if you slay him you do one of the most sinful deeds in the world, for of all knights he is wellnigh the best!'

'Get away, sir priest!' screamed Lionel, 'or I will slay you as well!'

'Indeed,' said the good old monk, 'I had rather you slew me than him, for my death will not be half such a loss to this realm as his would be.'

'Have it your own way!' shouted Lionel wildly, and he smote so hard that the monk's head flew from his shoulders and went rolling across the grass. Then Lionel reared up his sword once more to kill Sir Bors, but at that moment a cold blast of wind seemed to blow between them and a voice said:

'Stay your hand! For the fiend has gone out of you!'

Then Sir Lionel knelt trembling and weeping on the ground, and there was Naciens the Hermit of Carbonek standing a little way away, leaning on his staff.

'For God's love, fair sweet brother, forgive me my trespass,' sobbed Lionel; and Sir Bors rose slowly to his feet and embraced his brother, saying: 'May God forgive you, as I do gladly.'

Then Naciens led them both into the abbey; and there Bors lodged for many days until he was whole again. Lionel remained there for a year and a day doing penance; but Bors rode away through the forest until he came to the sea-shore.

And there, floating quietly on the still waters he saw a mysterious ship hung with white samite which glowed and gleamed with the red and golden lights of the evening.

Leaving his horse Sir Bors entered the Enchanted Ship and immediately it moved away from the land, sailing as swiftly as a bird across the waves, out of the daylight and along the glimmering path of the setting sun into the darkness of the night.

Sir Bors slept; and when he woke he found another knight lying near him in the ship, fully armed except for his helmet, and he recognized him for Sir Percivale of Wales.

'You must have come here by God's especial guidance,' said Percivale; and they rejoiced in each other's good fortune.

Over the morning waves sailed the Enchanted Ship, and Percivale told Bors of all his adventures and of the temptations which had beset him; and his sister the holy nun of Carbonek ministered to them, and instructed them in many divine truths which she had learnt from Naciens the Hermit.

'And now,' said Sir Percivale to Sir Bors as the Enchanted Ship carried them swiftly over the bright waves round the coast of Britain, 'now we lack nothing except Sir Galahad the good knight!'

5

The Adventures of Sir Launcelot

FAST and far rode Sir Launcelot on his quest, seeking to find his way back to the Castle of Carbonek where once already he had seen the Holy Grail passing dimly through the hall in the hands of the Grail Maiden. After many days' journey he came to the Waste Lands which had lain desolate ever since Balyn struck the Dolorous Stroke in the first year of King Arthur's reign; but though he rode hither and thither through the desolation he could not find any trace of the mysterious castle.

One night as he rode wearily along he came to a stone cross at the parting of two ways and saw by the cross a slab of white marble. But it was so dark that Sir Launcelot could not clearly see what it was. Not far from the cross there stood an old chapel, its battered walls half hidden in dense folds of ivy. A light shone through the windows, and, thinking to find people there of whom he could ask the way, Launcelot dismounted, tied his horse to a tree, and leaving his shield beside it, went to the chapel and tried the door. But it was firmly locked and no one came when he hammered at it. At last he climbed up the ivy and looked in through the window, and inside he saw an altar covered in shining silk on which stood a great silver candlestick with seven branches, each holding a tall candle which lit up all the chapel. Then Launcelot desired greatly to enter, but he could neither open the door nor climb in through any window, so at length he gave up sadly. Returning to his horse he unsaddled it, and taking off his sword and helmet, lay down to sleep near the stone cross.

And so he fell asleep; and, half waking and half sleeping, he saw drawing near two white horses bearing a litter in which lay a sick knight; and when he was near the cross the horses stopped.

Then Launcelot, half waking and half sleeping, heard the sick man say:

'Ah, sweet Lord! When shall this pain leave me? When shall Thy holy vessel draw near to me and heal this pain which I have endured so long?'

Then Launcelot saw the door of the chapel open and the ancient hermit, Naciens, who had brought Galahad to Camelot, came out carrying the silver candlestick, which he set upon the marble block which now seemed like an altar in front of the cross.

Then, as Naciens stood beside the altar in prayer, suddenly the Holy Grail, covered in a fair white cloth, came gliding on a pure moonbeam and rested awhile near the candles – and their light seemed as dim as if the sun shone, and dim also was the light of the full moon in the glorious brightness of the Light within the covered Grail.

The sick knight, crawling painfully on his hands and knees, drew near to the altar, and then, reaching out his hands he touched the Holy Grail, and straightway he was cured of his sickness.

Then, as he knelt in prayer, the Holy Grail rose from the altar and passed on its way like the brightest star of Heaven, and was lost to view.

The knight rose slowly to his feet and bowed reverently to Naciens the hermit.

'Indeed I am well once more!' he cried joyfully. 'Thanks be to God who has cured me by means of His holy vessel! But I am amazed to see this sleeping knight who did not wake even when the Holy Grail drew so near to him!'

'He is held to the earth by his sins,' answered Naciens. 'This is Sir Launcelot of the Lake, a noble Knight of the Round Table.'

'Heavy indeed must his sin be,' said the knight, 'for surely he is in quest of the Holy Grail.'

When he had said this he took Sir Launcelot's helmet and sword which Naciens held out to him, mounted upon

Launcelot's horse, and rode away. Then Naciens took up the silver candlestick and went once more into the chapel, closing the door behind him.

All this while Launcelot had lain unable to move, half sleeping and half waking. But presently, when the moon shone out again, he woke completely, and, wondering whether he had dreamed or not, he went towards the stone cross. When he found that his sword, helmet, and horse had all disappeared, he knew that it had been no dream, and he said sadly:

'My sin and my wickedness have brought me into great dishonour. When I sought only after worldly adventures there was no quest too hard for me to accomplish; but now that I seek for holy things, my great sin comes between me and them, and I had no power to stir or speak when the Holy Grail drew near me.'

As he stood lamenting thus, the chapel door opened again, and Naciens the hermit came out to him and said:

'Launcelot, you ought to thank God more than any other knight now living; for in worldly fame no man can equal you, no, nor in beauty, strength, and honour, for great deeds. But come now and lodge here with me, so that I may instruct you in spiritual things; and we will speak of your sins and examine how you may be forgiven them.'

'Alas,' said Launcelot, 'all my great deeds of arms have I done for the sake of Queen Guinevere, without stopping to think if they were right or wrong. And in loving her, who is the wife of my lord King Arthur, I have committed the great sin which keeps me from the Holy Grail.'

So for many days Launcelot remained with Naciens, confessing to him all that he had done wrong, and especially how he had married Elaine thinking her to be Guinevere; and how, since then, he had never ceased to make love to the real Queen Guinevere.

'You must forswear all such thoughts,' Naciens told him. 'Elaine is dead long ago, and out of the evil of your marriage with her God has brought good: for Galahad, the Holy Knight of Logres, is her son and yours.' Then he gave

Launcelot a horse and a helmet, and sent him on his way once more.

Many days after this Launcelot came to the sea-shore, and there, riding among the desolate sand-dunes, he met a knight who carried a white shield with a great red cross on it.

'Noble sir,' said Launcelot, 'it is many a long day since I met with any knight: here is a fair open shore, let us joust in friendly fashion!'

Launcelot had thought to make easy conquest

The stranger set his spear in rest at this, and the two of them rode together at full gallop like a white flash of lightning and a red thunderbolt. Now Launcelot had thought to make easy conquest of his adversary: but what was his surprise and annoyance to find himself struck out of his saddle and sent sprawling on his back in the sand, while the stranger rode away down to a little bay where a strange ship was waiting for him.

'By my faith!' exclaimed Launcelot suddenly, 'that must be none other than Sir Galahad! He is the only knight in the world who could overthrow me thus in a fair joust!'

Then he sprang on his horse with all haste and rode to the bay side. And there he found the Enchanted Ship in which

Galahad, Bors, Percivale, and Percivale's sister were waiting for him.

As soon as he came aboard the ship moved by itself out of the bay and went floating away across the sea. Then the four knights rejoiced together, and told each other of their adventures and of all the temptations which had beset them. Percivale's sister also told them many strange things which Naciens had told her; about Joseph of Arimathea who had come to Britain in the Enchanted Ship, bringing with him the Holy Grail; and of the sword which Galahad wore; and many other things. But always when she spoke of the future it was of what was to happen to them, never of herself, and at last Percivale said:

'Fair sister, what of you, when we come to the Waste Lands and draw near to Castle Carbonek?'

'I shall leave you before you come thither,' she said, 'though I know not how. But first we must visit the Castle of the Maiden which we draw near to even now.'

Not long after this the Enchanted Ship came into a deep bay with high cliffs on either side, and the four knights went on shore together with Percivale's sister, whom they followed up a little path among the rocks until they found themselves in a forest beyond the cliffs.

They had not gone far through this when they came to a castle. But before ever they reached it an armed knight rode up to them and said:

'Lords, this gentlewoman that travels with you: is she a maid, or the wife of one of you?'

'Sir,' replied Percivale's sister, 'I am a maid, and vowed to the service of God, to be a nun all the days of my life.'

When he heard this the knight seized hold of her, exclaiming: 'By the Holy Cross! You shall not escape me before you have fulfilled the custom of this castle!'

'Let her go!' cried Sir Percivale. 'Know you not that a holy virgin is free to wander where she will?'

While they spoke a troop of a dozen knights or more had come from the castle and closed in about them; and a little way behind came a damsel who carried a silver dish.

'Nevertheless,' repeated the first knight, 'she must fulfil the custom.'

'What then is the custom of this castle?' asked Sir Galahad.

'Sir,' said the knight, 'every maid that passes this way must fill this dish with blood from her right arm.'

'A wicked custom indeed,' cried Galahad, 'and this lady shall never suffer from it while I am left alive to protect her.'

'So help me God,' said Sir Percivale, 'I too had rather be slain.'

'And I,' said Sir Launcelot and Sir Bors in one breath.

'By my faith,' said the knight, 'you shall indeed die, all of you, even if you were the best knights in the world!'

Then a terrible battle began: the four knights of Logres stood back to back with Percivale's sister in the middle, and the knights of the castle rode at them from every side, seeking to slay them. And they had come very near to it when there came out from the castle a knight clad in golden armour, who cried in a loud voice: 'Cease this strife!'

Then he said to the four who still guarded Percivale's sister: 'Sirs, if you will come and pass the night in this castle, I promise you on my honour that you will suffer no harm, nor the lady either.'

'Let us go in,' said Percivale's sister.

'We will go with you,' said Galahad to the Golden Knight.

When they had rested and eaten, Galahad asked his host about the custom of the castle, and the Golden Knight led them to an upper chamber where a lady lay upon a fair couch, very wasted and ill, and so feeble that she could scarcely move.

'Sirs,' said the Golden Knight, 'this lady was a king's daughter of great virtue; but she was stricken by a wicked enchantment from which she may never be healed save with the blood of a pure virgin, the noblest in the world. And for this reason we have stopped all maidens who pass this way and forced them to yield us this silver dish full of blood. But as yet our lady has not been healed.'

'Now,' said Percivale's sister when she heard this, 'I see that it is for me to cure this lady if I may.'

'But if you bleed too much,' cried Percivale, 'you will die!'

'Yet must I chance that,' she answered.

Then she fulfilled the custom of the castle and the lady rose from her bed as well and strong as any in the world.

But Percivale's sister grew weaker and weaker, and nothing which any of them could do would stop the flow of her blood.

'This is my fate,' she said gently as Percivale and his comrades knelt weeping about her. 'But I die worthily for the healing of this lady. Set me in a litter now and bear me to the Enchanted Ship and lay me therein when I am dead and let the Ship take me whither it will.'

So they made a litter, and the lady of the castle gave a horse to each of them, and two white horses to bear the litter, and rode with them to the sea-shore and laid Percivale's sister in the Enchanted Ship.

But as they went towards it they saw a wounded knight without armour riding desperately through the forest and behind him an evil knight who sought to slay him. When the wounded man saw them he cried out:

'Help me, for God's love, or I shall be slain.'

'Truly,' said Sir Galahad, 'we must help him, for His sake on whom he calls.'

'Fair son,' said Sir Launcelot, 'let me ride after him, for there is but one knight striving to kill him.'

'Go you then,' said Galahad, 'and we shall meet at Carbonek if God wills it.' So Launcelot rode away into the forest, and the rest continued on their way. And when they had seen the Enchanted Ship sail out to sea with Percivale's sister lying dead in the midst of it, Percivale said to them:

'Fair friends, this night I will kneel upon the sea-shore and pray for the dear soul of my sister. But ride you back to the castle with this lady, and to-morrow I will follow you and meet you there if I may. But if not, we meet at Carbonek, for I, who have been there before, know well that it is not now far to seek.'

So Galahad and Bors rode away with the lady and came in the late evening to the Castle of the Maiden. But when they drew near they found that the fire of Heaven had fallen upon it, and there stood nought but an empty shell of black, hollow walls, with never a living thing within them.

'This is the vengeance for shedding the blood of maidens,' said the lady of the castle; and she led them to a little chapel where were many tombs of maidens who had died from the custom of that castle. 'Alas,' sobbed the lady, 'through no will of mine I have brought this evil upon many.'

Then she departed from them and came after many days to the Court of King Arthur and told there of all that had chanced.

But Sir Galahad and Sir Bors rode forward side by side through the Waste Lands towards the mysterious Castle of Carbonek.

6

◣◤◢◥◣◤◢◥◣◤◢◥◣◤◢◥◣◤◢◥◣◤◢◥◣◤◢◥◣◤◢◥

How Launcelot and Gawain
came to Carbonek

AT the beginning of the quest Sir Gawain rode out from
Camelot alone, and alone he continued for many, many
days, until he drew near to the Waste Lands. And there one
day he met Sir Hector de Maris, Launcelot's brother, and
they greeted each other with great joy.

As they rode on through the forest of dead trees and across
the bleak uplands where there was never a blade of grass to be
seen, Sir Gawain said:

'Truly I think that I have ridden nearly far enough, for I
feel certain that I am one of those who is not worthy to see the
Holy Grail.'

'One thing surprises me much,' remarked Sir Hector. 'I
have met more than twenty of our friends, all Knights of the
Round Table, and all of them complain also that they can
find no trace of the Grail, nor news of any who have seen
it.'

'I wonder where your brother Sir Launcelot is,' said
Gawain thoughtfully.

'Truly,' answered Sir Hector, 'I can hear no news of him,
nor of Sir Galahad, Sir Percivale, and Sir Bors.'

'Those four have no peers,' said Gawain, 'they are indeed
the truest and worthiest knights in all the realm of Logres.
If they cannot achieve the Quest of the Holy Grail, then no
man in all the world can do it.'

So talking, they rode out of the dead forest and came to the
little chapel by the stone cross. As the darkness was falling
fast they tied their horses to a tree and went into the chapel,
where they made themselves as comfortable as they could in

two of the pews. And there, between waking and sleeping, they beheld strange things.

First, in the darkness they saw a single candle moving slowly towards them; and as it came near they saw that a hand held it, and an arm covered in red samite on which hung a bridle. But beyond the arm there was nothing, and yet it moved just as if someone were walking through the chapel carrying the candle and the bridle.

In front of Sir Hector the arm stopped, and a voice spoke out of the empty air, saying:

'Knight, full of evil faith and poor belief, these two things have failed you: you have not followed the Light nor bowed your neck to the Bridle: and therefore you may not come to the Holy Grail.'

Then the arm with the candle passed on into the sanctuary and faded from sight.

'I must go,' said Sir Hector sadly; and when he had bidden farewell to Sir Gawain he went out of the chapel, mounted his horse, and rode sorrowfully back to Camelot.

But Gawain knelt in the darkness in front of the altar; and presently as he raised his face from his hands he saw a great silver candlestick with seven lighted candles in it standing on the altar in a great halo of light. But in spite of it, all the chapel was as dark as ever. Then, as he watched, there came a great clutching black hand out of the darkness and extinguished the candles one after another, until all was dark once more.

'So shall the darkness fall upon Logres,' thought Gawain sadly, and he bowed his head in prayer once more.

In the morning Naciens the Hermit came to him, heard his confession, gave him absolution, and counselled him in many things.

'Ride forward through the Waste Lands without any fear,' he said, 'for you shall come to Carbonek and see the Holy Grail, though the full quest is for others to achieve. But, noble Gawain, you may free this land from the evil that is upon it if you be found worthy. Go now to Carbonek, and when all is accomplished, return swiftly to Camelot, for you have still duties to perform in Logres. But I charge you to be

They rode quietly through the Waste Lands

moderate in all things, and to speak only in due season: more I am not permitted to reveal. Go now, and the blessing of God be with you.'

Then Gawain mounted his horse and rode once more into the dead forest and so continued for many days until at length he found Sir Launcelot wandering there alone. For when he had saved the wounded knight and slain the cruel robber, he had tried in vain for long to find Sir Galahad once more.

Gawain and Launcelot greeted one another, and then rode quietly through the Waste Lands and up into the barren mountains; and at length they came to the mysterious Castle of Carbonek.

This time there were many people moving about in it, who welcomed the two knights and led them into the great hall where old King Pelles lay upon a rich couch, still tortured by the wound which Balyn had given him so many years before.

The floor of the hall was strewn with roses, and a great feast was laid out on long tables at which all the knights and ladies of the Waste Lands were gathered. Yet amongst them all no one spoke a word except to the two strangers, and then it was in quiet, sad tones.

'Welcome again, Sir Launcelot of the Lake,' said King Pelles in a feeble voice. 'It is many years since you were here: then it was a sad coming, for in sin my daughter Elaine was wedded to you – she who had been a maiden of the Grail – and so she was lost to me and died not long after her son was born.'

Then Launcelot knelt before King Pelles and begged his forgiveness for the wrong he had done him. And King Pelles forgave him and blessed him, holding his thin and trembling hands above his head.

After this they sat down to dinner and fair maidens tended on them, offering them rich dishes and strong wine. After a little while Launcelot ate of the banquet and drank from the goblet which the loveliest of the maidens offered to him; but Gawain spoke never a word and drank only clear water in a silver cup. Then the maidens tempted him more than ever with the goblets of sweet-smelling wine; but still he would not taste of them. After this many strange things were shown to him; but he spoke never a word, nor asked any questions.

Then all who sat at the banquet taunted him and mocked him, calling him a coward and a craven, a knight without manners or courtesy. But still Sir Gawain sat quietly in his place, speaking no word; but Sir Launcelot lay with his head on the table and slept.

Presently the strange silence fell once more upon the hall, and all those who sat at the tables became still. Then on a sudden the doors flew open and there entered a procession of maidens clothed in white: shadowy figures scarcely human were the first three, who carried one a silver candlestick with seven candles shining in it; the next the Spear from the shining point of which the red blood dripped ever and vanished before it touched the ground; and the third a golden dish on which was Bread more white and bright than the clear light of the sun. But behind them came the Grail Maiden herself, the loveliest maiden in all the world, and she carried the Holy Grail in her hands, covered in a fair white cloth, and the light of it was all about her so that her white garments seemed to be made of the very sunlight.

All those who sat in the hall bowed their faces into their hands with one rippling movement which travelled up the lines of knights and ladies like the wind passing over a field of corn. Only Gawain did not bow his head: but he rose from his place at the table, stepped forward to meet the Grail procession, and cried in a loud voice:

'Maiden of the Grail, tell me, in the name of God, what these things mean!'

'Follow, and you shall learn!' said the Grail Maiden in a low clear voice; and Gawain rose and followed the procession like one in a dream.

Down the hall it went and through the door: and then on a sudden Launcelot raised his head from the table, rose slowly to his feet, and followed also, with outstretched arms, but walking like one in a sleep, with wide-open eyes that yet saw nothing.

Through the castle they went, by many a dark passage and empty room; then up a winding stairway in the keep, and so to the Chapel of the Holy Grail near the top of it.

Launcelot reached the doorway, and on a sudden the great door came to with a crash, shutting him out from the room; and he woke from his strange sleep.

And as he stood without the door he heard the sweet voice of the Grail Maiden within singing: 'Glory to God in the highest!'

Then Launcelot knew that the Grail was in that room, and he fell on his knees and prayed, saying:

'Fair sweet Saviour, if ever I did anything that was pleasing in Thy sight, let me see at least something of what I seek!'

Then the door opened slowly and Launcelot saw the chapel filled with light, the Grail, still covered in white samite, standing on the silver altar between the Bleeding Spear and the candlestick. He saw also how Sir Gawain knelt at the altar, with the Grail Maiden upon one side and Naciens the Hermit upon the other; and how Naciens drew back the cover from the Grail, so that the light shone from it more gloriously than ever.

'Sir Launcelot!' cried Naciens in a great voice. 'Come not

here, for you are not worthy to draw near. Behold now the Holy Grail! But from it you may not drink!'

Then it seemed that the light within the Grail filled the room with fire and Launcelot fell to the ground like one dead, and all his senses forsook him.

But Gawain rose from before the Grail, came through the blinding light unhurt and knelt by Launcelot, while the door of the chapel closed, shutting out the sight of the Holy Grail from their eyes for ever.

Very tenderly Gawain carried Launcelot down into the hall of the castle and laid him upon a couch; and in a little while Naciens the Hermit came to where he was and said in a loud voice to all who were assembled there:

'King Pelles and all you people of the Waste Lands, rejoice and be exceeding glad. For Gawain has taken away the Curse of Desolation which Balyn brought upon you when he struck the Dolorous Stroke. Therefore be sure that the Grail Knight draws near, and the long penance will soon be ended.'

Then a mighty shout of joy rose from all those in the hall until the very roof shook with the noise. For Gawain had resisted the temptations of the hall and had asked the question which would loosen the curse. But still King Pelles was unhealed of his grievous wound and still the Castle of Carbonek and all those who dwelt in the Waste Lands must remain a people cut off and apart from the rest of the land of Britain.

But Gawain remained at Carbonek with Launcelot, who continued for twenty-four days insensible. And when at last he recovered and asked where he was, King Pelles said:

'Sir, you are still within the Castle of Carbonek.'

'I have seen great marvels,' said Sir Launcelot, 'and no tongue can tell of them, nor can my heart remember them clearly. And had it not been for my sin I would have seen much more. But now that may never be.'

'I saw these things too,' said Sir Gawain, 'and many other wonders that cannot be told. Yet, though I saw the Holy Grail clear and unveiled before me, it was not for me to drink from it. For the Grail Maiden told me that from that very cup which I held in my hands Our Lord gave the First Sacrament to His disciples at the Last Supper, but that, though she is its guardian and with her Naciens the Hermit, no one may touch the Grail with their lips until the Grail Knight comes.'

Then Launcelot and Gawain bade farewell to King Pelles, and rode away towards Camelot. And as they passed through the Waste Lands they saw the first green buds on the forest trees, and the first blades of grass showing through the barren earth. And all the people blessed Sir Gawain and sped him on his journey.

'And now,' they said, 'we wait only for the Grail Knight himself!'

7

The End of the Quest

WHILE these things were happening to Launcelot and Gawain, Percivale had overtaken Galahad and Bors, and was riding with them through the forest of dead trees towards Carbonek. At length they came out of the forest and after a month of wandering among the bare hills they came one evening through a narrow pass in the rocks and found themselves near to the castle.

Then they went forward swiftly, Percivale leading the way, for he remembered his visit to the mysterious castle when he had found and lost the lovely maiden Blanchefleur. Before it was dark they came in through the broken courtyard and, threading their way among the shattered walls, came to the great hall and left their horses outside.

Up the steps they went, and within found King Pelles still stretched upon his couch by the high table on the dais, while the silent company sat once more at the long tables in the lower part of the hall. But now Naciens, the divine Hermit of Carbonek, stood at King Pelles' side; and he welcomed the three knights, saying:

'Sirs, we greet you in the Name of God. Your wanderings are ended, for in this castle is the Holy Grail, and this night all things shall be accomplished.'

The three knights took their places at the table, and the feast began. But each of them declined the rich fare and the strong wine offered to them, eating only bread and drinking clear water.

Then, when the moment was due, the doors opened of themselves, and in a beam of clear light the procession of the Grail came in for the last time. There were the ghostly maidens carrying the Bleeding Spear, the Silver Dish and the candlestick, and then came the Grail Maiden herself carrying the Holy Grail covered in white samite: and Percivale trembled as he saw her, for he knew that she was Blanchefleur his lost love.

When the procession drew near Galahad rose to his feet, and holding up the sword which so long ago Merlin had placed in the floating stone, he cried:

'In the name of God, stay a moment!'

The procession paused, and a great gasp of wonder went up from all those who were gathered in the hall. Very slowly Galahad went down from the dais and took his place in front of the procession, holding the sword before him by the blade so that the handle made a great shimmering cross above his head. Then, walking like a man in a dream, he went by the high table, down the hall, and away through the dark

'In the name of God, stay a moment!'

passages of the castle; and behind him followed the Grail procession. Then, at a sign from Naciens the Hermit, Percivale and Bors took up the couch on which King Pelles lay and followed behind the Grail Maiden; and last of all came Naciens himself.

Through the castle they went, the light shining all about them, up the dark stairway, and so at last into the chapel. And there the candles and the dish were placed on the silver altar, and the Bleeding Spear hung once more in the air above it, the blood-drops falling and vanishing as before.

Percivale and Bors set down King Pelles below the steps of the altar and knelt one at either side of him; but Galahad knelt on the first step, and the Grail Maiden went up and placed the Holy Grail in the centre of the altar. Then Naciens the Divine Hermit came and took the Grail in his hands and after he had prayed, he brought it to Galahad and said:

'Holy Knight of God, I who have been the Priest of the Grail these many years give the Holy Grail into your hands that all things may be fulfilled. Now, Sir Galahad, my trust is ended, let me depart in peace. For I, many years ago, sinned deeply against the good Joseph of Arimathea who brought these wonders into Britain. And when he died this penance was laid on me: that I should live beyond the span of mortal men to be the Priest of the Grail until the coming of Sir Galahad the Good Knight.'

Then Galahad took the Holy Grail in his hands, drew away the cloth, and drank of the Holy Wine. After this he rose from his feet and set the Grail upon the altar: and it seemed to all who saw him that his face shone with a great light. Next, he knelt down beside Naciens, took him in his arms and kissed him upon the forehead; and with a happy little sigh Naciens the Divine Hermit fell asleep and woke no more in this world.

Then Sir Galahad turned to King Pelles, and went towards him carrying the Bleeding Spear in his hand. And King Pelles raised himself on his elbow and said:

'Sir Galahad, good Knight of Logres and my grandson, you are right welcome and long have I desired your coming. For such pain and such anguish have I endured these many years as surely no man ever suffered. But now I trust to God that the end of my pain is at hand, and so I shall pass out of this world and be at peace.'

Then Galahad held the Spear so that the drops of blood fell into the wounds of the Maimed King: and at once Pelles was cured of his sufferings, and his flesh was as whole and unscarred as if Balyn had never struck the Dolorous Stroke.

While Pelles returned thanks to God, Galahad knelt once more beside the altar; and now the Grail Maiden came forward suddenly, carrying in her hands a sword which was broken into three pieces.

'Percivale,' she said gently, 'take from me this sword, and see if you can place the pieces together. Many knights have tried to do so, but only he who shall be the first king of freed Carbonek, and my husband, can mend it.'

Sir Percivale took the three pieces in his hands, and when he had prayed to God, he placed them together: and at once they were joined, with only one small crack.

'If you had spoken the words which would release the spell when you first came to Carbonek,' she said, 'there would be no crack in the sword.'

Percivale rose to his feet and taking her hand he said:

'Lady Blanchefleur, I have loved you these many years, and to you I have been true in thought and in deed – though I did not believe that I should ever see you again.'

Then he took her in his arms and kissed her; and there in the Chapel of the Holy Grail Sir Galahad, who now was the Priest of the Grail, blessed them and made them man and wife.

Sir Percivale and the Lady Blanchefleur knelt before the altar, and beside them Sir Bors, who had seen all these things. And Galahad took the Holy Grail once more and gave them the Holy Sacrament out of it; and they were filled with divine peace and joy.

Then Galahad set the Grail upon the altar and knelt once more in prayer. And as he knelt, his life was accomplished, and his soul was taken up to Heaven so that his body lay dead before the altar. Then the sunbeam descended from above, striking clean through the roof of the chapel, and the Bleeding Spear and the Holy Grail passed up and vanished from sight, nor were they ever again seen upon this earth.

When all these things were accomplished, Percivale and Blanchefleur became king and queen of Carbonek and of all the wide lands which surround the castle and which were never more waste or desolate. And the castle itself was no more a mystery, nor was it set apart any longer from the rest of the land of Britain. But when the last battle had been fought and the realm of Logres was no more, Percivale's kingdom made still a little light in the darkness of a Britain conquered and laid waste by the barbarians. Long and happily Percivale and Blanchefleur lived at Carbonek, and when they died their son Loherangrin the Swan Knight became king.

But meanwhile Sir Bors de Gannis remained with them only long enough to see Galahad buried before the altar in the chapel where the Holy Grail had been, with Naciens on his right and Pelles on his left. Then he bade farewell to Percivale and Blanchefleur, and rode away towards Camelot.

He came there upon the Feast of Pentecost two years after the beginning of the Quest of the Holy Grail, and found King Arthur and his court gathered about the Round Table. But now many of the places were empty, for many knights had died on the Quest.

That day there was no need for King Arthur to wait until any other marvel or adventure was shown to him before the feast began, for Sir Bors told the whole tale of the Holy Grail as he and Galahad and Percivale had seen it, and of how they had succeeded in the Quest. Gawain and Launcelot told of their adventure also, and presently Sir Bors said to Launcelot:

'Sir Galahad your son sent you greetings by me before he was taken from us, and to King Arthur and his whole court. And the good Sir Percivale greets you also, where he dwells with his lovely wife Blanchefleur, who was once the Grail Maiden. And for you, Launcelot, they pray, that you may escape from the sins of this world.'

'I trust to God that their prayers may help me,' sighed Sir Launcelot. But in a little while his eyes travelled back to Queen Guinevere, and he forgot how he had failed when he came so near to achieving the Quest of the Holy Grail.

BOOK FOUR

The Departing of Arthur

I

Launcelot and Guinevere

THE Quest of the Holy Grail was ended, and all those
knights who were left alive had returned to Camelot. King
Arthur rejoiced greatly to see them sitting once more about
the Round Table, but he was sad also, for he knew that the
time was drawing near when the realm of Logres should be
lost again in the darkness. For there was a change after the
Quest was over: many seats stood empty at the Round Table,
and now no new names grew in letters of gold upon these
seats, for there were no new knights to take the places of those
who were dead.

Now too the evil which had never quite been rooted out of
Logres began to stir once more, and in a little the fellowship
and harmony of his court was to be broken.

Yet for a little while the sun shone as brightly as ever, and
only Arthur, who remembered the words of Merlin the good
enchanter, knew that the end was near.

Now that Sir Galahad was dead Launcelot was once more
the greatest knight in Logres, and for a little time he was the
noblest too, for he remembered how he had failed to achieve
the Holy Grail by reason of his sinful love for Queen Guinevere. And the Queen noticed that Launcelot avoided her now
and rode away from Camelot on every quest that offered, and
one day she sent for him and said:

'Sir Launcelot, I see and feel daily that your love for me
grows less, and you ride ever to help damsels and gentlewomen. Have you perhaps found one of them who is dearer
to your heart than I am?'

'Ah madam,' said Launcelot sadly, 'I love you only and no
other woman in all the world. But for many reasons I strive
to flee your presence. Lately, when I followed the Quest of

the Holy Grail, it was shown me how sinful was my love for you – for you, the wife of my dear lord King Arthur: and had it not been for this love I would have seen what Sir Gawain saw, and partaken from the Grail itself with my son Sir Galahad and with Sir Percivale and Sir Bors: and that I may not lightly forget. Moreover I think also of your good name – for there are those about the Court who wait only some such chance as this to bring sorrow to King Arthur, and shame and dissension to the whole realm of Logres.'

Then Queen Guinevere was angry with Sir Launcelot, and cried:

'These are all lies – and now I understand your falsehood clearly enough. You are tired of me and you have found someone else! Therefore go hence and never come near me again!'

In great sadness Sir Launcelot took his horse and rode away from Camelot, far into the forests of mid-Britain, and no one knew where he was. But in a little while Queen Guine-vere was sorry and wished very much for Launcelot to return. However, she could not show this to anyone, so instead she called to her ten Knights of the Round Table and told them that she would ride a-maying with them into the woods and fields near Camelot: for now it was the month of May when trees and flowers were growing and blossoming in the sun-shine, and the hearts of men and woman should be filled with love and joy also.

'You must come on horseback,' she said, 'dressed all in green; and I will bring with me ten ladies, so that one may ride by the side of every knight; and each lady shall have a damsel to tend on her, and each knight a squire. For I would have all of you that be lovers to call ever to your remembrance the month of May!'

Away they rode into the green wood, their bridles flashing in the sun and jingling in tune with their merry laughter and songs.

But on that very same day there came to King Arthur's Court a knight called Sir Urry, carried in a litter, with three grievous wounds in his head which no man could heal. For many years Sir Urry had been in great pain, for no doctors could cure him; and at last his mother and his sister had set out on pilgrimage to take him into all the Courts of Europe to see if there was any man who could help. And at length they had come to Britain, to the Court at Camelot, and as they drew near they met with the lady Nimue, and she came with them to King Arthur and said:

'Lord King, this man Sir Urry may be cured only by the touch of the best knight in the world.'

'If any man may heal Sir Urry,' answered King Arthur, 'surely it shall be one of my Court: for there are none better in all this land, unless it be the good knight Sir Percivale who is King now in Carbonek. And to encourage all men, I myself will lay hands upon him first – though I know that I am not worthy to heal him – and then all my subject kings, dukes, earls and knights shall try.'

Then all the fellowship of the Round Table, one hundred and ten of them, laid hands in turn upon Sir Urry: but none might heal him.

'Where is Sir Launcelot of the Lake?' asked King Arthur then. 'For if he cannot do this thing, then surely there is no knight worthy enough.'

And while they stood speaking of these things Launcelot came riding back to Camelot. Arthur told him what had chanced, and begged him to attempt the cure of Sir Urry.

'Not so,' exclaimed Sir Launcelot. 'It were but evil pride in me to think that I might succeed where so many noble knights have failed.'

'You shall not choose,' said King Arthur, 'for I lay my command upon you.'

'Then, my most noble lord,' answered Launcelot, 'I will not disobey you.'

So Launcelot knelt down beside Sir Urry, and when he had prayed a while he laid his hands on the three cruel wounds: and at once Sir Urry was as whole and well as if he had never been wounded at all.

All the knights, and King Arthur among them, shouted aloud for joy and thanked God for His mercy. But Launcelot wept as if he were a little child that had been beaten. Then King Arthur grew silent too, for he remembered how upon the day when he first came to Camelot, Launcelot had healed a wounded knight in the very same way, and how Nimue, the Lady of the Lake of Avalon, had prophesied that Launcelot would do just such another deed, his very last before the passing of Logres.

While these things were happening at Camelot, Guinevere with her knights and ladies rode a-maying deep into the forest. But there was a knight called Melliagraunce, who had long loved Queen Guinevere, and now when he saw her riding with so few attendants, and knew that Launcelot had been missing from Camelot for some time, he thought that his chance had come. So he set out with twenty armed men and a hundred archers, and laid an ambush for her, and surrounded her and her following suddenly.

'You traitor knight,' cried Queen Guinevere when she realized what had happened. 'Remember that you are a king's son, and a Knight of the Round Table: you bring dishonour upon all knighthood, upon your lord King Arthur, upon King Bagdemagus your father, upon me your Queen – and upon yourself.'

'As for this talk,' cried Sir Melliagraunce, 'I care nothing for it. For know, madam, that I have loved you long, but never before found such a chance as this.'

Then the ten knights who rode with Queen Guinevere strove to defend her, but they had no armour with them, and before long all of them were stretched wounded on the ground.

'Sir Melliagraunce, do not slay my noble knights!' begged Guinevere. 'I will go with you if you promise not to harm them further: but if you do not promise I will slay myself forthwith.'

'Madam,' said Sir Melliagraunce, 'for your sake I will spare them, and they shall be carried into my own castle and well tended – if you will ride with me.'

So Guinevere and her knights were taken to Sir Mellia-graunce's castle; but on the way one of the squires, a boy young and daring, broke away suddenly and galloped at full speed towards Camelot; and although the archers shot at him, he got safely away and came to the Court of King Arthur not very long after Launcelot had healed Sir Urry.

When they heard the tale, Launcelot, who was still armed, leapt immediately upon his horse. 'I will go thither at once!' he cried to King Arthur, 'and do you follow with many men as soon as you are armed. You will find me at the castle of Sir Melliagraunce – if I am still alive!'

Then he set spurs to his horse and galloped away in a cloud of dust. But before he had gone very far a band of archers appeared in front of him with their bows bent, and bade him stand.

'You pass not this way!' they cried. 'Or if you do, it shall be upon your feet, for we will slay your horse!'

'That will be little advantage to you!' said Launcelot, and he charged at them full tilt. Then they loosed a flight of arrows and the horse fell to the ground, pierced to the heart; but Launcelot leapt clear and attacked the archers, who broke and fled in every direction so that he could not overtake any of them.

So he continued along the road on foot: but his armour and his spear and shield were so heavy that he could only move very slowly, and yet he did not like to leave any of them behind, for fear lest Melliagraunce had prepared any more snares for him.

But presently he met two woodmen who were driving a cart along the road.

'Fair friends!' cried Launcelot, 'let me ride in your cart, I beg of you!'

'Whither would you go?' asked one woodman.

'To speak with Sir Melliagraunce at his castle,' answered Launcelot grimly.

'He is our master,' said the woodman, 'and he has sent us out to gather wood in the forest. We will not let you ride in our cart!'

Then one woodman struck at Launcelot with his whip, and spoke evil words; but Launcelot smote him on the side of the head with his fist, and his skull broke into pieces so that he fell dead to the ground.

'Fair lord,' said the second woodman, 'spare my life, and I will take you wheresoever you wish to go!'

'Then turn your cart about,' said Launcelot, 'and drive me to the Castle of Sir Melliagraunce more swiftly than ever you drove before!'

'Jump in!' cried the woodman, 'and you will be there in no time!'

So away they went at a great speed; and presently Queen Guinevere's damsel, who was looking out of the window of Melliagraunce's castle, exclaimed:

'Ah, look, madam! Here comes a cart such as hangmen use, and in it rides a goodly knight!'

'Where?' cried Guinevere; and then she looked out and knew Sir Launcelot by the device on his shield. 'Oh, I knew he would come!' she murmured. 'I knew he would come!'

Meanwhile Launcelot arrived at the gate; and there he descended from the cart and cried out in such a voice that the whole castle rang with it:

'Where are you, false traitor Sir Melliagraunce? Come out and fight, and all your treacherous curs with you – for here am I, Sir Launcelot of the Lake, ready to do battle with you all!'

Then Melliagraunce took fright, and he came and grovelled at Queen Guinevere's feet, and begged her forgiveness; and at length she said that she would ask Launcelot to spare his life, for she would rather have peace than war. So the gate was opened and Launcelot came rushing in like an angry lion, but Guinevere managed to persuade him to make peace with Sir Melliagraunce; but not until they had agreed to do battle together in full armour, knight against knight, at Camelot in the presence of King Arthur.

Then Guinevere took Launcelot by the hand and led him to her room, where she unarmed him and bathed the hurts he had received from the arrows which had been shot against him.

That night they stayed in the castle; and early the next day King Arthur arrived with a great company of knights. But when Queen Guinevere had told him all that had happened, he too agreed readily that no vengeance should be taken on Melliagraunce or any of his people, but that Melliagraunce should fight with Launcelot.

'This day week the battle shall be,' said King Arthur, 'in the meadow between Camelot and the river. And if either knight keeps not his tryst, then he shall be called the shamefullest knight in all Logres.'

After this King Arthur led Guinevere back with him to Camelot, and the wounded knights were carried there in litters.

'Sir,' said Melliagraunce to Launcelot, 'there is not hate between us now, I trust? For this day week our honours shall be satisfied. Therefore I pray you, abide with me in my castle this day and I will feast you royally.'

'I am content to do so,' said Launcelot.

But when the evening came Melliagraunce went to Launcelot's room and led him down towards the hall; and he brought him by a passage in the midst of which was a trapdoor, and when Launcelot trod upon it, it opened under his feet and he fell a great way into a dark vault filled with straw.

There he lay for seven nights and days, and each evening a fair damsel brought him food and water; and each evening she said:

'Noble Sir Launcelot, if you will but promise to be my lord and love, I will set you free from this prison. But if you do not promise, here you shall stay until your honour is gone for ever.'

'Far greater dishonour would be mine,' said Launcelot, 'if I were to buy my freedom at such a price. King Arthur will know well that only some treachery could keep me from Camelot when the day of battle comes.'

But on the morning of the day when he was due to fight with Sir Melliagraunce, the damsel came to Sir Launcelot weeping, and said:

'Alas, noble Launcelot, I have loved you in vain. Give me but one kiss, and I will set you free.'

'There is no shame in one kiss such as this,' said Launcelot. Then he kissed the damsel once and hastened from the prison, stopping only to put on his armour which she had brought to him, sprang upon a horse which stood waiting in the court-yard, and galloped away to Camelot.

But the damsel stood weeping softly in the gateway: 'Alas,' she sobbed, 'my kiss meant nothing to Sir Launcelot: he thinks only of Queen Guinevere!'

Meanwhile the king and queen with many knights and ladies were gathered in the great meadow by Camelot to see the battle. The hour came – but there was no sign of Sir Launcelot, and Sir Melliagraunce swaggered about, boasting that he was the best knight in all the realm of Logres, while Launcelot was a coward and a runaway.

And he was about to ride home, leaving all the fellowship of the Round Table shamed for ever, when suddenly a cry was raised, and Launcelot came into sight, spurring his horse desperately.

When he was come before King Arthur he told of how treacherously Melliagraunce had tricked him – and all those present began to cry shame upon Sir Melliagraunce until at length he seized his spear and cried: 'Have at you!' to Sir Launcelot.

Then the two knights drew away to the ends of the meadow, and at a given signal came together like two thunderbolts; and Sir Launcelot struck Sir Melliagraunce so hard that he fell backwards over his horse's tail. Then Launcelot dismounted, drew his sword, waited until Melliagraunce was on his feet again, and attacked him fiercely. Melliagraunce tried to escape in many ways, and to have the better of his enemy by unfair means; but the end of it was that Launcelot smote him such a stroke with his sword that helmet and head were split into halves. And that was the end of Melliagraunce the traitor.

There was great joy after this in Camelot, and King Arthur thanked Launcelot before all the court for rescuing his Queen. Guinevere, however, said little, only she looked upon Launcelot with shining eyes, and she whispered to him:

'Come to me in my garden at sundown, for I would thank you alone.'

It chanced that Agravain, Sir Gawain's brother, heard her words; he was one of the wicked and disloyal knights who hated the Queen and were jealous of Sir Launcelot's fame and renown. Agravain told Sir Mordred, his cousin, Queen Morgana le Fay's son, who was the evilest knight of all, hating all things good as his mother had done, and seeking ever to bring shame and ruin upon King Arthur and the whole realm of Logres.

Mordred now saw his chance, and he and Agravain hid themselves in the Queen's garden that evening when the sun was casting long shadows under the apple trees; and presently she came, walking among the flowers, more fair than the fairest rose in the world.

Guinevere walked in the garden alone for a while; and then Sir Launcelot came, the goodliest knight in the world. He

He knelt before Queen Guinevere

knelt before Queen Guinevere, and she thanked him for saving her from Sir Melliagraunce, and asked his forgiveness for her harsh words.

'Oh Launcelot, Launcelot,' she said softly, 'since the first day that you came to Camelot, when I was little more than a girl, the bride of King Arthur, I saw you and loved you.'

'I loved you on that day also,' said Launcelot, 'and all these years I have striven against that love – but in vain.'

'Launcelot,' said Guinevere, her voice trembling, 'I wish above all things in the world that you would be my lord and my love, even though it must be in secret ... I would that you might come and visit me secretly in my room this evening ...'

'My lady and my love,' said Launcelot in a strained voice, 'wish you that with all your heart?'

'Yes truly,' answered the Queen.

'Then for your love, it shall be so!' cried Launcelot.

Guinevere drew near to him and kissed him on the lips: then she turned and glided away through the twilight, passing amidst the flowers from which all the colours had gone, leaving them grey in the dying light. But Launcelot stood quite still with the last sunbeam on his face, and he trembled from head to foot, and sighed with joy as he remembered Guinevere's kiss.

Presently he also turned and went out of the garden in the gathering darkness.

'And now,' said Sir Mordred, 'my time has come. These two have given the whole realm of Logres into my hands.' And the look in his eyes was not good to see as he and Agravain stepped out into the night.

2

The Plots of Sir Mordred

IN an upper room of the Castle of Camelot that same evening, while the candle light threw black, flickering shadows on the bare stone walls, Sir Agravain spoke with Sir Gawain his brother, and Mordred stood near the door, his dark eyes shining strangely.

'Brother Agravain,' said Sir Gawain, much moved, 'I pray you and charge you speak no more to me of such matters, for be assured that I will have no share in this business.'

'I marvel that you can let this shame be!' cried Agravain, his weak face working nervously. 'We all know that Launcelot loves the queen and would bring shame upon King Arthur and all the realm of Logres if he could ... We have but to tell King Arthur and this night Launcelot may be taken in the queen's chamber, and put to death for treason.'

'If you are afraid to speak,' said Mordred quietly to Agravain, 'then I will go alone to the king.'

'That I can well believe,' said Gawain, 'for you, sir, are ever ready to stir up any unhappiness. But you, my brother, think before you do this thing of what will come of it.'

'Whatever may happen!' cried Agravain, 'I *will* tell the king!'

'Alas,' said Sir Gawain sadly, 'now is this holy realm of Logres about to be destroyed, and the noble fellowship of the Round Table broken by civil war.'

But Agravain and Mordred went from the room and found King Arthur.

'Take twelve knights and do what must be done,' said King Arthur when he had heard all the tale. 'But woe to you if you have come to me with lies and slanders in your mouths – for this is the saddest night's work that ever has been in this land.'

Then the two conspirators went to choose their followers. But some hours later Sir Gawain found King Arthur sitting all alone in the great empty hall in his place at the Round Table, with the tears running from his eyes and trickling unheeded through his grey beard and on to his hands.

Sir Launcelot sat up late in his room with Sir Bors; and at last he rose to his feet and said:

'I bid you good night, fair cousin. I go to speak with the queen.'

'Sir,' said Bors, 'I counsel you not to go this night.'

'Why not?' asked Launcelot.

'I fear Sir Mordred,' answered Bors, 'for he and Sir Agravain are ever about to do you shame and bring ruin upon us all.'

'Have no fear,' said Launcelot, 'I shall go swiftly and silently, and return at once.'

'God speed you well,' said Sir Bors, 'and bring you safely back again.'

Then Launcelot took his sword under his arm, wrapped his long furred gown about him, and went through the dark castle to Queen Guinevere's room.

And they had not been together for many minutes when Sir Mordred and Sir Agravain, with their twelve knights, came to the door and cried:

'You traitor, Sir Launcelot, now are you caught!' This they shouted with a loud voice so that all the castle might hear.

'Alas!' sobbed Queen Guinevere, 'now are we both betrayed!'

'Madam,' said Launcelot, 'is there any armour here that I can put on? If so, these cravens shall not take me easily.'

'Alas, no,' said Guinevere, 'I have no armour, nor a helmet, nor even a shield: wherefore I fear that our long love is come to a sad end.'

But Launcelot turned to the door and shouted: 'Fair lords, cease from all this noise and I will open the door quietly.'

'Come quickly, you traitor knight!' they shouted back. 'If you yield yourself quietly we will take you prisoner and bring you before King Arthur.'

Then Launcelot wound his cloak about his arm, unbarred the door with his left hand and opened it a little way. Immediately a knight – his name was Sir Colgrevaunce – rushed forward, striking at Launcelot with all his might. But Launcelot warded the blow with the thick folds of his cloak and struck Sir Colgrevaunce such a stroke on the head that he fell down and never moved again. Swiftly Launcelot dragged him into the room and barred the door once more. Then, with the queen's help he stripped the armour from the dead man and put it on himself.

'Traitor knight! Come out of the queen's room!' shouted Sir Agravain, beating on the door.

'Cease your noise, I am coming!' replied Launcelot. 'I advise you, Sir Agravain, to run away and hide!'

Then Launcelot flung wide the door and stood there a moment, as fine a knight as ever this world has seen. Next moment he was among them, and the swords flashed like lightning among dark clouds: at the first stroke he slew Sir Agravain, and then he laid about him with such blows that before long all his foes lay dead on the ground except for Sir Mordred, who ran wounded from the place.

'I go now!' shouted Launcelot to the queen. 'But if you are in any danger for this night's work be assured that while I am a living man I will rescue you.'

Then Launcelot rode away in haste from Camelot, and with him went Sir Bors and Sir Lionel and many another knight; and they hid themselves in the forest near by and waited to see what would happen.

Meanwhile Sir Mordred came, all wounded, to Arthur where he sat with Gawain in the great hall.

'How comes this to be?' asked the king. 'Did you not take him in the queen's chamber?'

'He was there indeed,' gasped Mordred, 'and all unarmed. But he slew first Sir Colgrevaunce, armed himself in his armour, and killed all those who came against him, except for me, who escaped thus wounded.'

'Ah,' said the king sadly, 'he is indeed a marvellous knight! Alas that ever Sir Launcelot should be against me, for now I am sure that the noble fellowship of the Round Table is broken for ever, for many knights will side with him.'

'What of the queen?' asked Mordred. 'She is guilty of high treason, and by the law she must die at the stake!'

Then Arthur covered his face in his hands and wept.

'Be not over hasty, my lord,' said Gawain gently. 'How do we know that Launcelot and the queen are guilty? Perchance she sent for him merely that she might thank him for saving her from Sir Melliagraunce.'

'The queen must die according to the law,' said King Arthur. 'But if Launcelot comes here again he shall suffer a shameful death.'

'Then God forbid that ever I be by to see it!' exclaimed Gawain.

'Yet he slew your brother Agravain,' said King Arthur.

'Often I warned Agravain,' answered Sir Gawain, 'for I knew what his plots would bring him to. Moreover he was one of fourteen armed knights attacking a man unarmed ... Therefore I pardon Sir Launcelot his death.'

'Make you ready in the morning to lead my queen to the fire,' said King Arthur.

'Not so, my most noble King,' cried Gawain, 'it shall never be said that I was of your counsel for her death.'

'Then,' said the King, 'call before me your brothers Sir Gaheris and Sir Gareth.'

And when they were come, King Arthur gave them his commands.

'Sir,' they answered, 'what you bid us that will we do. Nevertheless, it is sorely against our will, and we will go there unarmed and dressed in robes of mourning.'

'Then make you ready,' cried the King, 'for the hour has come!'

'Alas,' said Sir Gawain, 'that ever I should live to see this day!'

So Guinevere was led to the stake, dressed only in her smock, and many followed her in mourning garments. But Sir Mordred was there fully armed and with him a band of knights armed also.

When the torch was already lit, suddenly Sir Launcelot came

But when the torch was already lit, suddenly Sir Launcelot came, with his followers, cut his way to the stake, slaying many knights as they went, and carried off Queen Guinevere. But, without knowing it, Launcelot killed both Gaheris and Gareth who stood near the stake unarmed and in mourning costume.

Then Sir Launcelot and all those who favoured his cause rode away into his own lands of Gwynedd in North Wales and fortified themselves strongly in his Castle of Joyous Garde.

Now indeed the realm of Logres was broken, for Britain was split with civil war, and there was hatred where of old love and faith had been. When his anger passed, King Arthur repented sorely that he had condemned Queen Guinevere to the flames so speedily, and rejoiced that Launcelot had saved her. But now the lifelong friendship between Gawain and Launcelot was ended, and a sudden hatred and a desire for revenge grew in its place.

'I swear before God that I will never rest,' cried Sir Gawain, 'until Launcelot and I meet face to face and one of us is slain. For never can I forgive him for slaying my dear brothers Gaheris and Gareth the good knight – slaughtering them unarmed and defenceless. And you, my uncle, I charge by the sacred order of knighthood, and as you are true king of this land, to make war forthwith against Sir Launcelot, both to avenge my brothers and to rescue your queen.'

All the knights who remained faithful to him also begged King Arthur to make war; and at length he gathered together his forces and marched north until he came to Joyous Garde and laid siege to it.

After fifteen weeks of fruitless siege it chanced on a day that Sir Launcelot spoke from the gate-tower with King Arthur and Sir Gawain:

'My lords both,' he said, 'you cannot take this castle.'

'Come forth then,' cried King Arthur, 'and fight with me in single combat!'

'God forbid,' said Launcelot, 'that ever I should fight with the most noble king of all time, he moreover that made me a knight.'

'Now fie upon your fair language!' cried the king. 'Know that I am now your mortal foe, and ever will be. For you have robbed me of my wife, slain my knights, and broken this goodly realm of Logres.'

Then Launcelot begged King Arthur to make peace, offering to give up Queen Guinevere and defend her innocence against all her accusers. And the king might have listened to him had not Sir Gawain persuaded him against making any truce with Launcelot.

And on the next day Launcelot led his men suddenly out of the castle, for he was angered at length by the cruel taunts Sir Gawain had heaped upon him the day before, and a terrible battle ensued.

In it Sir Gawain, seeking for Launcelot, struck down Sir Lionel and slew him; but Sir Bors smote King Arthur to the earth and stood over him with drawn sword crying to Launcelot:

'Sir, shall I make an end of this war at a single stroke?'

But Launcelot answered: 'Strike not, or I will slay you myself. For I will never see our most noble lord King Arthur slain or shamed by any man.'

And then Sir Launcelot sprang down from his horse and very tenderly helped King Arthur to his feet, and so on to his own horse, saying as he did so:

'My dear lord king, for God's sake make an end of this war. Take back your queen with all honour, and I will promise to leave this land of Britain and never return until you may need me.'

Then King Arthur was deeply moved, thinking of the great courtesy of Sir Launcelot and of all the noble deeds he had done in the past. And in spite of all that Sir Gawain could do he made peace with Launcelot.

And when all was agreed, Launcelot came unarmed before the king, leading Queen Guinevere by the hand, and he said:

'My most noble lord, I bring hither your queen. And if there is any knight who dares say that she is false to you, then I will fight with him to the death. Whatever I have done, or sought to do, this lady is innocent: but you have listened to liars and quarrel-makers,' and as he said this he turned and looked towards Sir Mordred, 'and by their evil mischief-making the goodly fellowship of the Round Table is broken in sunder.'

'The king may do as he will,' broke in Sir Gawain, 'but never while we live shall I make peace with you: for you slew my dear brother Sir Gareth, and Sir Gaheris and Sir Agravain also.'

'You know well that I loved no man better than Sir Gareth,' began Launcelot, 'and all my life I shall lament that I slew him, not knowing what I did –'

'I will never forgive my brothers' death,' interrupted Gawain passionately, 'and in particular the death of my brother Gareth.'

'And now,' said Launcelot, 'I must bid farewell to this dear land, and to the holy realm of Logres, and go overseas into Armorica, in the land of France.'

'Be sure that in time I shall follow you there!' cried Sir Gawain.

Peace reigned in Britain for a little while after this, but it was a broken and a troubled peace. For ever Sir Gawain brooded on his brothers' deaths, and ever Sir Mordred stirred up hatred against Sir Launcelot. And at length so many knights sided with Sir Gawain that Arthur was forced to declare war on Sir Launcelot; and he gathered together a great army and went into France, leaving Mordred to rule Britain while he was away.

They marched into Armorica, to the Castle of Benwick where Launcelot had taken up his abode, and they remained there for a long while. And three times did Launcelot and Gawain fight together, and each time Launcelot overcame Gawain and wounded him almost to death. But it seemed now that Gawain was mad, for even when he lay desperately wounded he ceased not to cry:

'Traitor knight! Coward! When I am whole again I will do battle with you once more. For never will I forgive you for Gareth's death, and never will I rest until one of us is slain!'

Meanwhile in Britain Sir Mordred continued with his plots. And when he had won enough knights to his side, he announced that King Arthur had been killed in the French wars, and he persuaded the people to choose him as their king, and even had himself crowned at Canterbury.

Then he seized Queen Guinevere and tried to force her to marry him. But she managed to escape from him and came to London. Thence she sent messengers to find King Arthur and meanwhile she and those who remained faithful to her retreated into the Tower of London and fortified it.

Presently Sir Mordred came and tried to force his way into it, but it was too strong. He tried to persuade Queen Guinevere to come out, but she answered him bravely: 'I would rather die by mine own hand than be wife to you!'

Then the Archbishop of Canterbury, the same who had crowned King Arthur so many years ago, and who was now a very old man, came and warned Sir Mordred:

'Do you not fear the vengeance of God?' he cried. 'King Arthur is not slain – and you do great harm to the queen and to all this land.'

'Peace, you false priest!' shouted Mordred, 'for if you anger me more, I will strike off your head!'

'Sir,' answered the archbishop, 'if you leave not your sin, I will curse you with bell, book, and candle!'

'Do your worst,' cried Mordred, 'I care not for you or your curses!' So the archbishop left Sir Mordred and gathered all the clergy together and cursed Sir Mordred, putting him outside all the rites and blessings of the Church.

Then Mordred sought to kill the archbishop; but he fled away to Glastonbury in Somerset and there became a hermit at the abbey.

Queen Guinevere's messenger had reached King Arthur by this time, and swiftly he marched to the sea coast with all his men, and set sail for England. But Mordred was waiting for him at Dover, and a terrible battle had to be fought before he and his men could land. At length, however, they were all ashore; and then they charged the rebels, and sent them flying over the downs, Sir Mordred leading the flight.

When the battle was over King Arthur found Sir Gawain lying mortally wounded, for the last wound which Sir Launcelot had given him had broken out afresh.

'Alas, my beloved nephew,' said King Arthur, kneeling beside him, 'here now you lie dying, the man whom I loved best in all the world. And now all my joy is gone. For you and Launcelot I loved best of all my knights: and I have lost you both.'

'Ah, my dear lord,' said Gawain, 'all this is my doing. Oh, I have been mad of late – mad with wicked pride and anger. ... If the noble Sir Launcelot had been with you this war would never have come about. I forgive him now – would that I had forgiven him sooner ... Can he ever forgive me ?'

Then Gawain asked for pen and ink, and he wrote a letter to Sir Launcelot:

'Oh, Launcelot, flower of all noble knights that ever I saw or heard of, I Gawain, dying by your hand – and by a nobler man might no one be slain – beg your forgiveness ... Come again, noble Launcelot, come with all the speed you may, for the realm of Logres is in deadly peril, and our dear lord King Arthur has need of you ... This day we landed at Dover and put the false traitor Sir Mordred to flight, and by misfortune I was smitten again upon the wound that you gave me. And now I write this in the very hour of my death. And oh, I beg you, the most famous knight in the world, to come swiftly. Of me you will find only the grave: but come at once before Mordred can gather fresh rebels ... Noble Launcelot, I salute you, and – farewell.'

Then Sir Gawain died, and King Arthur wept at his side all the long night through.

3

The Last Battle

KING ARTHUR and his army were encamped upon the Plain of Camlann not many days later, and scarcely a mile away Mordred waited for him with a great gathering of knights and men-at-arms who had thrown in their lot with him, choosing rather his easy and lawless rule than the high service of Arthur the good King of Logres.

After the Battle of Dover, Mordred had fled away defeated; but in a very little while news came that he was marching into the west country, harrying the lands of all those who would not fight for him. Then Arthur marched swiftly towards Cornwall and Lyonesse, and came one night to Camlann near where, so many years before, Merlin the good enchanter had brought him to receive his sword Excalibur from the Lady of the Lake.

That night Arthur could not sleep: for he knew that on the morrow there would be a great battle in which many more of his knights would fall, and he feared that this was the last of all his battles, which Merlin had foretold, when the realm of Logres should pass into the darkness. For already the Saxons, hearing of the strife and civil war, were pouring into Britain from the north and east – for the first time since the battle of Mount Badon twenty-one years before – and now there was no fellowship of the Round Table ready to ride behind King Arthur at a moment's notice and drive out the barbarians wherever they might chance to land.

Arthur tossed and turned upon his bed in the royal tent until, near morning, he grew still. And then, neither sleeping nor waking, he beheld a strange thing. For suddenly it seemed to him that Sir Gawain, who lay buried in Dover Castle, came to him attended by a train of fair ladies:

'Welcome, dear nephew,' King Arthur said, or seemed to say, 'I thank God that I behold you alive whom I thought was dead. But tell me whence you come, and why attended by these ladies.'

'My dear lord king, my very dear lord king,' Sir Gawain answered, or seemed to answer, 'all these are ladies in whose cause I fought when I was a living man: for ever I fought in righteous quarrels only – and for this cause God has been very merciful to me, and has sent them to bring me hither to warn you of your passing. For if you fight with Sir Mordred this day, both of you will fall, and the most part of your people also. But I come to warn you, by God's grace, not to fight this day, but to make a truce with Sir Mordred, whatever his terms – a truce for one month. For within a month Launcelot will come with all his noble knights, and you and he together will slay Sir Mordred and overcome all that hold with him.'

Then Sir Gawain and the ladies vanished away, and in a little while King Arthur arose from his bed and called to him Sir Lucan and Sir Bedivere. And when he had told them of how Sir Gawain had visited him, and what his counsel had been, he bade them take two priests with them and go to make a month's truce with Sir Mordred.

'And spare not,' added the king, 'but offer him lands and goods as much as you think reasonable.'

So they came to where Mordred was with his great host of a hundred thousand men, and they treated with him for a long time. And at last he agreed to have Cornwall and Kent to be his at once, and the rest of Britain after King Arthur's death.

It was arranged that Arthur and Mordred were to meet midway between the two armies each attended by fourteen men only. Then King Arthur gave orders to his men: 'If you see any sword drawn, charge fiercely and slay that traitor Sir Mordred, for I do not trust him.'

And Sir Mordred spoke likewise to his army: 'If you see any sword drawn, come on and slay them all! I do not trust this treaty, and I am sure that King Arthur is eager to be revenged on me.'

So they met as had been arranged, and the agreement was

drawn up and signed by both of them. Then wine was brought, and they drank together. But while this was happening an adder came out of the heather, as evil as the serpent which tempted Eve, and stung one of Mordred's knights on the heel. When the knight felt himself stung he looked down and saw the adder; and then, without thinking, he drew his sword and killed it.

But when the two armies saw the light flashing on the drawn sword, a great shout arose from either side, and in a minute they were charging at one another across the Plain of Camlann.

'Alas, this unhappy day!' cried King Arthur. Then he and Mordred leapt each upon their horses and rode into the battle.

Never since that day in any Christian land was there seen a sadder or more dreadful battle. There was rushing and riding and striking; and many a grim wound was given, and many a deadly stroke. And ever King Arthur rode in the heart of the battle doing mighty deeds; and this time Mordred fought well also, and did not think of flight. But every man there fought only to kill: and thus the battle lasted through all that long day, and never ceased until all those noble knights were laid upon the cold earth.

The evening fell, dark and ominous, and the dreadful hush of death spread over the battlefield; and King Arthur wept to see all his people slain. For he looked about him and could see only two of all his knights left alive – Sir Lucan and Sir Bedivere – and both of these were sorely wounded.

'Oh God!' cried King Arthur, 'what has become of all my noble knights? Alas that ever I should see this doleful day! But now I know that the end has come ... Yet I would that I could find that traitor Sir Mordred, the cause of all this sorrow and destruction.'

Then, as King Arthur looked about him, suddenly he saw Sir Mordred, who stood leaning upon his sword among great heaps of dead men.

'Now give me my spear,' said King Arthur to Sir Lucan, 'for yonder I see the traitor who has brought about all this woe.'

And when Mordred saw King Arthur, he ran at him

'Let him be, my lord,' answered Sir Lucan, 'for he is accursed. And, moreover, if you can pass this unfortunate day, you shall be right well avenged. And, noble sir, remember your night's dream and what the spirit of Sir Gawain told you: for God of His great goodness has preserved you through this battle. By His blessing you have won the field – for there are three of us, while Sir Mordred stands alone. If you leave him now this wicked day of destiny is safely past.'

'Come life or death,' cried King Arthur, 'I will do justice upon this man who has brought destruction upon the realm of Logres.'

'God speed you well,' said Sir Bedivere.

Then the King took his spear Ron in both his hands and ran towards Sir Mordred shouting:

'Traitor, now is your death upon you!'

And when Mordred saw King Arthur, he ran at him with drawn sword; but the king smote Sir Mordred under the shield with a feint of his spear and ran him through the body. But when Mordred felt that he had his death-wound, in his hatred and fury he thrust himself forward upon the spear and gripping his sword in both hands smote King Arthur upon the head so hard that it cut through the helmet and deep into the head beneath. Then Sir Mordred fell to the ground and died screaming.

But King Arthur fell without a sound, and Sir Lucan and

Sir Bedivere came to him and raised him with difficulty between them. And so by gradual stages, for they were both sorely wounded, they carried him to a little deserted chapel not far from the mysterious sea where the mist lay red like blood in the last rays of the setting sun. And then Sir Lucan fell down and died, for the strain of lifting was more than he could stand with a mortal wound already tearing his vitals.

'Alas,' said the king, who had recovered from his swoon, 'this is a heavy sight to see this noble knight die for my sake – for he had more need of help than I had.'

And Sir Bedivere knelt by Sir Lucan and wept, for the two were brothers and had loved each other dearly.

The sun had sunk and now the moon flooded the field of battle with cold white radiance and grim shadows; and the mysterious waters were veiled in long bars of silver mist.

Then King Arthur said to Sir Bedivere:

'Now leave your weeping and mourning, gentle knight, for it is of no avail – and my time is short. But now, while yet I am with you, you may do me one last service. Take my good sword Excalibur and go up over yonder ridge; and there you will come to a dark lake in the mountain pass; and when you come there I charge you to throw my sword into that water and come back and tell me what you saw.'

'My lord,' answered Sir Bedivere, 'your commandment shall be done, and I will bring you word at once of what I see.'

So Sir Bedivere departed, carrying the sword Excalibur. And as he went he looked at the sword, admired the precious jewels in the handle, and said to himself: 'If I throw this valuable sword into the water no good will come of it, only harm and loss.' So, when he came to the dark lake in the mountain pass he hid the sword amongst the rushes and hastened back to King Arthur, saying that he had thrown it into the water.

'And what saw you there?' asked King Arthur.

'Sir,' answered Sir Bedivere, 'I saw nothing but the wind stirring the dark waters of the lake.'

'Then you do not speak the truth,' said King Arthur. 'Therefore go quickly and throw the sword far out into the lake!'

So Sir Bedivere returned again and took the sword in his hand; but again he thought what a shame it was to throw away such a noble sword. So he hid it once more and returned to the king.

'What saw you there?' asked King Arthur.

'Sir,' answered Bedivere, 'I saw nothing but the dark waters stirred by the moaning wind.'

'Ah, traitor and liar!' cried King Arthur, 'now you have betrayed me twice! Who would think that I had loved you so well, and that you had been so noble a Knight of the Round Table, when now you would betray your king for the value of this sword. Go again swiftly and do my bidding; for this long waiting puts me in danger of my life, and I grow cold in this chill night air.'

Then Sir Bedivere was ashamed, and he ran swiftly over the brow of the hill to the dark lake in the pass of the mountains. He came to the waterside, took the sword in his hands, and flung it as far out from the shore as he could. And as the blade flashed away in the moonlight there came a hand and an arm up out of the dark waters, the arm clothed in shining white samite, mysterious and wonderful, and caught the sword by the hilt. Three times it brandished the sword on high, and then vanished with it beneath the water, and the lake grew dark and still once more.

So Sir Bedivere came back to the king and told him what he had seen.

'Now help me hence,' said King Arthur, 'for I greatly fear that I have tarried here too long.'

Then Sir Bedivere supported the king down the grassy slope, where the dew glimmered like magic diamonds in the moonlight; and they came to the shore of the mysterious sea. And then out of the white mist came a barge as if to meet them; and in it were many fair ladies, all veiled in black. And among them was Nimue, the Lady of the Lake, and the Lady of the Isle of Avalon was there also, and Queen Morgana le Fay, Arthur's sister. And a sad, low cry rose from them when they saw King Arthur.

'Now place me in the barge,' said King Arthur to Sir Bedivere.

And so he did as he was commanded, and the three ladies received him tenderly, and laid him down with his head resting in the lap of the Lady of the Isle of Avalon.

And then Queen Morgana le Fay, who knelt at his feet, wept softly, and said:

'Ah, my dear brother, why have you tarried so long from us ? Alas, the wound in your head has caught over-much cold.'

Then the barge moved slowly out from the land and Sir Bedivere stood alone upon the shore and cried aloud:

'Ah, my dear lord King Arthur, what shall become of me now that you go and leave me here alone ?'

'Comfort yourself,' answered King Arthur, 'and do as best you may. For you remain to bear word of me to those who are yet alive. For I must go into the Vale of Avalon there to be healed of my grievous wound. But be you sure that I will come again when the land of Britain has need of me, and the realm of Logres shall rise once more out of the darkness. But if you hear never more of me, pray for my soul.'

Then the barge floated away into the mist and was lost to sight. But a strange low cry of mourning came over the waters until the sadness passed from it and it was lost in a quiet whisper beyond the distance.

Avalon

SIR LAUNCELOT landed at Dover and asked of the townspeople where King Arthur was. They showed him the grave of Sir Gawain, and there he knelt long in prayer, sorrowing for the death of a very noble knight who had been his friend: but of King Arthur they had no tidings, except that he had marched westward nearly a month before.

Then Launcelot left all his men at Dover under the command of his cousin Sir Bors de Gannis, and rode away alone to the west. And after eight days he came to Almesbury and, as the night was falling, sought shelter in the great nunnery there. The abbess received him kindly and led him towards the guest-chamber. But as they passed by the cloisters there came a nun who cried aloud when she saw Sir Launcelot, and fell down in a faint. And when they bent down beside her, behold, it was Queen Guinevere!

That evening she told Sir Launcelot of a message that had come to her from Sir Bedivere telling of the dreadful battle of Camlann on the day of destiny; and of how he had seen King Arthur borne away sorely wounded into the unknown land of Avalon. And Sir Bedivere had made his way to the Abbey of Glastonbury which was not very far from the battle-field, and had there become a hermit, meaning to spend the rest of his days as a monk.

And Guinevere told Launcelot of her sorrow and repentance:

'For it is through our love that my lord King Arthur is slain, and with him most of the noblest knights of the world. And this land of Britain is laid open to the heathen Saxons, and the holy realm of Logres is no more. Therefore I came secretly hither and made my vows to dwell a nun all the days that are left to me, praying God to forgive me my grievous sin.'

'Now, my sweet lady,' said Launcelot, 'I will never be false to you. For here I swear that I too will take the vows that you have taken, and pass the rest of my days in prayer and fasting.'

Then they said good-bye to one another, knowing that this was the last time they would ever meet on earth. And in the morning Launcelot rode away until he came to Glastonbury; and there he found the ancient Archbishop of Canterbury and Sir Bedivere who had become a monk. Gladly they welcomed Launcelot to their company, and in a little while he had flung away his sword and armour and was clad in the coarse robes of a simple friar.

There, many months later, Sir Bors came to join him when he had sent away the great army which had come over from France. For Constantine the Duke of Cornwall was king now: but little of the land of Britain could he keep from the Saxons.

Years passed, and one night Launcelot dreamed that Guinevere lay dying and called to him. In the morning he and seven of his fellow monks set out to Almesbury and found that she had died quietly during the night. Then Launcelot brought her to Glastonbury and himself spoke the burial service over her when she was laid in her deep grave near the high altar.

But within a few weeks he too fell sick, and passed away quietly as one who had no longer any will to live.

And when he lay waiting for burial his brother Sir Hector de Maris came and stood beside his bier.

'Ah Launcelot,' he said, 'you were the best knight in all Christendom. You, Sir Launcelot, who lie there never had nor never will have any to rival you. And you were the most courteous knight that ever bore shield, the truest friend that ever bestrode horse, you were the truest lover that ever loved woman, and the kindest man that ever wore a sword. You were the finest man that ever was seen in a company of knights, and the meekest and most gentle among ladies, but the sternest knight to your mortal foes that ever put spear in rest.'

And when Launcelot was buried, Sir Hector and Sir Bors, Sir Blamour and Sir Bleoberis, the only knights left living of all the fellowship of the Round Table, set forth on pilgrimage to the Holy Land and there ended their days.

So ended the realm of Logres and all those who had lived and fought for the glory of God and the spreading of His Will on earth. For very soon the Saxons had conquered the whole of Britain and the Dark Ages descended upon all the western world.

But never was King Arthur forgotten, and always the belief endured in Britain, and in Wales particularly, that he would come again to save his land in the hour of its deadliest danger; that once more Britain should become the holy realm of Logres, the land of peace and righteousness and of true Christian living.

Round about the year 1200 it was announced suddenly that King Arthur was indeed dead – for the monks of Glastonbury had found his bones laid in a stone coffin buried in their precincts near to those of Queen Guinevere. This must be true, they reported, for beneath the coffin was a stone with a leaden cross sunk into it and a Latin inscription saying: 'Here lies King Arthur in this tomb with Guinevere his wife, in the Isle of Avalon.' The bones, they said, were of more than mortal size, and there were many more signs and wonders proving that here indeed lay King Arthur.

This story, it seems, was invented by the monks to bring fresh glory to their Abbey – and also to please the Norman kings of England, who did not like their conquered subjects to believe that King Arthur might return any day and release them from their new overlords.

But we may think, if we like, that it was Launcelot and not Arthur whom the monks dug up in the reign of Richard Cœur de Lion and reburied with all honour in a marble tomb.

And we may believe, too, that King Arthur still sleeps in some enchanted cave – perhaps in some 'Vale of Avalon' in the deep mountain fastnesses of Wales. For there, so the legend is told still in the haunted land of Gwynedd, a shepherd once met with a strange and mysterious man.

'Beneath the tree from which that staff was cut,' said the Stranger, pointing to the hazel crook in the shepherd's hand, 'lies hidden a vast hoard of treasure!'

And when the shepherd enquired further, he was told the secret of the cave:

'In the doorway hangs a great bell,' the Stranger told him, 'and you must not touch it, for if you do the Sleepers in the Cave will wake.' And when he had said this the Stranger vanished mysteriously and the shepherd rubbed his eyes, thinking that he had dreamed a dream.

But not long afterwards, while seeking for a lost sheep high up among the mountain crags, he came to a little valley, and recognized the hazel tree at the head of it as that from which he had cut his crook when climbing among the rocks as a boy.

So he went up to the tree, and there under its roots, sure enough, was a narrow cave entrance. Into it he went on his hands and knees, and presently found himself in a great, dark cavern. Here he struck a light and lit a candle which he happened to have in his pocket, and holding it above his head, he beheld the marvels of the place. All around in a great circle lay warriors sleeping, each of them clad in old armour and with a sword by his side; and upon a couch in the midst lay an ancient king who wore a golden crown and held in his hand a shining sword with a jewelled cross-hilt, while at his feet lay great heaps of gold and silver.

Amazed at what he saw, the shepherd stepped backwards suddenly and by ill luck struck against the great bell which hung over the doorway. And as its deep tones echoed through the cavern the old king on the couch woke out of his sleep and sat slowly up.

'Is it day?' he asked.

And the shepherd, trembling in terror, cried, he hardly knew why: 'No, no! Therefore sleep on!'

And then the king said: 'You say well; I will sleep once more until the day comes when I shall rise and bring victory to the people of Britain. Take of the silver and gold that lies before you, and get you gone speedily: for if my knights awake before it is time they will slay you – and then there will be none to speak the words which you have spoken, and which send me now back to my long rest.'

Then the king slept once more; and the shepherd took up as much gold and silver as he could carry and fled from the place. But never again, though he sought for it often, could he find the cave under the hazel tree which led to the mysterious cavern where sleep King Arthur and his Knights of the Round Table.

ON THE NEXT FEW PAGES

THERE ARE DESCRIPTIONS

OF SOME OTHER

FAVOURITE BOOKS IN THE

PUFFIN STORY BOOKS

SERIES

*

ADVENTURE

Five Proud Riders (PS 70). The five proud riders, who were boys and girls between ten and fourteen, were on New Forest ponies, and this is the story of their first riding holiday alone in the New Forest. Their mounts were every bit as varied in character as the riders themselves. The story, which is by Ann Stafford, is full of the delights of riding, but especially of riding on, day after day, instead of always having to turn tail for home. Each stranger met suggested possibilities of adventure, and the children did actually run into some bad men planning evil deeds, and found rather more happening than they had bargained for. (2s)

The Young Detectives (PS 47). This is a family story by R. J. McGregor with more than a mere spice of adventure in it. The five Mackie children had the rare good luck to find, in a house taken for the holidays in Devonshire, a secret passage leading to a smugglers' cave. There was a mysterious intruder who slipped round doors too quickly for recognition, footprints where no footprints should have been, and a wreck off-shore with something curious about it too. *The Secret of Dead Man's Cove* is another first-rate adventure story by the same author, available as Puffin Story Book No. 42. (2s)

Treasure Island (PS 36). This, the best of all adventure stories, was inspired by a thirteen-year-old boy and mostly written under his eye. It is the story of a boy's adventures with pirates, beginning in the *Admiral Benbow* public house on the Devon coast, and continuing with a tale of hidden treasure, an expedition, a map, a mutiny, and a derelict ship. The author, of course, is R. L. Stevenson, whose other great adventure story, *Kidnapped*, is also a Puffin Story Book (PS 34). (2s)

MAGIC AND ROMANCE

The Secret Garden (PS 69). It is forty years since Frances Hodgson Burnett wrote this book, but the magic of the story never fails. Poor Mary! She was a forlorn, unwanted, disagreeable child when, after cholera had carried off her nurse and both parents in one day, she was brought from India to live at the great lonely house (most of it shut up) on the bleak Yorkshire moors. Wandering in the gardens, she found one that was walled in. There seemed no way to get inside it – except as the robin flew, over the wall. How she got inside and what happened to her there is the sort of magic that can still happen. (2s 6d)

Ditta's Tree (PS 57). This is a deliciously fantastic fairy tale by Jean Hughes with India as its setting, and a rich, unusual flavour behind all its magic and mischief. Ditta was a sprite who lived in a tree and made Magics. The villagers regarded him with great respect and brought him flowers and fruit, rice, and even small sugary cakes which he liked best of all. But on the day that Ram Bux brought his shiny red motor car to the village, they forgot him altogether and just stood still and stared at the great marvel, till Ditta made a Magic and sent hornets in clouds to sting them into a better state of mind. (2s)

Fairy Tales from the Isle of Man (PS 59). On the Island the gold of gorse comes right down to the sea; the hills are purple with heather, and the banks thick with primroses in spring. Gulls flash in the sunlight and seals bask on the rocks or slip silently into the sea. But in winter storms lash the coast and the waves leap up in columns of spray, and the cries of the gulls echo on the wind. This is the scene against which Dora Broome tells the stories of the Little Fellows, the Giants, the Phynnodderee and the Bugganes. (1s 6d)

POEMS AND VERSES

A Puffin Book of Verse (PS 72). This anthology, which has been compiled by Eleanor Graham, is intended simply to give pleasure, and it is hoped that every boy or girl who browses among its pages will find something to enjoy. It ranges from nursery rhymes and nonsense poems to verses whose meaning has to be thought about: but, whether the poems are simple or more difficult, they have been chosen partly for that beauty of rhythm and language which makes lines linger in the mind after the book that contains them has been put aside. (2s 6d)

Walter De La Mare: Selected Stories and Verses (PS 70). Walter de la Mare is one of the greatest writers who has ever used the greatest gifts for the delight of children. Everything he writes comes to us in a crystalline perfection. Every word is deliberate, significant. The stories have far more than their obvious tale to leave with the reader, and reveal rich hidden treasure on successive readings. His poetry, particularly for young readers, can be a world of adventure, a browsing ground in which to discover what words can say and do. It is rich in subjects, moods, feeling; original in the use of rhyme and rhythm; full of humour, full of meaning. (2s 6d)

A Child's Garden of Verses (PS 22). There are more than sixty famous verses by Robert Louis Stevenson in this book, and they are illustrated with many drawings by Eve Garnett. 'These are rhymes, jingles,' the author wrote to a friend, 'I don't go in for eternity and the three unities.' They are rhymes about his childhood, divided into three sections – *The Child Alone*, *Garden Days*, and *Envoys*. (2s 6d)

FAMOUS MEN AND WOMEN

The Radium Woman (PS 68). This is the story, written by Eleanor Doorly, of Madame Curie, the great scientist who discovered Radium. It gives a picture of her strange childhood experiences in Poland under the Russian Tsar – the gay dancing days and sleigh rides, a secret society for the patriots, and exile to Siberia for anyone who was found out. Then comes Paris and University life, her marriage and the exciting days of her famous research for Radium. (2s)

Elizabeth Fry (PS 65). Elizabeth Fry was one of a large family, 'wide' Quakers with scarlet cloaks and gay ways, riding ponies and playing all over their big, rambling house. They kept lively diaries of their daily doings, so there was plenty of material for Kitty Barne to draw on for this story. Elizabeth married a city merchant and came to live in London, where her thoughts turned persistently to a deeper purpose in life, one which took her to Newgate Prison in the dark days of our inhuman treatment of prisoners. The story of her work there is exciting: she succeeded against such heavy odds, and never neglected her home and eleven children. (1s 6d)

The Insect Man (PS 50). Henri Fabre is the 'Insect Man', and his story is told here by Eleanor Doorly in a way that shows you not only how he earned that title, but how and where he spent his days. It describes how an English family set out in a car in France to discover something about Fabre for themselves. They tracked him from the village where he was born, seeing the fields in which perhaps he had first watched the doings of the insects whose life story he has written, to the town where he went to school, on to Avignon and further. (1s 6d)